FLOWERS AND CORPSES

"Time to hand out the shovels and spades," Delia said to Ernie.

"Good enough," Ernie said. "I put the tools in the shed this morning and put the lock on, but I don't think I shut it. You know the combination, though, right?"

"When this morning?" Lilly asked.

"Around five," Ernie said. "I've marked off some of the bushes that may be worth saving and just need some strong pruning. Only folks who are good at pruning should try their hand at it."

"Agreed. There are some clippers in the shed. Maybe you can give lessons—"

Ernie was interrupted by Delia's bloodcurdling scream. Lilly and Ernie both ran over to her. Ernie took her by the shoulders and turned her around to hold her close and try to calm her down. She screamed some more into his barrel chest, and then she started to sob. Lilly stepped around them both and looked in the shed.

Merilee Frank was lying on bags of mulch, staring up, hedge clippers protruding from her chest . . .

PRUNING THE DEAD

Julia Henry

KENSINGTON BOOKS
www.kensingtonbooks.com

To Pat Spence, who helps many gardens grow.

CHAPTER 1

Goosebush was a place where most residents preferred that folks from outside didn't know it existed. The town had squared-off borders on three sides. The fourth side encompassed the jagged coastline of the south shore of Massachusetts, including inlets and marshes, a small harbor, and the great Atlantic Ocean. The town was one of the first incorporated after the Pilgrims displaced the indigenous tribe off the land when they started to expand their settlements. The upper corner of Goosebush belonged to the tribe, a settlement of sorts that the town had arrived at after years of legal and moral delays were finally resolved at the turn of the last century. At that time, the land seemed to be useful for its views only, since it was surrounded by water, and it felt the force of Mother Nature too often to make investments in infrastructure make much sense. But in recent years, the folks who still lived on the spit of land had reseeded oyster beds and leased a portion of the bayside beach to a research institution in Boston. That thrust of activity put Goosebush in the news for a bit, a state that made a few folks cranky, but that storm soon passed.

Unlike other towns that required and benefited from being historical sites and tourist destinations, Goosebush did not. Not that there wasn't a rich history—there was—and the folks who volunteered in the Goosebush Historical Society were more than pleased to talk about that to anyone who came by during their office hours in the town library twice a month. But there were no scheduled tours or town reenactments or guidebooks available. That wasn't the Goosebush way. It made planning the quadricentennial celebrations, which were two years away, challenging. To say the least.

Besides, there are some disparities with the history. "Facts are facts, but the truth depends on the teller," the late Alan McMillan used to say. He'd married into Goosebush when he fell in love with Lilly, a descendant of one of the original settlers of the town. For many generations, the Jayne family was property rich and cash poor. But the most recent descendant, Lillian Rose Jayne, changed that by establishing herself in the finance industry, making her family and many others extremely wealthy. The Jayne family, like many Yankee families, did not flaunt their wealth. But neither did they hide it if you took a good look around Windward, their family home.

The center of Goosebush was a rotary—called a roundabout or a circle in other parts of the country and known as the Wheel in Goosebush—from which well-traveled roads flowed, each of which ended in a rotary themselves. Someone had suggested they looked a bit like a flower, when all the side roads were included, so each road was called a petal. The southern petal led to Route 3. It was mostly residential, with a couple of churches settled along it. The east petal led to the shoreline and the town beaches. North was a shortened petal, due to the filling in of a marsh years ago that resulted in a lumberyard being located there, blocking the road. The Frank family had run the lumber business for years. Pete Frank Junior, PJ to most people, had struggled in recent years to keep the business running, but thanks to some new investors, he was on his feet again. Good thing. The lumberyard employed twenty people—not insignificant in a town of Goosebush's size.

The north petal was the main drag of Goosebush and included the most desired addresses in town. It ended in the Wheel, which was as close to a commercial district as Goosebush got. The Wheel, short for Captain's Wheel, included access to the police station, hardware store (Bits, Bolts & Bulbs), Paul's Grocery Store, and Spencer's Package Store. Directly on the Wheel was the Star Café, the post office, a real estate office, the local pharmacy, and a gas station. There wasn't a single national chain store in Goosebush. Folks liked it that way.

Schools, restaurants, and other stores were between the petals. On the north petal there was one spot, across from the boatyard, with an unobstructed view of the harbor and a distant ocean view. It was a triple lot raised higher than its neighbors, set back from the street edge. If you were new to town, you could be forgiven for not thinking there was a house up there at all, so difficult was it to see from the street and through the perfectly maintained privet hedge. But Windward was there, behind the reinforced stone wall. It was named after the ship of a very long ago Jayne relative. Access to the house and garage were granted through a gap in the wall and an electric gate. Not that it was used much. At least not much these past few years.

But today the gate would be open, as would the front door. Today Lilly Jayne was hosting a garden party, and she had invited over a hundred people to come. Lilly's friend and housemate, Delia, suspected double that number would show up, since guests would likely bring their curious friends as their plus ones. Lilly thought the number was more likely to be close to fifty. Considering that her best friend Tamara's family counted as ten people, including the grandchildren, Lilly was showing a pessimism her young friend did not share. The women split the difference and ordered enough food for a hundred people, but only after Delia assured Lilly she had found a place to donate the leftovers.

CHAPTER 2

Lilly was wrestling with a rosebush in her back garden. Well, not actually the rosebush. The weeds from her next-door neighbor's overgrown garden had begun to creep over the garden wall, through her privet hedges, and into her rosebushes. Lilly hoped that the new owners cared about getting their garden under control, and soon. Rumor had it that they were moving in this weekend. Lilly would give them a day, maybe two, to settle in, and then go over to discuss the matter and offer help. She'd take blueberry cake with her. Delia's blueberry cake might win them over, even if her "gardens being a reflection of the soul of a home" argument did not. If nothing else, the food would help mitigate her cranky Yankee demeanor. Lilly was aware that she could be a formidable presence, and when she was younger, she had tried to mitigate that. Ever since she'd turned sixty, though, she didn't worry about it as much. As long as she had kindness in her heart, and she usually did, she didn't worry about how people perceived her. In fact, keeping folks off balance gave her tremendous pleasure.

She finally beat back the weeds and backed out of the bush slowly. She straightened up carefully and stretched backward, loosening her joints as best she could. Next, she rotated her hips back and forth a bit. Back in the day, she would get down on her knees, squat, stand up, and bend in all directions with great ease and no aftereffects. She was still in good shape for a woman in her mid-sixties, but she was a woman of a certain age. Attention must be paid, and her back appreciated her concern.

Lilly looked down at her arms. Minor scratches. She wasn't going to stay out much longer. There was just a bit more cleaning up that needed to be done in the garden before the party. The party. How did she ever let Tamara and Delia talk her into this?

"It will be good for you," Tamara had said, when she'd first brought the idea up to Lilly. "Let folks know you're back."

"Back from where? I grew up in this house. I traveled a lot in the past, but I've stayed put for the past few years." Since Alan got sick was the unsaid explanation.

"I was being metaphorical, Lilly. I meant you're back among society. And it's about time."

"Don't sugarcoat it, Tamara."

"I never do," Tamara said. "Do I, Delia?"

"No, you don't. That's one of my favorite things about you," Delia said. Delia had been Lilly's husband Alan's, graduate assistant. When he first got sick and everyone assumed he'd bounce back, Delia had helped him keep up with his class preparation and grading. After a few months, when it became clear he wasn't going to get better, he'd taken a leave from the university, but Delia hadn't taken a leave from Alan. She still came by every day to visit, caught him up on gossip, and supported Lilly however she could. Delia also helped Alan with his research, which allowed him to get most of the work done on his final book.

Delia was a brilliant researcher but did not get along with many people. Lilly and Alan were exceptions. When Alan died two years ago, Delia moved into the house, getting room and board in exchange for helping Lilly with repairs, shopping, and running the household. Alan had suggested the arrangement, knowing that the house was too big for Lilly to live in alone. It was the last kind thing that Alan had done for Lilly after twenty years of marital bliss. The women had become great friends despite their forty-year age gap.

Lilly took the pile of weeds and added them to the paper bag she'd been filling all day. Normally she liked to compost, but these weeds were insidious. Better to take them to the town compost pile, where they couldn't spread back into her garden. She ran her hands down the front of her legs. She was tired, but it was a good tired. The gardens were coming back after a couple of years of neglect. Some of the flowering bushes made her fight for their love, refusing to bud last summer after she'd neglected them all spring. She'd won them back over by protecting them with hay and burlap over the winter and feeding them her special fertilizer mix as soon as the ground began to thaw. She looked around and saw the color forcing itself out of the tips of the branches. She'd be rewarded with flowers this spring and summer. Her garden was welcoming her back. They were both coming to life.

There was always something to be done in the garden, which is one of the reasons she loved it. Her backyard was never going to be perfect, but she knew her attentions would pay off. Some of the time, the work she did was more of a long-term investment, like the herb garden she'd just put in and the tomato seedlings she was nurturing in the greenhouse. But sometimes, like today, the rewards were immediate. Weeds were gone. Mulch was down. The gardens looked beautiful and befitting the house they adorned.

Windward had been built over one hundred and fifty years ago. It was, at the time, the largest house in town, a Victorian monstrosity inside with elaborate gardens surrounding it. For many years, the inside of the house faded in glory, but the Jayne family always kept up with the outside. Lilly believed that gardens weren't just decorative, they were a life force. It didn't escape her notice that every member of the Jayne family died during the dead of winter, when gardens were fallow. Even Alan had rallied through the blooming season despite his illness. Sitting on the back porch, looking at the gardens, had been a tonic for him; he'd told her that every day when she took a break and went up to hold his hand while sipping her iced tea.

Lilly missed those days, hard as it had been watching the love of her life disappear. She looked over at the koi pond she'd created in his memory. Having one of his favorite statues in the middle—a modern piece made of twisted steel that looked a little like a woman from a certain angle—made her smile. She'd hated the piece when he'd bought it from a former student and had relegated it to the side of the house for years. He'd insisted on putting his hammock where he could see it. "It reminds me of you, Lilly, my love," he'd always say. Now it reminded her of him and had a place of honor in the center of her magnificent backyard.

"Earth to Lilly. Where were you?" Delia Greenway bounded down the stairs carrying two large glasses of an indefinable liquid. Delia didn't often see Lilly daydreaming. She stepped down, stood next to Lilly, and followed her gaze. Alan's pond, of course. Alan's memory still loomed large for both women. Delia hip-checked Lilly lightly and handed her a glass. "You've been out here a long time. The midday sun is strong, even if it doesn't feel it. Where's your hat?"

Lilly took a tentative sip and smiled in relief. Lavender lemonade. Phew. Lilly elected to ignore the green tint. Delia had been given to creating drink concoctions that she promised would cure whatever ailed Lilly and prevent what didn't. Some of them were delicious. Others were bracing. A few were not potable, though Delia insisted Lilly drink up. She'd only do so if Delia matched her sip for sip. Battles of will were commonplace in the Jayne house. They always had been.

"I'm coming in soon," Lilly said. "I found a few weeds that I'd missed earlier in the week."

"The weeds are growing quickly this spring, even if the rest of the plants aren't." Both women looked around. The winter had been long and brutal. Spring was always a loosely defined term in New England, but this spring had been cold and damp.

Lilly knew that real spring and summer would eventually arrive, but she had to agree. That bright green surge had yet to happen.

"I think we're ready for tomorrow, don't you?" Lilly said. The party was planned for Saturday afternoon, when the sun would be warm enough for people to be outside and enjoy the gardens. Lilly had obsessively been checking the weather, and it seemed like it was going to cooperate.

"We are. Tamara is coming over in the late morning to help us set up. Tables and linens were delivered a little while ago."

"Really? Oh dear, I didn't hear the bell. Good thing you were home."

"Friday is a half day," Delia said. Delia was still working on her masters at the university but hadn't found another mentor like Alan. Her graduate assistantship hadn't been renewed, and she was taking one class each semester. Lilly had offered to help her pay for school, but Delia had resisted. Both women were stubborn, one of the reasons they got along so well.

"Well, good thing you were here. I'm hopeless, aren't I? I lose track of everything when I'm in the garden."

"You've got the magic touch out here. That takes concentration."

Lilly smiled and nodded her thanks. "I'm thinking about putting more container gardens around the yard this summer," Lilly said. "A couple of varieties of mint, rosemary, thyme. Anything else you need for those concoctions of yours?"

"I knew I'd win you over. Don't wince like that; they're good for you. I've got a list of plants upstairs I'd love to be able to use," Delia said. She ran her finger around the condensation on her glass, not looking up. "Hey, Lil, I have a friend who could source some interesting planters for you to look at. He was telling me about them yesterday. Concrete. They're made by a local artist who's trying to figure out ways to make money with his art. If you like them, it could help him build up his confidence and maybe build his business."

"Then by all means, I'm happy to take a look," Lilly said. "I love the idea of more art in the garden."

"Thanks, Lilly." Delia looked around and had to smile. The garden had dozens of nooks and crannies with statues, painted tiles, trellises, planters, and benches that were unlike anything she'd ever seen in another garden. She knew that Lilly liked to rotate items. She'd helped her more than once, but only moving the heavy things. Deciding where things should go was not Delia's forte. If it was up to Delia, she'd line everything up in even rows and group items by color. Lilly's artistic eye was second only to her gardening skills.

Maybe third. Lilly's ability to help folks—or put things right, as she said—was her best skill, in Delia's opinion. She'd known Lilly would be willing to help her artist friend. She also knew that her friend would never feel like he was on the receiving end of charity or that his talent wasn't appreciated.

"Your phone's been ringing off the hook," Delia said. She pulled the house phone out of her pocket to hand it to Lilly, who ignored it.

"Let it go to voice mail. And stay there, for all I care. The only people who call the house phone are bill collectors, people who found my number on voter rolls, and acquaintances to whom I have not given my cell phone number." Lilly moved her hips around in a figure eight and stretched backward as far as she could, which wasn't far.

"Lil, how come you're moving your hips like that? You okay? I told you to take it easy."

"I'm hardly an invalid," Lilly said, stiffening her spine a bit. Lilly was proud that she still measured five feet ten inches tall, even now, when many of her friends had lost an inch or two. She kept active, did yoga, and ate reasonably well. Except for Delia's baked goods. Cookies were her biggest vice, and one she had no plans to give up. Life was too short. Way too short.

"So I heard," Delia said.

"Heard I wasn't an invalid? What are you talking about?"

"I was at the Star Café this morning, checking on the food for tomorrow. I went to get a cup of coffee, and folks were talking about the party. Someone asked me if you'd bagged any robbers lately. I asked what they were talking about."

"Honestly, that was years ago. I can't believe people are still talking about it."

"Good thing Ray Mancini was there. He filled me in on how you helped foil a robbery at a Christmas tree stand a few years back. He said you chased a guy who stole the money box."

Lilly laughed. "That was, what, six years ago? Probably longer. Ray was still the chief of police. Anyway, I chased him, but I didn't catch him. The kid slipped and fell on the ice. Broke his ankle. What made that story come up in conversation?"

"A few folks said that they were glad you were back in fighting form, and the adventures of Lilly became the talk of the Star for a minute. Interesting thing. Ray said he never could figure out how the kid found the only patch of ice in Goosebush," Delia said. "He remembered that it was almost forty that day."

"It was odd," Lilly said, taking another sip of her drink.

Delia watched her friend and shrugged her shoulders. How did things just happen when Lilly was around? Icy patches were only one item in a long list that Delia had questions about. But asking the questions? Where to start? She'd probably start with questions about the magical concoctions Lilly sprinkled on her gardens.

"You do have a voice mail," Delia said, looking down at the phone she was holding out to Lilly.

"Who from?" Lilly asked, not taking it.

"I don't know," Delia said. Lilly took another sip of her drink, so Delia looked through the display. "Woops."

"Woops? Who called?"

"Pete Frank," Delia said. "Sorry, I should have checked the messages. I'll erase it."

"No, give it to me," Lilly said. She punched in her code and listened to the message.

"What does he want?" Delia asked. She kicked herself. She *should* have checked the messages.

"He wanted to let me know that he heard Tamara mention the party, and that they are going to stop by," Lilly said.

"Wow, he's got some nerve," Delia said.

"He does. Always did," Lilly said. "I still can't believe he moved back to Goosebush. I thought he'd left his hometown for good."

"He says he's glad to be back, though his fourth wife—"

"Third."

"Fine, third wife, Merilee, is a horror show who hates the town. Merilee. What a joke of a name for her. Does she ever smile? Can she smile? Maybe she had bad plastic surgery that makes the scowl permanent. Kinda like the Joker."

"Merilee," Lilly said. "She is something else, isn't she?"

"You're never going to say anything mean about her, are you?" Delia said.

"I don't see what I would gain," Lilly said.

"You know she doesn't play by the same rules you do, right? She bad-mouths you every chance she gets."

"That hurts her much more than it hurts me," Lilly said. "She would be much better served to help Pete charm folks. There are a lot of long memories here. A lot of ruffled feathers. Rather than smoothing them down, she is just ruffling more."

"And how," Delia said. "Did I tell you about—"

"I do wonder why Pete moved back," Lilly said. "Why is he putting her through living here? She is so obviously miserable."

"I've heard they burned so many bridges in New York, then Boston, then Providence, that they really didn't have a lot of choice. Between his ex-wives, and her ex-husbands, Pitiful Pete and Merilee had to go somewhere. He was hoping for local boy makes good, goes home to a hero's welcome."

"Pitiful Pete?"

"That's Ernie's nickname for him. Sort of fits, don't you think?"

"Does Ernie have nicknames for everyone?"

"No, not everyone," Delia lied. Lilly didn't need to know that Ernie called her the Lovely Lillian.

"You aren't going to tell Pete he can't come, are you?"

"I'm not, no," Lilly said. She held the phone all the way out, trying to focus on the number. "Can you help me call him back? There's got to be a way, right?"

"You have a soft spot for Pete," Delia said, taking the phone from Lilly and scrolling to Pete's number. She waited for Lilly to answer before she dialed the number. "Why?"

"Ah, Delia, here's what you need to understand. Pete and I were kids when we got engaged. It was what was expected of both of us, and neither of us considered not going forward with the marriage. We were twenty-one, going into our senior year of college when we walked down the aisle. I fell into this groove of expectations, and into a life I'd never decided I wanted. Then Pete wanted out, so he left me. Guess what happened then?"

"What?"

"Rather than my life ending, it began. I moved back into this house, but I also got an apartment in Boston. I went back to school and explored a career for myself. It was glorious. And then I met Alan. If I'd stayed married to Pete, I would have missed out on Alan. That would have been a real tragedy. In a way, I owe Pete. He'd never understand that, but that's how I feel."

"I wish you and Alan had had more time together," Delia said, reaching up and putting her hand on the taller woman's shoulder, squeezing gently. Lilly reached up with her free hand and put it on Delia's for a moment, then she let go and straightened up.

"We had twenty wonderful years. That makes me luckier than most people I know. We both know that Alan would be furious if I lived in the past. Or if you did. We'll keep missing him, but we need to live life. Which, as it turns out, is awfully short. Choosing a kinder path is important. It makes the journey easier." Lilly looked over at the statue and smiled.

Delia took Lilly's glass and raised hers toward the koi pond. "You're a better woman than I am."

"No, I'm not. I see Pete with Merilee and thank my stars that I got another chance at love. Third time isn't the charm, poor man."

CHAPTER 3

The party was supposed to start at three. At two forty-five, Lilly was in the front foyer, waiting for the doorbell to ring. This area, like much of the rest of the house, had undergone a face-lift over the past two years. Lilly had found it difficult to keep still and had tackled projects like no Jayne had since the house had first been built. Floors were sanded, stained, and polished. Faded wallpaper was removed. Walls were refreshed, windows were cleaned, curtains were replaced, furniture was moved. She added her own twist, including the eclectic art and artifact collection she and Alan had acquired over twenty years of travel and adventures.

The kitchen and bathroom renovations that had been dreamed of for years finally came to fruition. Lilly didn't even attempt to be faithful to the era of the house if it meant giving up her vision. Throughout the process, Ernie Johnson, owner of Bits, Bolts & Bulbs, the local home and garden store, became Lilly's right hand. She'd known him for years, but it was during this time, the time of Lilly's deepest grief,

that Ernie became her friend. He'd lost his own
husband three years earlier and recognized the
pain in Lilly's eyes when she'd first come in to order
a new sink for the downstairs bath. He'd gently per-
suaded her that the utilitarian sink might not be the
best choice, and he helped channel her energies
with good taste. She was grateful for his help and
came in several times a week to discuss choices. She
insisted on ordering things through his store, and
he supported her efforts by connecting her to good
local tradesman who were looking for work.

Lilly had lived in Goosebush for her entire life.
She'd worked in Boston and had traveled a great
deal, but she was a Goosebush stalwart. Alan Mc-
Millan had opened her heart to joy while they
were married. In death, he'd given her a final gift.
He'd opened her up to the town of Goosebush. He
made her promise to have a big garden party every
May, around their anniversary. She'd avoided it last
year but honored his wish this year.

"I'm proud of you, Lil," Tamara O'Connor said,
gliding up to Lilly's side and grabbing her hand.
Tamara was the same height as Lilly when she was
wearing heels and had been her best friend since
they were both four years old and met at nursery
school. Tamara's short-cropped curly hair was flecked
with gray, but her African American face was unlined.
Tamara gave Lilly's hand a squeeze and held it tight.

Lilly squeezed her hand back. "I'm a nervous
wreck. I hate giving parties."

"But Alan loved them, bless his soul. He threw
some great ones. I think this is your first solo party.
Ever."

"Not ever. I've had two wedding receptions—"

"Both completely taken over by your mother. If it

weren't for Viola, you would have ordered takeout both times."

"True enough." Lilly smiled at the memory of her standing in dressing rooms trying on the dresses her mother chose, tasting food and shrugging her shoulders, knowing that the menu was already decided. "I seem to recall you standing next to my mother both times, egging her on."

"Of course," Tamara said. "Someone had to stand up for you. You still owe me. A wedding in the mid-1970s and another one in the 1990s? You came this close to fashion disasters both times. I fought to keep you classic."

"And classy. You've always been fighting that fight for me, Tam. I wouldn't have gotten through these past two years without you."

"The great thing about being friends for sixty years? You don't have to." Tamara let go of her hand and looked around the foyer. "The place looks great. Our mothers would be proud."

"They would, wouldn't they? Lord, I miss them both," Lilly said.

"So do I, so do I. Now, enough of that. We'll both start crying like babies if we keep that up. Let me look at you." Tamara stepped back and took a long look at her friend. She adjusted the pearls, moved the belt around her shirtdress so that it was centered, smoothed the blush against Lilly's cheeks. Lilly Jayne had grown into a real beauty as she aged. Finally—finally—Tamara saw a spark coming back in her oldest and dearest friend.

"Is Warwick coming by?" Lilly said. Warwick was Tamara's husband. In addition to being a high school coach, he reffed games for different leagues on the weekends.

"He's got a game this afternoon, but he'll come by afterward. Rosie is coming by with her kids."

"That's lovely," Lilly said. "I'm surprised she's venturing out so soon after Alan's birth. She must be exhausted."

"She wouldn't miss her godmother's party for anything. Besides, once she walks in here, she has a dozen built in babysitters for both Alan and Hank. She'll probably sneak upstairs for a nap."

The doorbell rang. Lilly checked her watch. Three o'clock on the dot.

"Smile, Lilly. It's showtime," Tamara said.

Pat French stood to the side of the back porch, lips curled, a determined frown on her face. While some saw the extraordinary beauty of Lilly's garden, the whimsy of its design, and the wonderful incorporation of art and artifacts from her travels with her late husband, Pat saw only waste. Lilly paid her fair share of taxes. As town clerk, Pat could attest to that fact. In fact, she paid more than her fair share of taxes, not taking the long-term-resident or senior-citizen exemptions most folks availed themselves of. It was just that, well, this garden was a huge waste of space, in Pat's less than humble opinion. Two, or possibly three, houses could fit on this lot, easily.

Pat glanced over to her left. The large garden wall was not up to town code but had been grandfathered in. The back addition to the house, including the porch Pat was standing on, was built over the course of a hundred years as the family fortune waxed and waned. There was no specific style to the house; it was just a three-story hodgepodge of architectural

imagination, with additions, porches, a greenhouse, and a widow's walk. Were Pat a less judg-
mental soul, she would've appreciated the elegance
of the furnishings, the flow of the rooms, and the
quality of the craftsmanship. But she sat in judgment, as she always did in the presence of wealth,
and tapped her foot impatiently as she watched the
crowds wind around the garden, clustering in groups
to laugh, greeting one another as old friends. Pat
would not give Lilly the pleasure of seeing her enjoy
the gardens. No, she would remain on the porch,
near the food buffet. She picked up another sandwich and darted her eyes about before sliding it
into her overstuffed pocketbook.

Delia watched Pat French slide the sandwich into
her bag and resisted the urge to call her out on it.
Instead, she channeled Lilly and went back into the
front kitchen to get more fruit punch and ginger
ale mix. She'd lost count of the guests, but there
were well over a hundred people there already.
After she refilled the punch, she'd find Lilly. It was
time for more food reinforcements. Especially if Pat
kept standing at the buffet table.

Ernie Johnson came in through the side door of
the house, depositing bags of ice in the kitchen.
"Where did that come from?" Warwick O'Connor
asked. Tamara had sent Warwick into the kitchen to
find another bottle of wine, but Warwick had gotten
distracted by the empty bags and bottles strewn
about and had stopped to clean them up. It was
part of being a high school coach. Warwick under-

stood that messes begat messes, and you needed to stay on top of them.

"I parked my delivery van out there," Ernie said. "Delia called in an order to Spencer's for more beverages and ice. Then she called me and asked me to pick it up."

"Let me help you get it in the house," Warwick said.

It took the two men three trips each to get everything loaded into the kitchen. Warwick started to load up the freezer, while Ernie sat at the kitchen table to take a deep breath. Warwick handed him a glass of water, and Ernie accepted it gratefully, taking a large sip. Warwick and Ernie were around the same age, but whereas Warwick was fit and trim, Ernie had a round belly, bad knees, and asthma.

Ernie looked around the kitchen. He had been there dozens of times and had helped Lilly design the remodel, but he had never seen the room used like this—to its fullest potential.

"Why are you stuck in the kitchen?" Ernie asked. He got up and put his glass in the dishwasher. He noticed it was full, reached under the sink to find the soap pellets, and put one in the dispenser.

"Not stuck, volunteered." Warwick said. "I got cornered by a few parents about the team's performance last year, and for Tamara's sake, I held my tongue. She sent me back here to find a bottle of wine and give me time to cool off. It's safer in here, for everyone."

"Football's a fall sport, right? Why are they still litigating last season?" Ernie asked Warwick.

"Second place isn't good enough for some folks," Warwick said, opening a beer and handing it to

Ernie. "Never mind that for a small school like ours? Nothing short of a miracle."

"I'm surprised they aren't offering families from other towns free housing if their kid plays ball for Goosebush High."

"Don't give anyone ideas," Warwick said, opening a beer of his own and taking a long swig. "You should probably head on back, help Lilly answer gardening questions. Folks have her cornered, asking all sorts of advice."

"I can only tell them what she orders," Ernie said. "How she gets her garden to grow like that? That's Lilly's special talent."

The party was supposed to end at five o'clock, but that wasn't going to happen. Lilly stepped out on her back porch and put down the last plate of sandwiches that Stan Freeland had delivered. She'd hired Stan to cater the party at Delia's suggestion. He'd responded to her panicked "We're running out of food!" call at four-thirty with quiet assurance that he would not let that happen. Lilly sighed. Running out of food? Her mother would have haunted her for days.

"Lovely party." Lilly turned to look at the owner of that deep voice, which was tinged with an Irish accent. She had to look up and saw a pair of large brown eyes looking right at her. The face was slightly lined, with a mop of gray hair that flopped over the man's brow. He swept it back with his left hand and offered her his right.

"Roderick Lyden," he said, shaking her hand. "I've just moved in next door. I hope you don't mind me crashing."

"Into the Colfer house? I didn't think you were living there yet, otherwise I would have come over to say hello. I'm so glad you came by."

"Tell me, will it always be the Colfer house? I understand they were several owners ago."

"Yes, well, the last owners, the Smythes, we didn't get along."

"So I heard. The real estate woman who sold me the house—"

"Tamara O'Connor?"

"Tamara, yes. She told me that I had to promise to take care of the gardens if I was going to buy the house. Interesting selling point."

"Tamara is a friend. The weeds from your garden have been moving into mine for years. Since she's been helping me tame them, I suspect it was in her own self-interest."

"The garden was a selling point. I think I'll enjoy gardening tremendously. My parents both did. Having a garden was one of the reasons I decided to move out of the city after I'd retired. That, and I wanted to be closer to the seaside."

"Goosebush is a good choice, then." Lilly had always lived close enough to the ocean to walk or ride her bike. She'd been landlocked a few times, on extended business trips, and always felt like she might explode inside. A daily dose of sea air was her tonic. When Alan was alive, every Sunday they would take their car down to the beach and drive on the permitted path to a secluded area with the paper, a thermos of coffee, and a picnic. They'd sit in the car, reading the paper, watching the water. When it got too cold, they'd turn the car back on to heat it up. It was a Sunday ritual she still missed but hadn't taken up again. It would hurt too much.

"You've retired? What line of business were you in? If you don't mind me asking," Lilly said.

"Not at all. I was a lawyer. International law. Came to the States thirty years ago and stayed."

Tamara came bounding up on the porch, her middle grandson on her hip. "Hello, Roddy! I'm glad you came over."

Roddy leaned down and gave Tamara a kiss on her cheek. "Thank you for letting me know about this," he said. "And who is this handsome young man?" He held his hand out, and Hank grabbed it, smiling broadly and saying hello quietly. He turned and saw Lilly, reaching both of his pudgy arms toward her. She reached over to take him from his grandmother, but Tamara turned her body aside.

"You don't want to do that, Lil," Tamara said, wrinkling her nose. "This is my grandson, Hank. He needs a diaper change. Desperately. Let me get this taken care of, and I'll be right down. Unless you want to do it, Lilly?"

"No, thanks so much for the offer," Lilly said. Though she'd never had children of her own, she'd changed hundreds of diapers in her time. Nieces, nephews, godchildren. Dozens of children called her Aunt Lilly. And now their children did as well.

She looked back at Roddy, who was surveying the backyard. "You have beautiful gardens," he said. "What an oasis."

"Thank you, but I can't take all the credit. I have some very talented friends who helped me tame the gardens back this year. I'd neglected them a bit for a couple of years, I'm afraid."

"Tell me, do your friends hire out? I could use some help."

"Do you see that man over there, by the koi

pond? The purple paisley shirt? That's Ernie Johnson. He owns Bit, Bolts & Bulbs, the local home and
garden store. Have you been there?"

"Not yet."

"Don't bother to go to a box store, go to the
Triple B. Ernie can and will match prices; more
than that, he'll connect you to folks who can help
you do the work."

"He seems like someone I should meet."

"Let me introduce you—"

"Thank you, but I've already taken up too much
of your time. I'll introduce myself, and then I'm
going to mingle and meet some more neighbors. It
was great meeting you."

Lilly watched him as he walked through the garden. He stopped to look at the different beds, bent
down to examine plants, ran his hand over the
lavender, and sniffed the fragrance. He introduced
himself to Ernie, who launched right in to showing
him the koi pond.

CHAPTER 4

Lilly walked back into the house, toward the kitchen. Stan was coming in the front door with more food.

"You're back," Lilly said.

"With four more platters of food. Sorry I keep coming in the front, Ms. Jayne, but the driveway was full."

"Call me Lilly, please. The front door is fine. It's chaos around here today. Do you need help? Warwick O'Connor is in the kitchen, and I could come out—"

"I'm all set, thanks. I'm going to head back to the Star. We've got a show tonight, so I want to make sure that's on track. Let me know if you need more food, and I'll bring it back with me."

The Star stood for Stan's Theater and Restaurant. It was more than that. On the first floor, there was a small bookstore and a café. In the back, there was a mid-priced bistro and bar that was open for lunch and dinner. On all the walls, Stan hung art from local artists, all of which was for sale. Upstairs there was more art, and a theater space that was scheduled every night with performances, readings, concerts, or meetings. The Star had been built in the old four-story Woolworth building, and Stan didn't try to pretend it wasn't an old five-and-ten-cent store. The ceilings were high and tin. The floors were pine, well worn by the thousands of feet that had trod them over a hundred years. While long-term residents of Goosebush still missed the store, few wanted to imagine life without the Star. It had become a hub of the community.

"I don't know how you do it all, Stan," Lilly said. "You're always working."

"Hey, I get all the credit, but I don't do it alone. I've got a great team. Most of my family is working for me now. Thankfully, business is going really well."

"Thankfully for all of us," she said. "I appreciate you for keeping us all fed this afternoon. I had no idea my little garden party would be so popular."

Stan laughed. "Well, I did. It's been the talk of the town all month."

"The month of May can be very boring, I guess," Lilly said. She glanced over to the stairs that led to the second floor. "Who's that young man by the stairs?"

Stan glanced over. "Benny Jacques? He's on security detail. Delia hired a couple of extra people from the Star to make sure no one took it upon themselves to wander around. Benny's been busy. Merilee Frank just tried to bully her way upstairs."

"Merilee is here?" Lilly asked. She'd been hoping she had dodged that particular bullet. Lilly prided herself on her civility, but Merilee pushed her to the limit.

"She went down the hall, to that room on the right. Stella Haywood followed her in."

"Stella? Does she work for you too?"

"She does, thankfully. She's awesome."

"That's great. Bash must be pleased that she found a good job."

"Even though they have the same last name, I can't believe they're related. She couldn't be more different."

Bash Haywood was the chief of police in Goosebush. He got the job more as a favor to his late father than based on his job qualifications. Fortunately, Goosebush was a sleepy town, and crime waves mostly consisted of bored kids breaking into summer homes and loitering at the beach. When there were bigger problems to solve, Bash came over to Lilly's for tea and conversation. These visits were their private business, and the secret to Bash's success.

"Stella's fifteen years younger than Bash. Stella took some time to find her path, but she obviously has. Listen to me, going on like this. Those trays must be heavy. What am I doing holding you up?"

"No worries," Stan said. "I don't get to see you that often, so I'm glad to have had the chance to say hello. And to offer you an invitation to the Star tonight. It's going to be quite the event—"

"I'll probably need a long nap after all of this, but thanks for the invitation. Maybe next time." They both let that hang there. Maybe next time. That had been Lilly's mantra for two years, ever since Alan died. For whatever reason, the phrase did not feel as settled for Lilly today. She shook herself and looked back at Stan. "Tell you what, I'll try to rally.

Now go take those trays into the kitchen. I'll check in with Stella."

"I'm going to save you a seat for tonight," Stan said. "Like I said, Stella's watching over Merilee. You can't miss Stella—she's got a pink mohawk these days."

Lilly's library wasn't for company. The back wall of the room was windows, and at the center was a French door that went out into the back porch, the screened-in part. Along the outside wall was a tiled fireplace, with large window seats on either side. The other walls were lined with built-in shelves that held collections of pottery, small paintings, glass, statues, busts, tapestries. All sorts of bits and pieces were on display because of their emotional resonance for Lilly. The room was right next door to the kitchen, and Lilly was the only person who used it regularly.

Lilly walked in just as Merilee Frank was picking up a piece of depression glass from the shelf. Lilly smiled at Stella and tilted her head toward the back door. Stella hustled out to the back porch but didn't move off it. She stayed within hearing distance. The Haywoods were very fond of Lilly, though Stella would never admit that aloud.

"Not even real," Merilee said to her husband. Merilee Frank was a few years younger than Pete but fought to appear even younger. Her skin strained over her cheekbones, and her eyes seemed very surprised all the time. Her lips didn't move a great deal and looked like they'd been bitten by a snake and swollen up. The ombre browns and yellows of her hair didn't even try to appear natural and were cut into an expensive bob. Her dress fit like a glove, though Lilly was certain Merilee couldn't sit down in it. She had a huge leather bag slung over her shoulder. The gaudy bling and bright color were all the fashion rage, but they both gave Lilly a headache. Lilly's style trended more toward cotton A-line dresses and sneakers, with cardigans on cold days.

Pete Frank had always been a handsome man, but his overly white teeth and dark tan showed that he was trying a bit too hard to recapture his bygone youth. He wore an untucked shirt over khakis, with a blue blazer and loafers without socks. Lilly smiled. Whenever she saw Pete, she saw a flash of the life that might have been had he not left her for Rhonda, wife number two, all those years ago. A deep feeling of relief always followed that flash.

Merilee turned and carelessly put the glass vase back on a shelf. It began to wobble, and Lilly moved quickly to steady it. Merilee walked to another bookcase and looked at the collection of vases Lilly had collected over the years.

"The glass is, in fact, very real," Lilly said, wiping Merilee's fingerprints off the purple vase. She carefully placed it back where it belonged. "Perhaps not terribly valuable, but very real. Left to me by my great Aunt Liz."

"I remember Liz," Pete said. "She was a real pistol. A suffragette, am I right?"

"You are," Lilly said. She turned to face Pete but kept a distance so he didn't feel the need to give her an awkward air-kiss. Not that she would have minded, but Merilee would have. And setting off Merilee was something Lilly tried to avoid at all costs. "Hello, Pete, nice to see you. Merilee. What a pleasant surprise."

"All this bric-a-brac, it must be a nightmare to

keep dusted," Merilee said, running her finger over one of the shelves. She looked down and made a face, then wiped the finger on her husband's arm. He had the good grace to look mortified.

"The place looks great," he said, taking a step away from his wife. "I don't remember those tiles around the fireplace. Are they new?"

Lilly turned to address Pete but tried to keep an eye on Merilee. Maybe she should have had Stella stay. "No, actually very old. There was a wooden façade that had been put there years ago. We moved it upstairs when we were doing some renovations and found the tiles. They are stunning, aren't they? They give the whole house a different feel."

"They do," Pete said. "I wonder why—"

"We didn't come here to walk down memory lane," Merilee said.

"Well then, by all means, join the party. It's out back, in the garden. Not in here," Lilly said, plastering a smile on her face. Merilee closed her purse and pushed her way out onto the porch.

Lilly followed Pete and Merilee back out to the foyer but stayed in the library to let them go onto the back porch alone. When Merilee made her appearance, the conversation stopped.

"Who does a girl have to sleep with to get a drink around here?" Merilee asked. Pete looked appropriately chagrined but gamely put his arm around his wife's shoulder, as if his presence justified hers.

After a few seconds, Lilly heard Ernie say, "The lemonade is to your left, Merilee. The stuff in the wineglasses has the kick you're looking for. Thanks for the offer, but you're not my type." Everyone laughed, and the party went back into full swing.

Delia stepped into the doorway, wiping her hands on a towel. "What just happened?" she asked Lilly.

Lilly shook her head. "Merilee's here."

"Enough said," Delia said. "I think we're all set for food. But Stan's still on speed dial just in case."

"Stan is taking good care of us," Lilly said.

The color rose on Delia's cheeks.

"Any particular reason for that?" the older woman asked.

"Stan and I are friends," Delia said.

"Friends?"

"Good friends."

"He's rescued us today. I look forward to getting to know him better," Lilly said. When Delia didn't answer her, Lilly didn't push the conversation. She'd learned over the years that Delia processed the world in her own, unique way. She'd let Lilly in, but in her own time.

"I think this is going well, don't you?" Lilly said, changing the subject.

"Too well," Delia said, surveying the party through the French doors. "We're never going to get people to leave at this rate."

"Folks do look entrenched, don't they?" Lilly said. "It's been a long time since we had a big party here at the house. I was never good at being a hostess. I ceded that to my mother, then to Alan."

"I remember that end-of-the-semester party he had, the first time I met you. I always thought you were responsible for it."

"No, those parties were all Alan. And some clever

caterers, but none as good as Stan. I just hope my gardens survive this onslaught."

Lilly and Delia both heard a loud laugh and saw Ernie, standing in the doorway, carrying two empty trays. "Leave it to you to worry about that. There have been a few of us on duty, making sure people stay on the path. Tamara and Roddy are double-dutying Merilee Frank right now. She's a bit unsteady on her feet, and Pete's ignoring her."

"Who's Roddy?" Delia asked.

"Your very handsome next-door neighbor," Ernie said. "He's out there charming everyone, including yours truly. Sadly, he's more likely to be interested in Lilly than he is in me. Story of my life."

"Handsome neighbors? Life is looking up," Delia said, elbowing Lilly in the ribs.

"Stop it, both of you. I'm well past the age where I'm interested in, or interesting to, anyone. Did he talk to you about his gardens, Ernie?"

"He did; thanks for sending him over. I told him I'd stop by and look at them this week. I also told him I'd try to talk the two of you into coming with me."

"Us—why?" Delia asked.

"Why? Lilly, you have the vision for gardens. Delia, you think creatively and can give him historical perspective about what the gardens may have looked like. Me, I know my way around getting work done. Add Tamara to the mix, and we're quite the team. It's only neighborly that we chip in and help him."

"I'm not sure—" Lilly said.

"Come on, Lilly," Ernie said. "How many times have I heard you complain about those wandering vines? You know you're dying to get your hands on those gardens. Besides, it's the neighborly thing to do."

"Well, maybe—"

Lilly was interrupted by the sight of Tamara coming up on the porch, drenched from head to toe. She made a "oh no" sound and rushed in the door, past Ernie, to meet Tamara in the hall. Delia followed her.

"What happened to you?" Delia asked, handing her the towel she'd been holding. It was not sufficient for the task, but Tamara took it and blotted her face.

"Merilee pushed me into the koi pond."

"Are the fish all right?" Ernie said.

Tamara glared at Ernie. "They're fine. That young woman with the pink hair—"

"Stella," Delia said.

"Stella? Stella Haywood?" Delia nodded. "So, she's back, is she? Anyway, Stella escorted them through the garage and then down the driveway."

"That's the long way out," Lilly said.

"But the quickest. Stella wasn't having it. She went right over, took Merilee by the elbow, and propelled her to the nearest exit. It gave me a chance to escape up here."

"Why don't you go upstairs and borrow something of mine that's dry," Lilly said.

"I'll do that," Tamara said, looking down at her drenched shoes. "Damn, first time I wore these babies." Tamara loved her shoes and wore the highest heel with a grace and ease that Lilly could never understand, never mind emulate.

"If we put newspapers in them, they'll dry out and keep the shoe shape," Delia said. "We can assess the color situation once they're dry. Let me have them."

"Delia, you are a lifesaver," Tamara said, slipping

out of her shoes and losing three inches in height immediately. Tamara picked them up carefully and hugged them to her briefly before handing them to Delia. "I'll never tell Warwick how much I spent on these, but suffice it to say, one wearing would not amortize them sufficiently."

"I still don't know how you walk in those things," Lilly said. Lilly never wore heels, ever. She wore Birkenstocks, canvas sneakers, and flat-heeled boots. She had fancier flats for events. All well-made, steadying, and supportive.

"Wearing shoes like these are the only way I can be as tall as you are, Lil," Tamara said. "I like looking at you eye to eye. And you don't stoop for anyone."

"Indeed, she does not," Ernie said.

"Did Merilee push you on purpose?" Lilly asked, ignoring them both.

"Yes, right after she accused me of having an affair with Pete," Tamara said. "As. If. What a train wreck that woman is."

"How ridiculous—"

"Right?" Tamara said, giving Lilly a meaningful glance. "Best thing Pete could do is to get rid of her. Lilly, I'm going to take you up on borrowing something dry."

"Help yourself to anything," Lilly said.

"Get rid of her? How?" Delia said, after Tamara turned to go upstairs.

"Divorce? Separation? Murder? Whatever it takes," Tamara said, turning back. "She's bringing him down, and he needs to make a move. If Warwick looks for me, tell him I'll be right down."

With that, Tamara went up the stairs, Delia went out to the porch, and Ernie went into the kitchen to drop the trays. Lilly looked around the now-empty foyer.

"Poor Pete," Lilly said. "Poor, poor Pete."

The student workers Lilly had hired to help with the party made quick work of the cleanup, and by six o'clock, Lilly, Tamara, Warwick, Ernie, and Delia were sitting on the back porch, finishing the punch, and nibbling on sandwiches.

"That food was outstanding," Lilly said, picking up a second sandwich. "Is Stan's food always this good?"

"Don't tell me you've never eaten at the Star Café?" Ernie said.

"I don't eat out that often," Lilly said. There was a pause in the room. Good friends acknowledge recent history with silence, not recriminations. Everyone in that room had invited Lilly to the Star Café dozens of times and had always gotten a polite excuse and refusal.

"This is his normal fare in the café, but he steps up his game in the restaurant," Delia said, smiling at Lilly. "Though I've got to admit, Stan outdid himself for this party. He wanted to impress you and your guests."

"Well, he did it," Lilly said. She took another bite of food and closed her eyes. "Hummus, avocado, cucumbers, and—"

"Beet relish," Tamara said.

"Beet relish? Really?" Ernie asked, picking up another sandwich and taking a bite. "This is delicious. What else is in this? Looks like mayonnaise but tastes like magic."

Tamara picked up the same sandwich, took a

bite, then pulled it apart. She shrugged her shoulders, slapped the sides back together, and took another bite. "That is the question, my friend. Delia, honey, you've got to get him to give you the recipes for that beet relish and this magic sauce. Then pass them on to me. It's so good it almost made me forget about my ruined shoes. Almost." Tamara looked down at her bare feet encased in a pair of flip-flops Warwick had had in his car. She sighed and crossed her legs. Warwick smiled at his wife. Only Tamara could make Lilly's yoga pants and sweatshirt look glamorous.

"Are you planning on making the beet relish?" Warwick said teasingly.

"No, babe, I want the recipe, so you can make it and we can all eat it," Tamara said. She nudged his knee with her foot and gave him a thousand-watt smile. Warwick was Tamara's second husband. Her first husband died right before her thirtieth birthday, leaving her with three little girls and a broken heart. She moved back to Goosebush, something she said she'd never do when she left for college. But her parents offered her a place to stay, and she needed their help. Within five years, she'd gotten her real estate license and was taking Goosebush by storm. Her business took off partly because of her personality. It also helped that her family had lived in Goosebush for generations. Over two hundred years ago, a distant relative who was a freed slave had moved to the town as a blacksmith. Later a few other African Americans had also moved to Goosebush, creating a community and adding to the rich history of the town.

Within a year, most real estate deals went through Tamara's office, rather than a chain. She brought on more business partners, but she still did a lot of the work herself. One day, twenty-five years ago, Tamara was showing the new high school coach some houses around town, and for the first time in what seemed like forever she looked at his left hand for a sign of a ring. She talked herself out of being interested at first. He was a few years younger than she was, and she came as a family unit with her daughters. But Warwick had noticed her as well and was instantly smitten. He met her girls and courted the entire family. Within a year, they were married. Since Tamara was over forty, they didn't think they would be adding to their family, but fate had other plans. At forty-two Tamara gave birth to their son Tyrone, now working on his master's degree in London. By this time, Lilly had married Alan. They were not blessed with their own children, but Lilly and Alan were Tyrone's doting godparents, and Tyrone loved them fiercely. Tamara always said he kept her young, but he had been a handful in high school, and didn't apply himself when he first went to college. It was Alan's illness that knocked some sense into Tyrone and gave him more of a purpose—to make Uncle Al proud. He e-mailed Lilly every week, and she always e-mailed him back right away. She also sent him care packages on a regular basis and encouraged him when he wanted to study abroad for the summer, even though she'd miss having him around. Tyrone had been a lifeline for Lilly in her darkest time.

Warwick and Tamara were finally empty nesters, and they had adapted to it well. Seeing Warwick and Tamara made Lilly smile. She and Tamara had been through a lot of life together, and Lilly thought of few others who deserved a happy ending more than her friend. She knew Tamara well enough to know that Merilee Frank's push was not forgotten, but there wouldn't be any retribution against Pete or Merilee from Tamara. "Keep it classy, even if it kills you," was Tamara's mantra, passed down to her from her mother, the wonderful Rose Spencer. Tamara would keep it classy, but no doubt the story was also racing through Goosebush.

"Let's double-team Stan at the Star tonight," Ernie said. "I'm putting some beets in my garden, and I'd love to be able to use them to make the relish if they come in this season."

"'If they come in,'" Tamara said. "Please. You have the magical powers over vegetables that Lilly has over flowers. Yeah, we'll double-team him. Of course, we could triple-team him if Lilly comes with us."

"I'm exhausted," Lilly said, making excuses by rote.

"We're all exhausted," Ernie said. "But this is going to be an event not to be missed."

"What is it exactly?" Lilly asked. "Some kind of poetry reading?"

"Some kind of?" Ernie said. Everyone had stopped and was staring at Lilly. "You know that Callisto Pace is going to be teaching in Cambridge next semester, right?"

"Cal is going to be teaching? I had no idea he was—"

"Cal? You call him Cal?" Delia asked. "You know him? Really?"

"Alan and I met him several years ago when Alan was doing some research in Florence. He was charming. We lost touch after that, and we haven't spoken for a couple of years. I had no idea he was in the area."

"Still is charming from what I understand," Ernie said. "He's not just in the area. He's renting the Brandon place out by the beach. He's been hanging out at the Star this spring, writing. It seems like the café inspired him; he eats most of his meals there too. Anyway, he's been working on a spoken-word performance piece and wanted to try it out. Stan talked him into a small public performance tonight. It's sold out, though, has been for days."

"Stan told me he'd save me a seat," Lilly said. "What time does it start? It's almost six-thirty."

"Eight-thirty," Tamara said. "Time enough for me to go home and get cleaned up. We'll pick you up on our way."

"I can walk from here," Lilly said.

"You can, but you probably won't. So we'll pick you up. Now, I don't want to hear it. Delia has to go in early to help Stan set up. You're coming with us," Tamara said. "Take a nap. Fix your face. By the way, I want an introduction to your friend Cal. Maybe he should buy instead of rent a place here in Goose-bush."

CHAPTER 5

The Star Café took up the most real estate of the Wheel. The old Woolworth had been the largest store in all of Goosebush for many years. It was in business until the mid-eighties, a four-story mecca where folks went to get their hardware, yarn, goldfish, stationery, health and beauty products, fabric, and other assorted sundries that made life easier. The lunch counter at the back of the store was the place to go for great diner food, and the ice cream parlor in the front was legendary for its homemade sauces. Those who remembered the old Woolworth still missed it. Some of the functions of the old five-and-ten-cent store had been replaced by several smaller shops, including Ernie's store a block away. But now there was no fabric store in Goosebush, and the closest yarn shop was two towns away. If you wanted a goldfish, you had to drive at least forty minutes.

Soon after the Woolworth closed, there was talk about leveling the old building and making it into "new and modern" shops. Lilly had been part of a movement to stop that path to progress, which would have paved over much of Goosebush's past and turned it into square stores with no unique personality. Sure, the old buildings could be challenging to operate a business out of, and many needed renovations to make them more accommodating, but they all had stories to tell. Stories that would get lost in the name of progress.

Lilly's mother was still alive then, and together they were a formidable duo, wearing down the most resistant members of the board of selectmen into submission. The old Woolworth building was deemed a historical site, and the town took over the upkeep and rental of it. For twenty years, it was used as a de facto town hall, with Christmas bazaars, book fairs, and different types of markets. Community theaters rented it for a reasonable rate. The building was maintained through a small fund that Lilly and her mother, Viola, established.

Three years ago, when Goosebush was five years away from the four-hundredth anniversary of its incorporation as a town, the board of selectmen was making decisions on how to mark the occasion. A historian had come to visit in preparation for writing a town history and had remarked on the faded beauty of the old stores on the Wheel.

"Faded beauty," Tamara O'Connor had remarked at a town meeting after the report on the costs of having the written history of Goosebush made into a book had been voted on. "Faded beauty. Is that how we want our town to be known, as a place of faded beauty? I, for one, am grateful that we are still a small town with the charms of our history still apparent. I, for one, am grateful that we have such strict zoning laws that our town character has remained, albeit by force when necessary. I, for one, am proud to be part of a family that has been in Goosebush for over two hundred years. But I do not like the idea of faded beauty in our beautiful town. It's high time we created a committee to spruce things up a bit and tend to our history. Who's with me?"

As it turns out, most of the town was with Tamara. A committee was indeed formed, but town funds were not diverted to the effort. "They just aren't there," Pat French had said at every town meeting from then until now. She'd point to the meticulous financial reports she provided at every town meeting to show where the funds were being spent. It was often said that if Viola Jayne were still alive, or if Lilly Jayne was around more, there would have been a lot more conversation around raising funds for the beautification and preservation of Goosebush. But Viola had been gone for years, and Lilly had been taking care of Alan, and then barely left her house after he died, so a fuss was not made.

But that didn't mean that the old Woolworth building was left to go to rack and ruin. Stan Freeland had lived in Goosebush for a few years, having come to the small town as an artist in residence for a year at the local museum. After his residency was done, he decided to stay. His work continued to sell, but he'd come to realize that he would need to do more to support his life as an artist. He had no desire to teach. Three years ago, he had rented the old Woolworth building for an exhibition and invited a friend to run a small café while his show was up. He revamped the old lunch counter and used the ice cream parlor to make coffee. Folks had flocked to the building. Stan knew that it was as much because of having a pleasant place to drink coffee and eat fresh baked goods as it was his art, and he decided to do more with this powerful combination. He signed a long-term lease with the town, and the Star Café was born.

On the first floor of the Star Café, there was a small bookstore that also carried stationery, board games, and some handcrafted items. The store was to the left as you walked in, and the café to the right. The back half of the store was blocked off by bookcases that went almost to the tin ceilings, with a two-foot gap upon which Stan placed a regularly rotated grouping of sculptures and other art pieces. Behind the bookcases, the old lunch counter had been turned into a bustling bistro with a retro vibe that opened at eleven o'clock in the morning for lunch and stayed open until ten o'clock at night. The menu was simple, the beer was local, and the décor was eclectic. It featured the work of local artists, all for sale.

Upstairs, Stan had created a small theater space. He'd taken out the ceiling between the second and third floor to make the room larger. The walls were all black, with a simple lighting grid on the ceiling. He provided chairs for an audience of fifty. A local community theater used the space four times a year. Additionally, it hosted readings, small solo performance pieces, karaoke nights, and music performances of all sorts. There was a lot of music at the Star Café, and its reputation for fostering new performers was growing.

Tonight, Stan had to rent extra chairs for the theater. He'd also set up some small café tables and hired extra staff from the restaurant to serve beer, wine, and snacks. Normally a poetry reading would not guarantee a packed house, but this was not a normal poetry reading. Callisto Pace was a well-regarded poet who rarely, if ever, did public readings. But he had become quite a fan of the Star Café and had been inspired by some of the artists he'd met. Rather than a regular reading, Cal decided to try out a multimedia performance piece he'd been working on. He agreed to do it as a fundraiser for Stan and the programming he was trying to do at the Star Café.

While Stan was working on renovating the space, Lilly had kept up with the work through Tamara and Delia. Though she was distracted and not involved with life outside her house at the time, stories of what Stan was doing had perked her up a bit. Lilly had a fund, a secret fund, that she used to help people like Stan do good things for Goosebush. She was a secret angel of many projects in her town, but the only people who knew that were Delia, Tamara, and Ernie. In the last three years, Lilly had been less involved than she might have been, but when Tamara told her that Stan needed help, Lilly wrote a check. But still, she hadn't stepped foot in the building until the night of Cal's poetry reading.

Walking into the Star Café that night, Lilly realized she needed to get out more often. The Star Café was alive. Lilly felt the energy as soon as she walked in. She inhaled deeply, half expecting to detect the musty smell of the old Woolworth. Instead she smelled coffee, books, faint traces of food, and people. It was not unpleasant. At all. She paused to look around. The old ice cream parlor was now a coffee bar, but the homage to its past was there, and Lilly pictured herself and Tamara there as young girls who had been allowed to walk into town to get an ice cream cone. She didn't wallow in memories for too long and followed Delia deeper into the building.

The staircase to the second floor was to the right, behind the coffee bar. The treads were wide, wooden, and worn. In the past, those stairs had been hidden behind a door, with a wall closing them up. Now they were a feature of the space. Back in the day, the second floor had been fabric, yarn, and other sundries. But now? Lilly was underwhelmed when she got to the top of the stairs. This is where the box office was located, along with the concession stand. There was no theatrical magic in the plain, functional lobby. Warwick went over and picked up their tickets. Sure enough, Stan had held one for Lilly, though they weren't sitting together. They went in to take their seats.

Here was where the magic lived, and when she walked into the theater, Lilly paused to catch her breath. Though simple in décor, a true black box, the room was artistically lit with a play of lights and shadows, creating an illusion of space and a place for endless possibilities. Delia stood up and gestured to Lilly. Their table was toward the front, but off to the side. Tamara and Warwick sat down a couple of tables over. Tamara caught Lilly's eye, and tilted her head backward. Lilly followed the motion and saw Pete and Merilee two rows back. There was an empty bottle of wine at their table, and a waiter was opening a new bottle. Lilly looked away, not wanting to catch Pete's eye. Poor Pete.

Lilly looked around and recognized most of the people in the room. Many of them had been at her house that afternoon. But there were a few who hadn't been there. One, Kitty Bouchard, hadn't been invited. Lilly caught Kitty staring at her and locked eyes until Kitty finally looked away. Kitty was, in Lilly's opinion, a piece of work. She'd married into Goosebush. Her husband, the late Bart Mallow, had been forty years her senior. Smitten by her great beauty, blond locks, and effervescent personality, Bart had showered his young wife with affection and all of his worldly goods, much to the consternation of his nieces and nephews, who had always assumed that they would be remembered in old Uncle Bart's will. Instead, Kitty had gotten it all. If rumors were to be believed, she'd also done a good job of running through Bart's fortune in the ten years since his death.

It wasn't because of her marriage to Bart that Lilly didn't like Kitty. It was Kitty's attempt to find a second husband in Goosebush, regardless of his current marital status, that bothered Lilly. Lilly knew of two marriages that Kitty had come close to destroying, and she was sure there were more. Kitty was in her mid-forties, but like Merilee Frank, she resisted the ravages of age by availing herself of expensive creams, occasional surgeries, and regular injections of Botox. Lilly was not an unkind person, but once in her bad graces, there you stayed.

Ernie arrived at the same time the waiter did, and he took it upon himself to order for the entire table. "You don't mind, do you?" Ernie asked. "I happen to know that Stan has an excellent Malbec I'd love you to try, and the flatbread pear and Gorgonzola pizza is sublime."

"No, please, I leave this to you," Lilly said.

"You've never steered me wrong on food, wine, or plants," Delia agreed. "I've been meaning to try that flatbread, but always wondered about the combination."

"It's divine, I promise. I wonder who Stan is going to seat with us," Ernie said, looking at the fourth seat at their table.

"Maybe Stan himself?" Lilly said.

"No, Stan never sits during events. He's too nervous," Delia said. "The show's sold out, so someone will be joining us, I'm sure."

"If so, we can get a fourth glass," Ernie said, looking around the room. "Who's missing, anyway? Seems like everybody who's anybody is here. Most of the poet's posse, anyway."

"Poet's posse?" Lilly asked. Lilly was never one to gossip, at least she told herself that. But she'd fallen out of many current event conversations about Goosebush, and she needed to catch up. Today had taught her that. She had to stop letting life pass her by.

"If I'd known you knew him, I would've told you that Callisto Pace was in town months ago," Delia said. "He's quite the ladies man."

"Always was," Lilly said.

"Well, Goosebush has not seen the likes of Callisto Pace in a long time, if ever," Ernie said. "Seriously, it's been like watching a soap opera. I've been eating more meals here, hoping to see the latest chapter of the show unfold. I'll give him this; if he's half as good a poet as he is a flirt, this is going to be a world-class reading."

"Don't you know his poetry?" Delia asked. "He's wonderful. Seriously, this is a thrilling opportunity—"

"You get thrilled by one opportunity, I get thrilled by another," Ernie said. "Poetry isn't my thing, usually, but if anyone can change my mind, it's probably Callisto."

"Sounds like Cal hasn't just been flirting with the women in town," Lilly said.

"Like I said, he's a world-class flirt. Straight as they come, but charming nonetheless. I've always been a sucker for charming men," Ernie said.

"As have I," Lilly said, patting Ernie's hand. "As have I."

She'd barely gotten the words out when the occupant of the fourth chair arrived. It was her new neighbor—what was his name again? As if sensing her need for name salvation, he leaned forward and stretched his hand across the table, offering it to her.

"Ms. Jayne, twice in one day. A fortunate day indeed. Roddy Lyden, your new neighbor."

"Of course, lovely to see you again. I believe you met Ernie at the party? This is Delia Greenway—"

"I've met them both, thanks to your wonderful party," Roddy said. "Thank you again for allowing me to crash. I suspect the introductions I got today would've taken me months otherwise. It's challenging moving to a new place and not knowing anyone."

At that moment, the waiter arrived with the wine. Rather than send him back for another glass, Delia went to fetch one. Lilly looked at Roddy and considered what he had said. He was right; moving to a new place at this stage in their lives would be challenging. She didn't think she'd be so brave. No, she'd left Goosebush for a while and traveled while her husband was alive. But Goosebush was, and always had been, home. She found herself hoping that Roddy liked it, but before she could think too much about her feelings, Delia came back with the glass, Ernie poured the wine, and Lilly found herself clinking with her tablemates.

A few minutes later, Stan stepped onto the stage

to introduce Callisto Pace. The poet had walked in behind Stan and stood to the side of the room, his hands holding a large notebook, his head down as he listened to the introduction. At one point, he looked up and gazed around the room. His eyes fell on Lilly, and he moved toward her.

"Good to see you, love," he said, squatting down beside her. "I'd completely forgotten, this is your town. I half expected you to be in Boston. We need to catch up. First, let me do this." He gave her a kiss on the cheek and stood up, sliding back to his waiting place.

Lilly felt her color rise and quickly looked around. Everyone was looking at her. The poet knew the town recluse. She had no doubt that she would be the fodder for much gossip over the next twenty-four hours. For the first time in her life, she didn't mind.

Cal walked onto the stage after Stan's introduction. He dove right into a poem, one of his older pieces. His deep baritone, slight lilt, and tremendous stage presence captured everyone in the room. You could hear a pin drop.

Cal took a deep breath, soaking in the adulation. He'd forgotten how much he enjoyed doing these readings. How much an audience meant to him. He hoped that they would be as transfixed when he got into his newer stuff. He was still nervous about that.

He did a few more of his older pieces, speaking a bit between them, talking about his process, his life, the source of his poems.

"But now, thanks in no small part to the magic of your lovely town, I've been inspired to try something new. Molding words has been my inspiration for years, but Goosebush has changed that a bit. You all know how lovely it is here, right?" A murmur of soft laughter encompassed the room. Residents of Goosebush did indeed know how beautiful it was there. They did their best to keep that secret to themselves, so as not to spoil it. "Between the town and sitting in this café and seeing the art that Stan has put up, I've been inspired to work with visuals. My paint box is this," Cal reached into his back pocket and pulled out his phone, holding it above his head, "and I've had some help in figuring out how pictures and words can come together. I'd like to show you some of the work I've done."

Stan and one of the waiters pulled a screen into the room and set it up behind Cal. Stan took a remote and pointed to the ceiling. A light flicked on, and he and the waiter adjusted the screen to fit the light box. Stan stepped to the side, and Cal stepped into the pool of light.

"I'm imagining that this will always be a live performance piece, a series of images narrated by me. Some of you have seen me around town, holding up my phone, snapping pictures. You've also seen me other places, doing the same thing. A few of you have even been kind enough to pose for me, as I explore my art. Without further ado, here it is."

For the next ten minutes, the room was completely silent while Cal recited a long poem. After a couple of minutes, Lilly realized that Cal would need to rethink this as a method to deliver his poetry. No one was paying attention to the words. But they were paying attention to the scenes of Goosebush, a Goosebush most people never saw. Or rather, never paid attention to. The trash left in a pile at the beach. The pulp of a tortured horseshoe crab. The overgrown weeds around the flagpole. The ruddy cheek of a man as he sipped a beer. An age-spotted hand carrying a grocery bag. Jeans-clad legs wearing worn canvas sneakers standing by while a dog peed on a doorstep. Dozens of body parts flickered on and off the screen. Including, briefly, naked flesh. The people in the images weren't recognizable per se. But the intimacy of many of the photographs could not be denied. If Cal was exploring expanding his art into photography, Lilly could not deny his talent.

When he was done, there was a stunned silence for thirty seconds. Then Roddy started to clap and called out "Bravo!" The rest of the crowd followed suit, though with somewhat less enthusiasm than Roddy had shown. Lilly looked around and noticed that Pete and Merilee were among those not clapping. Kitty Bouchard got up and left quickly, overturning her chair. Lilly looked over at Cal, who watched her go, a small smile of satisfaction on his face.

Cal read a couple more poems, thanked the audience for coming, and left the room.

"Well," Ernie said, "that was something." No one at their table had moved yet.

"It was indeed," Lilly said. "I can't help but feel as though I've been a Peeping Tom on some intimate moments. I've known his work and felt that way about his poems. But some of those photos were—"

"Very intimate," Delia said. "Did you see Kitty Bouchard leave? I think she was one of the naked ladies."

"Really?" Lilly asked.

"They've been having an affair on and off all spring," Ernie said. "More off than on lately. Three weeks ago, she threw a glass of wine in his face at dinner. He just laughed and kept eating."

"Not the first glass of wine he's had tossed in his face," Lilly said.

"Sounds as if you know that firsthand," Roddy said.

"I've known Cal for a long time," Lilly explained. "My late husband was a professor, and we traveled a lot, met many interesting characters along the way. Cal has always been charming, incredibly talented, and great fun to spend time with. He is a great artist. He can also be a selfish man, with a cruel charm. That I don't know firsthand. Far from it. Cal thought the world of Alan and has always been lovely to me. But I've seen the wake he's left. If I'd known he was here, maybe I could've—no, probably not. You can't warn people about the likes of a Cal Pace. Folks convince themselves that it will be different this time or that they can change him."

"He seems quite fond of you," Roddy said.

"I suspect he is. I'm the wife of his friend. Never was, and never would've been a conquest. I suspect for men like Cal I'm a bit of a relief, a woman who sees right through him and likes him anyway." Lilly drained her glass, and the others followed suit. They all stood up to leave, Roddy and Ernie leading the way, deep in conversation about some tools Roddy needed to start a new project.

"What did you think of the show?" Delia asked Lilly. "I loved it, but I also hated it, you know? Goosebush looked pretty grim."

"He showed a different truth about our town, one that I have never considered. The show made me feel—unsettled is the best word I can come up with. Still, I feel as if I've seen a bit of genius," Lilly said. "Dangerous genius, but genius."

CHAPTER 6

Lilly, Roddy, Delia, and Ernie walked down the stairs. A few people were milling about, making no move to leave the building. Tamara was waiting for Lilly at the bottom of the stairs.

"Let's have dessert in the restaurant," Tamara said.

"It's late," Lilly said.

"It's Saturday night, not even ten o'clock. Live a little," Tamara said. She took Lilly by the elbow and steered her toward the restaurant. The rest of the group tagged along. Delia held back a bit and made sure that Roddy followed. As they walked back behind the bookcases, Stan greeted Tamara and Lilly with a big smile. "You talked her into it," he said to Tamara. "I'm glad. Welcome, Ms. Jayne. I'm so glad you're finally here."

"You know, Stan, Tamara and I spent a great deal of our misspent youth in this building, when it was a Woolworth. That was what, fifty years ago?"

"Hush now with those numbers," Tamara said.

"I brought you in your stroller," Lilly said, smiling

at Tamara. "Anyway, I love that you didn't change the layout of this floor. The coffee counter is where the ice cream parlor was. This is where the lunch counter was—"

"Truth to tell, I kept the layout because it made economic sense. Moving the kitchen would have cost a fortune. We decided to pay homage to the past and keep as much of the old charm as we could. Why not? Tin ceilings, wonderful wood floors, built-in cabinetry here and there. I couldn't have asked for a better building to launch this crazy dream of mine."

"Well, I can't get over how wonderful it is. I'm sorry it's my first visit. I promise it won't be my last. I look forward to seeing this restaurant. I wonder, is there a table available for us?"

"Absolutely," Stan said. "Right over here, this corner booth. Let me bring over a couple more chairs. The specialty tonight is cobbler with fresh ice cream."

Stan led them over to the booth, and everyone sat down. Was this booth from the old lunch counter? Lilly couldn't tell for sure, but it looked like it. Refinished, of course. She looked around and had to smile. The ghost of the old lunch counter was there, but the spirit of the new restaurant was wonderful. Lilly turned to speak with Delia, but she'd given her seat to Roddy and was over talking to Stan. Ernie sat on Lilly's other side.

"The specialty is always cobbler," Ernie said to Lilly and Roddy. "Depending on the time of year, it's a different type of cobbler. Sometimes it's a cobbler you've never heard of. But trust me, you want the cobbler. Not sure what is in the crust, but it's divine."

"Sounds perfect," Lilly said. The waiter took the coffee orders and went to get their cobblers. Lilly looked around the room, packed with full tables and a double row of people drinking at the bar. She recognized a few folks from upstairs, but not many. She did see Pete and Merilee over in the corner, yet another bottle of wine on the table. Again, she averted her eyes.

"Pete and Merilee are here," Lilly said to Tamara, as much to warn her as to start a conversation.

"I should give her a bill for my shoes," Tamara said.

"Not tonight, sweetie," Warwick said. "Maybe Monday, at work, you can give it to Pete. Tonight, let's just have a good time."

"What a surprise, they're holding court again," Ernie said. "They practically live here. They must spend a fortune at this place."

"More like cost a fortune," Delia said, sitting down at one of the chairs at the end of the booth.

"What you mean?" Ernie asked.

"Never mind," Delia said, shaking her head. "Tamara, I know you work with Pete, and that you and Lilly have known him a long time, but I hate his wife. I know, I know, I shouldn't hate. But I do. I don't even feel bad about it." Delia looked around the table defiantly.

"She's easy to hate," Tamara said, shrugging. "She's a hot mess is what she is."

"Ladies, let's not let Merilee Frank ruin our night," Warwick said. "Pretend she's not here. The cobbler will be here soon, and I want to enjoy it."

"I'm going to try to, but I'm going to confess, I'm still thinking about some of those photographs from the show," Ernie said. "That was a pretty unsettling poetry reading. Not what I expected."

"Which pictures bothered you? The naked ones?"

Delia teased Ernie. Lilly smiled. Ernie was old enough to be Delia's father, but their relationship was more like siblings. They teased each other and argued incessantly, but they also held each other in very high regard.

"No, believe it or not, not the naked ones. Unlike you, my dear Delia, I do not dwell upon naked flesh. Oh, go ahead, deny it," Ernie said, smiling at Delia, who was blushing furiously. "No, I'm thinking about the pictures that made Goosebush look like every other town. He really dwelled on the underbelly, don't you think? The trash on the beach was particularly upsetting."

"Isn't there another beach cleanup day scheduled this month?" Tamara asked.

"There is. Three weeks from now. I wish there didn't have to be all these public cleanup parties," Ernie said. "Seems like a good job for somebody, going by and cleaning up the beach. There are folks who need the work, but—"

"No funds," Warwick and Tamara finished Ernie's sentence for him.

"The gospel according to Pat French," Ernie said. "I, for one, am sick of it. The flagpole looks terrible—"

"We should take care of that some weekend, Ernie," Delia said. "You supply the plants, I'll supply the labor. I know Stan will help."

"Good idea, but we'll probably need a permit from Pat," Ernie said.

Lilly laughed, but then stopped and looked around. No one else had cracked a smile. "Come on. A permit for weeding?"

"You laugh, Lilly, but this is dead serious. Pat has this town so tied up with permits and fines that folks are afraid to move. It took us three months to get permission to clear that public lot near my store. Between paying for proper disposal, guaranteeing that I'd looked for the owners of the garbage, and a hefty deposit for rodent abatement, it cost me a small fortune. I'm still not sure that come cleanup day, she isn't going to throw another wrench in the works."

The waiter came and served the cobbler all around, and everyone dug in. Lilly closed her eyes. Yum. Peach cobbler, not too sweet. Some kind of herb mixed in with the fruit. Ernie was right, the crust was to die for. Lilly took a small taste of the ice cream, vanilla with a hint of ginger, and then went back for a bigger spoonful. Delicious.

"Which public lot near your store?" Lilly asked.

"That parcel of land right across the street," Ernie said.

"You mean Alden Park?" Lilly asked. She turned toward Delia. "Is that why you were asking me questions about Alden Park?"

"That's why," Delia said, wiping the corner of her mouth. "I had to prove that that land had, historically, been used as a public park to the board of selectmen at the last town meeting. Next up, we need to get them to agree to let us do work on it."

"What kind of work?" Lilly asked. She took another bite of her cobbler.

"For starters, we're going to clear the land," Ernie said. "The tall grasses have become a teenage hangout spot during the day and a rat habitat at night. Honestly, if the rats hadn't started crossing into other people's yards, we probably wouldn't have gotten permission."

"Rats?" Lilly shuddered.

"The rats aren't that bad, but they did help make the point. Not good for Goosebush's image, rats running across the street at night. Anyway, Delia's research helped to show what the park used to look like, and folks got on board."

"Delia's research?" Roddy asked. He turned toward Delia, but she was focused on her cobbler, moving the ice cream to one side of the dish, the cobbler to the other.

"Delia was my late husband's research assistant," Lilly said. "He always said that she had a genius for research, and he was right. Her talent isn't useful only for academic fields though."

"Thank heaven for that," Tamara said. "More than once she's helped me find the history of the house I'm trying to sell. Adds a lot to be able to tell a story about a property, and there are a lot of stories in Goosebush."

"A lot of stories," Warwick said, nodding. "Sweetie, are you going to finish your ice cream?" he asked Tamara.

"It's all yours," Tamara said, sliding her dish toward him. "Warwick has a few students from the high school coming by to help with the cleanup."

"Ernie, let me know if you need more volunteers," Warwick said.

"We're in pretty good shape," Ernie said. "As long as we get past the town meeting on Thursday."

"Town meeting?" Roddy asked.

"That's how we work here in Goosebush. We have a board of selectmen, but everything comes up for a vote at a town meeting," Warwick said. "Democracy at work. It can be a beautiful thing, but it can also be a nightmare."

Roddy laughed. "How often do you have them?"

"There's one called for every month," Tamara said. "But sometimes there are special meetings called. Thursday is a special meeting about Alden Park, so that the use of the park can be discussed."

"Use of the park? Beyond being a park?" Roddy said.

"It's prime real estate," Delia said. "Some folks want to build on it—"

"That's not going to happen," Ernie said.

"It comes up at every meeting, and we'll keep voting it down," Delia said. "Most of the arguments now are about what type of garden to put in there. You'd be surprised, but gardening discussions can get pretty heated."

Lilly had stopped eating and looked around the table at her friends. "This sounds like a huge project," Lilly said. "Why haven't I heard about it?"

"We tried to tell you a few times, but you shut down the conversation," Delia said.

"I never—"

"You did so," Delia said. "I asked you if you wanted to be part of a town gardening project, and you said no."

"Well, that doesn't—"

"I asked you three times to be on the Beautification Committee. You said no, three times," Tamara said.

"You know I hate committees," Lilly said.

"They're the only way we're getting things done these days," Tamara said.

"Well, maybe if you'd explained—"

"Don't even start with me," Tamara said. "You've driven or walked by Alden Park almost every day. How have you not noticed how trashed it is?"

Lilly didn't respond, because she had nothing to

say. She hadn't noticed how Alden Park looked lately, not for years. "This is terrible. When I think about Alden Park, I see it as it was twenty years ago, when my mother was still alive and spent a few hours a month there with her garden club. I can't even picture it now." Lilly sat back in her seat and put her napkin beside her bowl. She sighed deeply.

"Lilly, you haven't been yourself these past few years," Tamara said gently. "We've all been giving you space since Alan died, maybe too much space. My old friend, Lilly Jayne, she never would've driven by that place more than three times without starting to fuss about cleaning it up."

"Who are you calling old?" Lilly said. She picked up her napkin and tossed it at Tamara. It landed on Ernie's empty dish. He picked it up, folded it, and put it on top of his own. Then he turned to Lilly.

"Lilly, we've got a group of folks who are going to clean up Alden Park, and then figure out what to do with it. Would you like to join us? You can start by coming to the town meeting on Thursday," Ernie said.

Lilly looked around the table. With the exception of Roddy, these people were her nearest and dearest friends. They'd been patient with her, nursed her through her grief, shared it in many ways. She thought about Alan, and how unhappy he would be that she hadn't noticed that Alden Park needed to be cleaned up. She shook her head, willing the fog she'd been living with to finally clear.

"I'm in," Lilly said. "I'll come to the meeting on Thursday. Delia, you'll need to catch me up. I hope you have notes so you can do that." Delia nodded, and Lilly laughed. "I'll join your damned Beautification Committee, Tamara. But I warn you, you may be sorry you asked, because I've got some opinions. Now, tell me about—"

Lilly was interrupted by the sound of glasses breaking. Everyone turned toward the noise. Merilee Frank had crashed into a waiter as she staggered out of the restaurant. Pete Frank had followed behind his wife and grabbed her by the waist so she wouldn't fall.

"Whoops," Merilee said, laughing loudly. "Oh Stan, you should clean that up. That's a real hazard, right there. Someone could slip and fall and sue you." She laughed again, and Pete dragged her out.

"Thanks for dinner," Merilee said over her shoulder. "See you tomorrow."

Lilly looked around. She found Stan standing by the kitchen door, watching them go. She saw a look on his face that she never expected. A look of pure hatred.

CHAPTER 7

Lilly got to the town meeting late, not to be dramatic, but because she had had a slight panic attack right before she left the house. Delia hadn't tried to pretend that Lilly wasn't having _it_, nor did she make a fuss. Instead, she made her friend a cup of tea, forced her to sit down and drink it, and talked to her about what she'd been able to find out so far about Alden Park. She also asked Lilly questions about what she remembered from when she was a little girl and asked what her mother's garden club was like and who else was in it. Delia took copious notes.

The cup of tea did its job. Also, the talk of the Alden Park of the past made Lilly more determined than ever to make sure it came back. She'd taken a trip to Ernie's store on Wednesday and forced herself to walk over to the park and really look at it. She could barely see the shadow of what it had been, it was so neglected. She'd come home and taken a nap; it was that bad.

Delia poured the rest of Lilly's tea into a travel

mug and packed herself a water bottle and some snacks. She'd learned the hard way that these meetings could go long. Very long. Ernie said they were designed as endurance tests for democracy.

By the time they got to the school gymnasium, the room was almost full. The bleachers on one side had been pulled out, with tables in front where the board of selectmen could sit. The meeting was just coming to order when Lilly and Delia came in. Ray Mancini paused, giving them a chance to be seated. There were seats at the top of the bleachers, but Lilly didn't like to climb bleachers. Instead Lilly and Delia found space dead center, in the first row. The six people sitting at the tables stared at Lilly, as did several people in the stands. Lilly had served on the board of selectman for years and was known around town. She'd also been missed in these meetings for a lot of reasons, and several people sat up a little straighter now that she was in the room. Lilly had that effect on people. Lilly looked at the town clerk sitting at one end of the tables up front and gave her a huge smile.

Pat French could barely hide her contempt. She'd always considered Lilly an entitled interloper, though she'd never admit that publicly.

Tamara, the newest member of the board of selectmen, beamed. Her ally on the board, retired police chief Ray Mancini, breathed a sigh of relief with the knowledge that the vote he'd estimated to be three to two could now be swayed, depending on what Lilly said or did. He wished he'd known she was coming; he would have made sure to have a conversation before the meeting.

Part of the meeting was listening to presentations of five proposals for Alden Park. To Lilly's surprise,

Stan was one of the presenters, suggesting a few community vegetable gardens around the edge of the park. Other proposals had water features, complicated paths, and dog-walking areas, and one even had a small amphitheater. Lilly didn't love any of them. For the umpteenth time that week, she wished she'd been more focused on what was going on around her these past few months. Years. But, as always, before she allowed herself to wallow for too long, she heard her mother's voice telling her, "What's done is done, and the only opportunity you have now is to do better." She would do better.

Pat French stood up and took the mic that the presenters had been using. She stood in front of the tables and addressed the crowd.

"And how, I will ask again, do we intend to pay for the upkeep of this park, never mind the initial work? Any one of these designs costs serious money, money we don't have. In addition—please, be quiet and let me speak—in addition, none of these designs are historically accurate. As you know, in my role as town historian—"

"Nobody gave you that job," a voice piped up from the middle of the crowd. Lilly turned, and couldn't see the speaker, though she recognized the voice. Portia Asher was here. Good.

"I've taken on the role as part of my job as Town Clerk. I take great pains to ensure that historical accuracy is maintained in the town of Goosebush," Pat said loudly. "Once again, I ask the board to table this discussion until—"

Ray Mancini stood up and went around the tables, taking the mic away from Pat. Ray, Tamara, and Lilly had gone to school together, and it always amazed her that he looked exactly the same as he had in high school. He had neither grown into his looks nor aged past them. He was just, as always, Ray. He glanced over at Lilly and smiled. She smiled back.

"Let's take the second point Pat made first. Historical accuracy. Now, a few of us grew up in Goosebush and can probably help come up with drawings of what it was. I don't necessarily mean that's what it should be now. But I'm just saying, as a point of reference, we can remember what was. Lilly Jayne, I'm going put you on the spot here. Nobody knows gardens like you do. Would you be willing to be on the committee to help draft up these memories?"

"Well, of course—" Ray walked over and handed the mic to Lilly, who stood up and turned to face the folks in the room. "For those who don't know me, my name is Lilly Jayne. I live over on Washington Street. I love gardens." Most people laughed. Even if they didn't know Lilly personally, everyone knew her house. And about her gardens. "I'm happy to serve. I'd also like to make a suggestion. My friend Delia Greenway is one of the best researchers there is. She's been considering the history of different parts of Goosebush for years. I imagine she can put together the history of Alden Park, what it used to look like, and what the original intent of it was. Delia, do you think that's possible?"

Delia looked up at Lilly from under her dark bangs and through her dark, horn-rimmed glasses. She nodded and smiled.

"I can do that—" Pat said.

"You have so much going on, so much on your plate, that you could use some help. That's not your official job anyway, is it, Pat? Your official job is to keep track of the taxes and fines and fees in this town, and let us know how the income is," Ray said. "What do you think, Lilly?"

"It seems to me if we're going to get this town back into shape in time for the quadricentennial, we have to find some money for these special projects and get some sort of plan in place. I'll admit I haven't had a chance to look over your reports for a few years, Pat, and I look forward to catching up. But even if it ends up being something we have to raise money for, that's a plan. Lack of money in Goosebush cannot be why we don't clean up Alden Park. There's money here in town; we just need to know who to ask." Lilly handed the microphone back to Ray.

Portia Asher stood up, and Ray walked over and handed her the microphone. Portia was one of the town elders and also a retired principal. Everyone stopped talking to listen to her. "Seems to me that one good cocktail party could get the funds for this raised quickly enough," Portia said. "It would be a damn shame if we don't recognize Goosebush being Goosebush for four hundred years in style. We need something to celebrate around here, that's for sure." She handed Ray back the mic and sat back down.

"A cocktail party? How quaint. I suggest you ask PJ Frank to ante up some cash. Maybe he should host the party. Especially since his house, his property values, are going to rise if Alden Park gets fixed up." Merilee Frank had stood up and started to walk down the bleachers. Nobody looks elegant walking down bleachers, and Merilee was no exception. Lilly and Delia both had the same thought: good thing she hadn't been drinking yet. "You all know that PJ shouldn't even have that house. It should belong to his father. But he sweet-talked his grandpa into leaving it to him instead of the next in line. Make them pay, that's what I say. He must have the money; what else has he got to spend it on?"

Lilly was so shocked she couldn't respond. Not at what Merilee had said. It was common knowledge that Merilee held her husband's son in very low regard, especially since PJ had inherited the family homestead after his grandfather's death five years ago. Lilly had often wondered if Merilee had stayed married to Pete because of the house. There were worse reasons to stay married. The monetary value, never mind the historical value, was well over one million dollars. Along with the house, PJ had inherited the family business, the Frank Lumberyard. No one except Merilee, and that included Pete himself, thought that PJ shouldn't have gotten the house as an inheritance. PJ had stuck around Goosebush, delayed any dreams he may have had in order to take care of his grandfather and the family business. The lumberyard and the house both took money to maintain, and it was only in the past year or so that PJ was able to feel as if he wasn't treading financial waters with weights on his ankles. Despite that, Merilee always made the point, publicly if possible, that PJ had stolen money from his own father and, by default, from her.

"What do you say, PJ? Ready to ante up—" Merilee said, turning toward Pete's son, hands on hips.

Pete had followed his wife down the bleachers, but it had taken him much more time. He'd finally gotten down to the gym floor and stepped quickly toward Merilee, grabbing her by her upper arm. "Let's go," he said.

"I'm not going anywhere. I have every right—" Merilee said, turning and twisting her arm out of her husband's grasp.

"You have no right. Do you understand me?" Pete said.

"Oh, Pete, please. Check with that lawyer of yours. I have every right. Go ahead, test me. I dare you." Merilee and Pete had a staring match for about fifteen seconds, and then she turned on her heel and walked out of the gym.

The spots of color on Pete's cheeks were the only sign of his seething anger and extreme embarrassment. "Sorry about the interruption, folks. She won't be doing that again. Ever." With that, Pete Frank followed his wife out of the room.

Ray Mancini ignored Pete, and stepped toward the center of the room again. He raised his voice to speak, but then he remembered the microphone. "Well, folks, as we were saying, we'll need to figure how to fund this park. First thing we need to do is to clear it, and we're doing that on Saturday. Then we've got to figure out the plan, as Lilly said. I, for one, suggest that we ask Delia Greenway to do the research on the history of Alden Park, so we can make some informed decisions about what to do with it. Maybe I should put that to a vote." Ray turned around and looked at the rest of the board of selectmen, all of whom nodded. Pat French sat at her seat at the table, seething.

"All in favor, say aye." A resounding "aye" echoed through the gym. Some folks liked the idea of Delia doing the job. But, truth to tell, most folks just liked the idea of Pat not getting her way for once.

"Okay, Delia, think you'll have something for us to look at by next meeting?" Ray asked. Delia nodded. "Good enough. Now, as to the money. Tamara, does this feel like something your Beautification Committee can take on, draft some recommendations for?"

"It does," Tamara said. "Lilly Jayne joined the committee over the weekend, and her financial expertise will help us with this."

"Good enough," Ray said. "Sounds like we've got a plan. Unless there's an objection, meeting adjourned. Do I have a second for the motion?"

Another set of "ayes" thundered through the gym.

CHAPTER 8

"Okay, we're here. Please tell me there's coffee somewhere in this place," Delia said. Six o'clock in the morning on a Saturday was way too early for Delia to be displaying company manners. She was abrupt at the best of times, never mind when she had lost several hours of sleep figuring out how to deal with Tamara's panicked call. Tamara had conference-called Delia and Ernie at ten o'clock the night before.

"Okay, team, we may have a situation," Tamara said. "Sorry to call so late, but you need to know about the call I just got from Ray."

"What situation?" Lilly asked. Delia had put her phone on speaker and gone into Lilly's room to have her listen in to the call.

"A Pat French situation. I have it on good authority that she plans to make a dramatic entrance at about eight-thirty, insisting the proper precautions for historical preservation are not being met. Doing that will make it look like Delia doesn't know what she's doing and suggest that Pat will need to save the day."

"Why would she do that?" Delia asked. "I've been so careful about keeping her in the loop."

"That woman is a menace," Ernie said.

"She really is," Tamara said.

Delia had brought her laptop with her and sat on the edge of Lilly's bed. Her fingers started to fly over the keyboard. "Sadly, for her, I'm a few steps ahead," Delia said. "I was planning on taking notes during the clean up anyway and keeping track of where people were doing the work. But why don't we make it a group effort and grid off the park? We would've done that anyway when it came to planting, later. That way it won't be just up to me to keep track of what came from where, and we can get everyone in on the historical preservation angle. Honestly? I don't think there's much to worry about, since this was always a community space. If we were digging the foundation of a building, I'd be worried. But, still, better safe than sorry." Delia had finished typing. "I'm sending you all the plan. Check your e-mail." After she'd hit SEND, she turned the computer for Lilly to look at. Lilly was used to seeing a grid pattern. It was how she planned her own gardens.

"This makes perfect sense to me," Lilly said. "Ernie, can you grab some stakes and string, and bring them over?"

"Sure can. I'll also grab some laser pointers to make it easier. I need to make sure I have my phone handy to catch the expression on Pat French's face. That's going to be all over social media, I can promise you that."

* * *

Ernie had asked a few people on the volunteer cleanup crew to come in early and help get ready for the big day. Finally, Alden Park was going to get its face-lift. He'd donated a toolshed that had been moved over to the park and assembled the night before. Several folks had volunteered to bring their own tools, but Ernie still wanted to get extras over to the shed before the day started, so that there weren't idle hands throughout the day. He'd spent a lot of yesterday spray-painting tool handles with fluorescent green paint so that people weren't tempted to walk off with them.

"There's fresh coffee in the office. Let's go back there. That's partially why I asked you to come in a little early."

"A little early? People aren't showing up until eight o'clock." Delia poured herself a cup of coffee and took a sip. She poured a second cup and handed it to Lilly. Both women took their coffee black, and Ernie made it strong, so the caffeine was delivered quickly, and Delia started to wake up a little bit. She looked over at Ernie's desk, where two new monitors were parked. "What's all this?" she asked. Delia loved technology and new gadgets almost as much as she loved research. Almost.

"New security systems I'm trying out."

"Systems? Plural? Isn't that overkill?"

"As you know, folks come over here to the Triple B to find all sorts of things. We've had a couple people coming in, looking at different security cameras. You know, the kind you can set up at home and monitor on the web. Nothing too fancy. Anyway, I thought I ought to give a few of them a test-drive so I can make better recommendations."

"What do you think? I've heard the—"

"Ernie, do you need security cameras?" Lilly asked.

"I'm sad to say, I think I do. Up until recently, I could leave things outside the shop overnight, chained up with a simple lock. But lately, things have been vandalized if I leave them out. In a couple of cases, things have walked away."

"That's terrible," Delia said. "Any ideas who's doing it?"

"I've been talking to Bash Haywood about it. He's had patrol cars drive by when they get a chance. And I've added lights to the outside. We both think it's probably some of the kids who have been hanging out in Alden Park. I've got a couple of cameras trained over at the park. But so far, we haven't caught anyone on camera. Thought maybe if we could get some decent footage, it might be fun to show the progress. Anyway, I set it up last night, and it doesn't seem to be working. I was hoping maybe you could take a look at it, Delia."

"You should have had me help you set it up," Delia said. "You know I love this kind of thing."

"To tell you the truth, I was hoping I could impress you with my expertise. No such luck. Here, all the camera names and passwords are on the sheet of paper taped underneath the keyboard."

"Baby Jane. Blanche. Jezebel. Interesting names for cameras," Delia said. "Great password security too."

"I was just thinking I might steal that idea," Lilly said. "The password idea. Not the naming. I'd probably go with Miss Marple and Hercule." Delia flashed her a dirty look, and Lilly smiled. She knew that her feigned ignorance on technical matters irked Delia. She also knew that if she didn't have Delia, she would figure them out herself. But, as she watched her young friend's fingers fly over the keyboard, she was grateful she didn't have to.

"Ernie, I'll get them set up for today. If we want good-quality footage, we may need to consider other cameras. Let me do some research for you. Sound good?" Delia said.

"Sounds great. Happy to invest in a few more cameras for you to take for a test-drive. We can even do a compare-and-contrast chart for the customers. Look at this camera," Ernie said, handing one to Lilly. "It's amazing how small they are these days. You can hide them almost anywhere."

"Well, I don't love that idea," Lilly said. "But I do love the idea of keeping a visual record of the work we're doing in the park. Might that be possible?"

Delia shrugged and nodded. "You mean like a webcam? Or higher quality?"

"Higher quality. Just in case we want to make the case for funding," Lilly said.

"To get a grant or prove the value of the community effort?" Ernie said. "Great thinking, Lilly."

"Should I set up another camera?" Delia asked Ernie.

"On it. I set up a camera in the front window to take time-lapse photographs. Put in a huge, brand-new memory card. I'll get it started around seven-thirty. It should be all set. It isn't on the web, but it will take time-lapse photographs."

"Is this the only reason you had us come over?" Lilly asked. "So that Delia could MacGyver your camera setup?"

"No, Lil, I want to show you something I found yesterday. Delia, you all set in here?"

"All set," Delia said. She barely looked up but did take another sip of coffee.

Ernie walked Lilly through the store toward the back. Ernie had a garden center built off the back of the shop, and they went in there. Ernie had opened Bits, Bolts & Bulbs—the Triple B, as it was known to locals—almost twenty years ago when he and his partner, Bruce, had moved to Goosebush. Lilly, who always believed in supporting local businesses, had immediately come in to talk to them about supplies. She and Ernie had bonded over garden plots, and Lilly was friendly with both men. Friendly, but not friends. More acquaintances.

Bruce had died of cancer eight years ago, and some people were afraid that Ernie would close the shop. But he kept it open. When Alan got sick, Ernie reached out to Lilly and offered to help her take care of her gardens while she took care of Alan. Ernie was one of the few people not afraid of sickness, and he became a regular visitor to the house. As she walked to the back of the store, she thought again how grateful she was that this kind, gentle man, who also knew loss, was in her life.

"Lil, I want you to look at this, tell me what you think," Ernie said. He led her to a corner of the garden center, the part closed off to customers. He picked up a plastic bin and put it on top of the workbench. Lilly walked over and looked in. She saw some grasses inside. They looked sickly and were shades of brown and yellow. She went to reach into the tub, but Ernie stopped her.

"Here, put these on," he said, handing her a pair of heavy-duty rubber gloves.

She did as she was told and reached in to pick up some of the grasses. She took a tentative smell of the soil and recoiled at the chemicals. "Is that bleach?" she said.

"Definitely bleach. If I was to guess, there may be some salt in this as well. You know, if you mix boiling water and salt, add liquid detergent, then add bleach, you've made a powerful weed killer. Problem is, it can kill more than weeds. I went over last night to lock up the shed. Someone's been pouring this all over the place."

"Recently? You think someone's been trying to get rid of the overgrowth themselves?" Lilly asked.

"Maybe," Ernie said. "Or maybe somebody's trying to destroy the soil, so we can't rebuild the garden."

"Who would want to do that?" Lilly asked. But she didn't answer her own question, nor did Ernie. There were a few folks who didn't want the garden to be rebuilt. Merilee Frank made it clear that she didn't want her stepson, PJ, to benefit from the raised property values. Then there were Pat French and other folks who didn't want the town spending money on beautification.

"I'm adding masks and rubber gloves to the stuff I'm donating today. I was wondering if you could do a speech before this all starts, let folks know they should be careful. I don't want to scare people off, but at the same time, I'm not one hundred percent sure what these chemicals are. I'm hoping these are enough precautions. What do you think?"

"I'm happy to talk to people," Lilly said. "You and I will survey the park beforehand, maybe mark off where we think folks shouldn't work until we've assessed the situation. There's a lot of work to be done. We're not going to finish today anyway. Does that sound like a plan?"

"Sounds good to me," Ernie said. He leaned forward and took a small whiff, screwing up his face once the bleach mixture hit his nostrils. "I've sent the soil samples out for testing, so we'll know more in a week or so."

"Well, we'll know what somebody used, but not who used the chemicals, or why. Your camera experiment might help with part of that in the future."

"Exactly what I was thinking," Ernie said. "I've never been a fan of surveillance, but I'd sure like to know who is poisoning the park."

Stan arrived a little after seven with two tables that he set up inside the park. Delia saw him on the surveillance camera that was focused right on the park and went over to offer her help. She also told him where to set up the food stations—in the field of view of the camera she had just set up so that she could have some action shots, even if it was just people going over to pick up a free cookie. He cleared an area near the shed where he could make sure the tables were steady, so the coffee wouldn't spill. Stella Haywood arrived at seven fifteen with a van full of refreshments, and Delia and Lilly went over to help unload. Many hands made light work, and then Stella drove the empty van back within ten minutes. Delia ran back to the store to help Ernie bring over a couple of wheelbarrows full of supplies.

It speaks a great deal to the excitement of the day that Alden Park were full at seven forty-five, though the start time wasn't until eight o'clock. All told, Lilly estimated there were fifty people milling around, drinking coffee, chatting with each other, waiting for

directions. Lilly looked around and saw Cal taking
pictures with his phone. He was walking around the
outer edge of the crowd, and people were giving
him a wide berth. Lilly wondered if Alden Park, or
the folks cleaning it up, were the objects of his next
photo essay. From the looks of things, people were
hoping it was the park.

Never one to not take the bull by the horns, Ernie
stepped forward and spoke to the crowd. "Welcome,
everybody. What a terrific turnout! The Star Café is
donating coffee and food today, so let's give it up
for Stan Freeland and his team." A roar erupted
from the crowd, and Stan beamed. "As you can see,
there's a lot to do. I'm very grateful to PJ Frank,
who rented a dumpster for us to use." Lilly scanned
the crowd and saw PJ near the corner with a group
of friends. One of the men punched him gently on
the shoulder, and Lilly saw PJ blush. She scanned
the crowd some more and saw Pete staring at his
son, then looking away. Merilee wasn't with him,
but that didn't surprise Lilly. Park cleanups didn't
seem like her thing.

"Lilly Jayne and I have been talking it over," Ernie
said. Lilly snapped her attention back to Ernie. Best
to know what he was saying about her. "We have a
plan to propose. We were thinking we should set up
a grid here at the park, using twine and stakes. That
way we can clear the space in a managed formation
and keep notes on what we find in each grid. Also,
Delia has created a map with the historical plan that
was approved by Pat yesterday afternoon, and she
laid the grid on it. If you are clearing square six-
teen, for example, you can mark off the part of the
path that needs to be cleared as well. Does that
make sense?" Delia had started handing out copies

of the plan, and folks were starting to discuss it among themselves.

"What's this blue dot in the middle of the park? I don't remember that," someone said.

"See where there's a circle sort of marked in the middle, right there?" Delia said.

"What? I can't hear you!" another voice called out.

Delia cleared her throat and raised her voice. "See that, right there? Those edge blocks? You can see where the grass is growing a little differently. There used to be a large, shallow pond in the middle of the field. It froze over in the winter, and folks used to skate on it."

"I never—" Ray Mancini said.

"Well, Ray, maybe you're not old enough," Delia said. Several people laughed, but Delia was serious. "Pat French requested a historically accurate drawing according to the records. This is what I came up with, and she approved. Right, Pat?"

Lilly didn't see Pat at first. No one did. But eventually the crowd parted a bit, and Pat was left standing alone, as far away from the crowd as she could be. She was wearing a black hoodie zipped up, hood on, and black jeans. Incognito Pat, that's just what everyone needed. She was probably there to shut down the first offense, or fine anyone who didn't mark the grid correctly.

"That's the approved plan," Pat said. She sounded hoarse.

"What is this, a ground clearing or an archaeological dig?" someone shouted. Everyone laughed.

"Funny you should ask," Ernie said. "It is, of course, a park cleanup and a clearing. But Delia's preliminary research shows that this has been a public park for many, many years. On the off chance we find something of historical significance, we want to know where we found it. I know this is a bit of a wrench in the works, but we feel like this extra step is an important one for the sake of preserving Goosebush's history."

Ernie and Delia exchanged meaningful glances. Truthfully, neither of them had thought about it until Tamara's call, but now they were prepared. And how.

CHAPTER 9

The group was quick getting started on the work of gridding out the grounds, but the grasses were so thick it was taking a while. Lilly looked around and took a mental note of who was missing. Roddy had been there early and was going around introducing himself to people while he was supervising a lot of the gridding project with Ray Mancini. Lilly saw Callisto Pace lying on a patch of debris and taking photographs. Great, the before of Alden Park was going to be part of his dystopian Goosebush piece. Lilly thought she saw PJ's mother, Rhonda, but she wasn't sure. Ever since Pete had left Lilly for Rhonda, Rhonda had always taken great pains to not cross paths with Lilly. Lilly appreciated the effort, though she expected that Rhonda had suffered more heartbreak at the hand of Pete than she ever had.

Kitty Bouchard was there and was even dressed appropriately and doing work, much to Lilly's surprise. It made Lilly wonder whether Kitty was a closet gardener. If she was, Lilly would feel compelled to reevaluate her judgment of the younger woman. In Lilly's opinion, all gardeners had redeeming qualities.

By ten o'clock, the grid work was done. The dumpster was set up on the edge of the garden, near the alley that ran along the back of the stores on the Wheel. A few people went over to move it closer to the park. During the lull, everyone gathered around the refreshment table to grab a drink of water or a cup of coffee before the next phase began. Lilly and Ernie were conferring with the map that Delia had created, blocking off areas that seemed to have been affected by the chemical spill, or whatever it was, having decided that it was probably better not to have people try to excavate that area until they knew what they were dealing with.

"Time to hand out the shovels and spades," Delia said to Ernie.

"Good enough," Ernie said. "I put the tools in the shed this morning and put the lock on, but I don't think I shut it. You know the combination, though, right?"

"When this morning?" Lilly asked.

"Around five," Ernie said.

"Five? Did you sleep at all last night?"

"Not much. I feel responsible for today, you know? The heads-up about Pat's plans made me nervous, so I kept reviewing everything over and over, to make sure there wasn't another loophole that needed closing."

"It seems to be going well so far," Lilly said. "Honestly, all I thought we'd get done is the gridding."

"I've marked off some of the bushes that may be worth saving and just need some strong pruning.

Only folks who are good at pruning should try their hand at it."

"Agreed. There are some clippers in the shed. Maybe you can give lessons—"

Ernie was interrupted by Delia's bloodcurdling scream. Lilly and Ernie ran over to her. Ernie took her by the shoulders and turned her around to hold her close and try to calm her down. She screamed some more into his barrel chest, and then she started to sob. Lilly stepped around them both and looked in the shed. She swallowed the bile that rose in her throat.

Merilee Frank was lying on bags of mulch, staring up, hedge clippers protruding from her chest.

Bash Haywood arrived within minutes of receiving the call from Lilly. The station was only a few blocks away, and luckily Bash had been in the office. As chief of police for the town of Goosebush, Bash's job was usually mundane. The occasional break-in, keeping kids off the beach at night, pulling over people driving under the influence, and an accident every couple of weeks. But murder? He'd never had to investigate a murder. The closest it had ever come to that was when they had found old Mrs. Ellicott with a gash in her forehead, sprawled out in her living room. He did assume she was murdered and came very close to arresting her daughter-in-law, until Lilly pointed out the rumpled area rug and the corner of the coffee table, and asked about Mrs. Ellicott's blood-alcohol level. Then Lilly talked the daughter-in-law out of a nuisance lawsuit against the police force. Everyone was grateful for that.

Bash Haywood was from a long line of folks who wore a uniform. His grandfather had gone to the US Naval Academy, the third generation to do so. His parents had met while they were serving in the Army. The assumption had always been that Bash would continue the lineage.

Bash may have had other ideas. In fact, he'd applied to art school in Boston. Lilly had written him a recommendation and was thrilled when he left town. But then Bash was orphaned at twenty and made responsible for his younger siblings. Most folks thought that Bash gave up his dreams when he moved back home to take care of his siblings, but they were wrong. He painted under a different name these days, and only Stan and Lilly knew his secret. Bash was as dedicated to peacekeeping and Goosebush as he was anything else, but he did thrive on the predictability of the post and did not like chaos.

"I don't suppose you got a list of who was here this morning?" Bash asked Lilly. He sighed and ran his left hand over his chin for the umpteenth time.

"As a matter of fact, Tamara and Warwick were signing people in, so long as they came in the main entrance here. I can add to it, so can Ernie and Delia . . . Delia. How is she holding up? Poor thing, quite the shock."

"I had Stan take her over to the Star Café. I'm going to go talk to her there. Stan's offered to make the café a holding pen until we get statements from everyone. I should get over there—" Bash said, looking toward the exit longingly.

"Once you have the scene secured and evidence collection is underway," Lilly said.

"Right, right, after that." Bash looked down and made a few more entries into his notebook.

"Are more folks coming in? To help?" Lilly asked.

"The police chiefs of Kingsbury and Marshton were happy to send people over. Thanks for the suggestion. Good thing it isn't beach season; otherwise, we'd all be stretched thin. I could call in the state police. Maybe I should?"

Lilly looked at Bash, who was clearly drowning in details he couldn't grasp. She'd need to keep an eye on him, set him up for success. Having the state police come in right away to help them solve this would not serve Bash's confidence well. Besides, they wouldn't know more than he did about the inner workings of Goosebush, and who was who. No, best to keep this local, at least for now. What happened in Goosebush stayed in Goosebush, hopefully. This was just the sort of publicity the town did not need or want.

Lilly looked around and saw Ray Mancini milling about at the edges of the crowd. She saw him hold his phone up and realized he was taking pictures. Pictures . . . Lilly made a mental note to talk to Cal Pace. "Maybe Ray can start to take some of the statements?" Lilly asked. As the retired police chief, Ray was in the Lilly camp of making Bash a success no matter what.

"Would those be legal?" Bash asked.

"Well, I'm not sure about that. I'm just wondering if this first step isn't about finding out who was where when and what they might've seen. You want to piece it all together. You'll have to follow up with more questions. And you must corroborate stories. Ray will know best, but maybe he can help?"

Ray Mancini and Lilly had known each other forever. In fact, Ray had been the first person to ask Lilly to marry him. She had said no, since she was already smitten with Pete Frank. He'd gotten over the heartbreak, such as it was, and married Megan Low a few years later, which had led to three kids, six grandchildren, and a happy life. Ray had never been unhappy that Lilly Jayne had said no to him all those years ago.

"You're right, Lilly. Ray is a good idea. Bringing him out of retirement seems like something that should be kosher. I'm going to go talk to him."

"Take him a copy of the grid," Lilly whispered. Ernie had given Bash a pile of them to distribute to the folks securing the scene.

"Will do. Thanks, Lilly. I don't know what I'd do without you at times like these."

"Don't second-guess yourself, Bash," Lilly said. "You're a good cop. Trust yourself."

"I promise, I'll get my head in the game," he said. "It's just that it's such a shock. I mean, Merilee wasn't one of my favorite people, but who'd want to kill her?"

"I suspect, Bash, that the list of folks who didn't like Merilee is pretty long. Who would want to kill her? That's a shorter list, I'm sure," Lilly said. But, she thought to herself, still substantial. She looked over at Pete Frank, who was standing off to the side with one of Bash's officers. He looked pale and shocked. Lilly gave herself a bit of a shake and then headed over to the Star Café.

"Are you all right?" Lilly asked Delia. Delia was relieved to see Lilly and let the older woman mother her a bit.

"No, not really," Delia said. Her hands were wrapped

around a mug, and she was staring straight ahead. "It was pretty awful."

"I'm sure it was," Lilly said. She sat down and moved her chair next to the younger woman. She put her hand on Delia's forearm and gave it a squeeze. Delia started to weep, so Lilly put her arm around her and pulled her into a half hug. She rocked her back and forth and told her everything would be all right. And at that moment, Lilly decided to do everything she could to make it all right. Somehow.

Delia was surprised at how comforted she felt by Lilly. She supposed it was to be expected after all this time. When it became clear that Alan wasn't going to win his race with finishing the work, he spent time training Delia so that she would be able to do the final edits and get the book published for him. It was a huge task, one that took Delia another year. Delia had moved into the house by then.

Delia promised Alan one more thing before he died. That she would take care of Lilly. "Mind you, you can't act as though you're doing it. Lilly would never stand for that. But just be around for a while, as much as she'll let you. Make sure she eats three times a day, gets some sleep. And no matter what, make sure she keeps up with her gardens. If she doesn't do that, be worried, and get Tamara involved. For heaven's sake, get on with your own life, but I would appreciate your keeping an eye on Lilly for a bit."

The thing of it was, Delia didn't really have much of a life before she'd gone under the wing of Alan McMillan. Until then, she had had interests, and tremendous abilities around research and making connections between seemingly disparate facts. But her connections were primarily academic. She'd been raised by indifferent parents and gone through over twenty years of school never having made a close friend. When Alan hired her, she knew of his work and admired it greatly. But it was meeting the man himself that changed her life. He was warm, brilliant, funny, and exacting. He demanded a great deal from her, and she tried her best to meet his standards. In Alan she found a mentor. But in his wife, Lilly, she found a friend.

Alan was a jovial personality, and Lilly was a bit reserved. But once you got to know the two of them, you realized the truth. Lilly was mostly shy, but her heart was warm and incredibly kind. Delia felt understood for the first time in her life. After Alan died, Lilly invited Delia to stay on to finish her work on Alan's book. Delia had her own set of rooms and continued to work on Alan's research. His final book was published last year, to great acclaim. When interviewed, Lilly always made sure to give Delia a lot of credit for the work. Delia began to write articles, started to get recognition in her own right, and continued work on her dissertation. She was on track to finish her degree soon. At Lilly's insistence, she applied for several teaching positions and got a few offers. She accepted a job at a school in Boston that was to begin this coming fall.

Lilly looked around the Star Café, and most people were looking at Delia with concern. If Lilly had given any of them a signal, they would have come over and helped console Delia. But for now, they gave the women privacy and broke into their own groups to gossip about the situation at hand.

Ray Mancini walked up to Lilly and gave her a nod. He sat on the other side of Delia and leaned close to her. "Delia, I'm going to need to talk to you. But tell you what. I can do it later if you want to go home and pull yourself together."

"No, sorry, I'm really fine—"

"Delia, I was a cop for over thirty years, the last ten here in Goosebush. Before that I worked for the state. I've seen a lot, more than my share, of dead bodies. Getting over it isn't something that happens right away. You have to give yourself time. Hell, I still think about some folks I only saw at a crime scene. You knew the victim. That makes it harder."

"Well, we weren't exactly friends," Delia said. "Quite the opposite, truth to tell. Maybe that's why it's hitting me so hard. I feel awful about how much I didn't like her. Does that make any sense?" Delia was, if nothing else, pathologically honest. It was part of her DNA and a major contributor to her abilities as a researcher. Facts were facts; she never felt compelled to sugarcoat or change them to make people feel better.

"Merilee Frank didn't have many friends, did she?" Ray asked. He looked toward Lilly, who gave him a half smile. Merilee and Ray had tussled more than once; everyone in town knew that. Ray may have retired from the force, but he was still a rule follower. Marilee was not and tried desperately to run over people to get her way whenever possible. More than once, Ray had stepped in on other people's behalf and stopped her. Most specifically, Ray always stood up for PJ Frank, Pete's son.

"One hates to speak ill of the dead, but it does seem to me that you will not be lacking suspects," Lilly said.

"If I was Bash, I'd put my name on the list. We ended up screaming at each other every time I saw her," Ray said.

"You? Screaming?" Lilly asked Ray. "I can't imagine that. I don't think I've ever heard you raise your voice."

"Something about that woman pushed me over the edge on a regular basis. She had this way about her. Finding your weak spot and exploiting it. In my case, it was smoking."

"Smoking?" Lilly asked. Delia had stopped crying but kept her head on Lilly's shoulder.

"Yeah. I promised Meg that I'd quit, but I lied. I still smoke a cigarette or two every day. Merilee caught me one day, made a big deal out of asking for a cigarette. I gave her one, and then another time I gave her another one. Next thing I knew, Merilee was making veiled comments in front of Meg. I told her to cut it out, and that's when she asked me to get their plans for adding on to her house through the red tape at town hall."

"All because you didn't want Meg to know you smoked."

"I don't smoke; I sneak cigarettes. Yeah, it was ridiculous. But when you watched her working a crowd, you realized that she probably tried that on a lot of folks—leveraging something that was a secret to get people to do what she wanted."

"If that's true, then there is going to be an epic list of suspects," Lilly said.

"Epic is right," Ray said. "Solving this one is going to come down to timelines and stories."

"And verifying those stories and timelines. Bash is going to need some help," Lilly said.

"From a lot of people," Ray said. "Tell you what, Delia, I'm going to talk to other people here and figure out what we've got. If you don't mind hanging around—"

"I don't mind," Delia said.

"Write down everything you remember," Lilly said. "Who got where when, who was working where, that sort of thing. I'd imagine Ray would find that very helpful."

"I can't imagine you'll remember all of that," Ray said.

"I remember a lot," Delia said. "It's part of what makes me good at my job. Plus, Ernie was taking pictures from his shop. And a lot of folks were using their phones. So I bet there will be a lot of ways to verify what was happening when. Would it be helpful if I started finding people's pictures too? Folks were using a couple of different hashtags. I can look at social media and download pictures." Delia said.

"Very helpful," Ray said. "What's this about Ernie's camera?"

"He was doing a time-lapse-photography project. He set it up to start this morning around seven-thirty."

"It's a pity it didn't start earlier," Ray said quietly. "That may have solved the case right away. Ernie's gone back to his store with one of the officers, to talk through the installation of the shed, when he brought the tools over, all that sort of thing. I'm going to give Bash a call to make sure they get the pictures from the camera. If you decide to leave, check in with me first, all right?"

"Do you have any questions for me?" Lilly asked Ray.

"I'm sure I do, and I'm sure you'll have questions as well. We'll talk soon."

CHAPTER 10

Delia got up from the table and walked over to the bookstore part of the Star. She grabbed two blank journals and took them back over to Lilly, handing her one.

"What's this?" Lilly asked.

"Lilly, don't pretend you aren't putting this puzzle together. But we both know you need to write stuff down, so here you go. I'll let Stan know we owe him. I'm going to start writing what I remember down. I can catalog what happened, write down the facts. But you see the truth. You know people and figure out connections. Start jotting down some ideas. I'm going to need you to help me make sense of this. I can't stop thinking about Merilee. She was staring up at me . . . the only thing I can think to do is try to fix this, whatever that means. I need your help."

Lilly and Delia looked at each other for a few seconds, and Lilly nodded. Delia went into Stan's office to gather her thoughts and pull herself together.

Lilly sat at the table and patted down her pockets until she found a pen. She took the plastic off the notebook and opened the first page. She looked around the room and started to take some notes. They weren't ordered notes by any means. Just Lilly's observations of the day, starting when she and Delia had arrived at Ernie's store. Lilly flipped forward a couple of pages and wrote down what had happened the day before, with the permit and Tamara's late-night call. Lilly wrote and wrote. Who knew what was important and what wasn't? In the past couple of years, Lilly had started to forget details unless she wrote them down, and she didn't want to risk that today.

Someone put a mug down beside her, and Lilly looked down at it and then up at the deliverer. Roddy smiled at her and asked if he could sit.

"Please do," Lilly said, picking up the mug and taking a sip.

"I hope you don't mind that I took the liberty of getting you some milk tea. It's my Irish background showing up. I always found tea to be of the utmost comfort during difficult times," Roddy said.

"This is perfect, thank you. You're right; tea with milk is much more comforting than a cup of coffee. I needed that."

"Terrible business, this," he said.

"It is," Lilly said. "I'm worried about Delia. It was quite a shock for her, finding Merilee like that."

"Well, you'll forgive me for saying this, but you seem to be holding it together quite well. Didn't you also see the body?"

"Is that a rebuke?" Lilly said, smiling slightly. Most people did not call Lilly Jayne out on her less-admirable traits. She found it somewhat refreshing that Roddy would, depending on how he continued the conversation.

"No, no. It's a compliment in its fashion," he said. "I admire a person who keeps her head about her when those around her are losing theirs. I have a reputation—earned, I'm afraid—for being able to stay dispassionately distant from the most wretched of circumstances. My three ex-wives would all agree on that, if nothing else."

"I'm sure you have other attributes that speak in your favor. Otherwise you wouldn't have three ex-wives," Lilly said.

"Fair enough," he said, laughing. Roddy looked around the room, taking note of who was there. He was at a disadvantage, not knowing most of the people. He did, however, have a memory that served him well despite the circumstances. Once he met someone, he remembered their name. He knew he should stay out of this situation; it really was none of his business. But he couldn't help himself. Old habits died hard. Roddy saw that Lilly was looking at something over his shoulder, and he turned around to see what she was looking at. He turned back toward Lilly.

"Who's she?" he asked.

"Her name is Kitty Bouchard," Lilly said.

"I've seen her about," Roddy said. "I haven't met her officially yet. Tell me, what's her story?"

Lilly looked at Roddy. His wavy hair was flecked heavily with silver and was receding a bit at the temples. Just a bit. His deep brown eyes focused on her, and the cleft in his chin was highlighted by the smile on his face. He was, with no possible exception made, a very handsome man. Lilly had no doubt that if Roddy had not met Kitty Bouchard officially yet, it was more his doing than hers. She sincerely doubted he could have lived in town for more than forty-eight hours without Kitty attempting to get her claws into him.

"Kitty was married to one of the town elders; he passed away a few years back. She stayed in town and has been working on finding her second husband ever since."

Roddy laughed. "Well, I see I have found a kindred spirit. Clinical observations tuned into human foibles. This could be the beginning of a beautiful friendship, Lilly." Roddy took another sip of tea.

"You may be a bad influence on me," Lilly said. "Usually, I'm a bit more discreet."

"It must be the shock," Roddy said. "You didn't know Merilee, did you?"

Lilly looked at Roddy. There was something about him. Something that made her trust him. Lilly was, if nothing else, a keen judge of human character. Something told her she could trust Roddy.

"I'm sure you've heard, or if you haven't, you will soon, that Merilee was Pete's third wife. I was his first."

Roddy's eyebrows went up. "I had not heard that, no."

"Really? Perhaps I overestimate my place in the annals of town gossip. We were very young. We knew one another in high school, went to the same college. We got married my senior year, much to my parents' chagrin. They wanted me to continue my education, but it all seemed to make logical sense at the time. Pete's family and my family had both lived in Goosebush forever; it seemed like destiny. When I look back now, I honestly don't know what I was thinking, except that I was supposed to get married, and Pete seemed as good a husband as any. Not fair to him, not fair to me. Anyway, as sort of a compromise, we moved to Boston, and I went to graduate school, for business. We made a good show of being a happy young couple in love, but it was just that. A show. I realize Pete may have been having affairs all along, but it wasn't until Rhonda moved to Boston as well . . . We'd known each other in high school, and she'd always carried a torch for Pete. They started an affair, and Pete decided he wanted to make a go of it with her. So he left me. Their son, PJ, was born a year later. PJ is Pete's only child."

"You didn't have any children?"

"Thankfully, no. That probably sounds terrible, but if we had had children we would have been tied to one another forever. No children, no ties. I dove into my career and built my life around that."

"You moved back to Goosebush at some point?" Roddy said. He looked right at Lilly, with curiosity mixed with kindness.

"Well, I always kept one foot in Goosebush," she said. "I did move around, lived in Boston, New York, London. But I came back to visit, and to take care of my parents as they got older. I met my second husband, Alan, twenty, almost twenty-five years ago. I brought him down to visit while we were dating, and he fell in love with the town. He let me see it through new eyes. We moved down here and made our lives." Lilly looked embarrassed. "Sorry, you can't be too interested in ancient history. Do you always have this effect on people? Ask someone a question and get their whole biography?"

Roddy smiled. "Well, my story is much less interesting. I fear I have more in common with Pete than

I do with Alan. No great love who helped me change my ways. As I said, I've been married three times. Best of intentions every time. But my work always took priority, and the marriages suffered."

"Any children?" Lilly asked.

"I had a daughter with my second wife. Her name is Emily. I tried to be a better father than I was a husband, but in that I fell short as well, I'm afraid. That's part of the reason I moved down here, to be closer to Emily and try get to know her. She's just had her first child, a daughter."

"Grandchildren are wonderful," Lilly said. "Of course, I don't know that firsthand, but I do borrow Tamara's."

"She is wonderful, though I have never been entirely comfortable around babies. Her birth made me feel both old and rejuvenated. Emily and I have reached a tenuous détente, and I'm hoping my retirement, in addition to a beautiful house near the ocean, will be an enticement to start afresh."

Roddy and Lilly sipped their tea in silence. Neither one of them were used to divulging personal stories, but somehow this seemed right. It was as if the time for small talk was short, and at this stage in their lives, their friendship needed to be built on a foundation, putting the past behind them.

"Tell me about Pat French," Roddy said after a bit. He pointed toward the front of the store with his chin, and sure enough, she was standing there. She'd changed out of her hoodie and was wearing more of a typical Pat outfit: a button-down shirt, cardigan sweater, and chino pants.

"I didn't see her much this morning, did you?" Roddy asked.

"No, I didn't," Lilly said. "I saw her when Ernie

was explaining the grid system, but she left a short while later, I think. She had planned to dramatically stop the work this morning, but we caught wind of her plan and took the wind out of her sails. Could be why she was dressed all in black, so she could slink around."

"She is an odd duck, isn't she?" Roddy said. "She seems to go out of her way to be miserable. Unkind of me to say, but there it is."

"I think her nose is a bit out of joint," Lilly said. "Delia stepped on her toes with the research on the park."

"Is she originally from Goosebush?" Roddy asked.

"No, she's a transplant. She's lived here in Goosebush for . . . oh, what? Ten years or so? She moved in with a distant cousin and inherited the house after she died. Anyway, Pat's worked at the town hall for years, keeping track of taxes, permits, that sort of thing. She's also deemed herself the de facto head of the Historical Society. But that's because most of the other volunteers left."

"Is that why Delia's research has been bothering her? Does she think that Delia is making a move on her turf?"

"Perhaps, though Delia doesn't have the temperament to go head to head with Pat, so she is unlikely to take over Pat's turf. You may have noticed that Delia is very forthright. She believes that facts are facts, and she respects facts more than anyone's truth. Does that make sense?"

"Sure, of course. Most people like to add their take on facts, tell their own story as the truth. But facts are stubborn things, and all that matters when it comes down to it," Roddy said.

"You and Delia agree on that. I will confess, I like facts, but more than once I've seen the value of letting folks hold on to their own truth despite the facts. It can be much kinder."

"Well, in that we are different," Roddy said. "Kindness was never one of my virtues. Anyway, how did Delia's fact-finding get her on the wrong side of Pat?"

"Delia's been doing some of her own research and started to discover some discrepancies in what Pat has been telling people. Nothing huge, just dates that were wrong. An occasional boundary line that is off by a foot or two. The history of a house that's a little off. That sort of thing."

"And she called Pat out on the errors?"

"No, that's not Delia's way. To her, for whatever reason, it made the most sense to tell Tamara what she'd discovered, probably because Tamara hires Delia to do research on houses for her. In any event, Tamara has started to call Pat out on the discrepancies. Pat's getting testy about it."

"Tamara seems to be a force of nature unto herself," Roddy said. "Where is she, by the way?"

"She and Warwick are with Bash, looking at lists of names," Lilly said. "Tamara and I have been friends forever, since we were in nursery school. She's had to be a force, for a lot of reasons. But she's also kind and hasn't called Pat out in public. She has let her know that there are issues, however."

"So, having Delia take over the Alden Park historical research?"

"A bit of a coup d'état by Tamara, I'm afraid. It should've happened earlier, but I wasn't paying attention."

"You weren't paying attention? To what?"

"To Goosebush. My husband, Alan, was sick for a

couple of years before he passed. Those years, and the years since, I've been in a bit of a state. I haven't been paying attention. No, not that, it's more like I haven't been engaged."

"It does get harder as we get older, don't you think?" Roddy asked.

"What's that?"

"To stay engaged. It all gets so exhausting."

"But how lucky are we to have lives worth engaging with and in. These past few weeks, getting my garden ready and caring about it for the first time in years? It's made me realize how blessed I am."

Roddy nodded, and they sat in silence for a few moments. Roddy didn't want to debate engaged versus exhausted. He hadn't felt truly engaged in life for years. Maybe Goosebush would be a tonic of sorts? Hard to tell, but it was time to change the subject. "I've heard nothing but wonderful stories about your gardens since I moved to Goosebush. As a matter fact, Tamara used them as a selling point for my house. She said that at one point, my back garden and your garden were part of the same plot."

"They were," Lilly said, smiling at the change of subject, relieved to be on a topic that felt safer. "My house was built by a ship's captain. He was a distant relative on my father's side of the family. He built your house for his daughter, and for a few years they shared a garden in harmony. But then there was a falling out. The details are confused, but my mother always said that it was because the captain's son-in-law was trading in things that the captain did not agree with. Anyway, the captain built the garden wall, which runs from the street to the back wall. He did put a door in the wall, which was keyed on both sides. Family lore has it that the captain always kept his side open, but his daughter never unlocked hers. A few years later his daughter sold her house, and she moved away."

"And the door has never been open since?"

"No, not that I remember. We were never so fond of the neighbors that we wanted to let them into our garden."

"So you haven't seen my garden lately?" Roddy asked.

"Not for years. From the weeds growing over the garden wall, I assume it's in disarray."

"Disarray is one term. Chaotic disaster is another. It's a wonderfully cathartic challenge, or so I keep telling myself. One of many I've found in Goose-bush." Roddy took another sip of tea and smiled over the rim at Lilly.

CHAPTER 11

Delia and Lilly got back to the house midafternoon. They probably could have left earlier, but Lilly didn't want to start a mass exodus that complicated the police officers' work. Luckily, Ray Mancini had come up with a system fairly quickly and got statements and contact information from everyone at the Star Café in short order. Roddy had gotten up to give his statement after Lilly assured him she would wait until the end. Delia rejoined Lilly at her table, and they both kept writing. Ray came over to the table and sat as the crowd thinned.

"What are you both doing?" he asked.

"Writing things down while they're still fresh in our minds," Delia said.

"It is the way we both process uncomfortable moments," Lilly said. "Delia had quite a shock, finding Merilee like that."

Ray nodded, but he didn't buy it for a minute. He'd known Lilly a long time. Her talent was creating order out of chaos, and not just in her garden.

He suspected, hoped to a certain extent, that Lilly was going to look into this.

"Tell you what," Ray said. "How about if you make copies of your notes and pass them on to Bash to help with his investigation?"

"Of course, that was the plan," Delia said. "I'll go home and put them into some sort of system that makes sense. A timeline maybe? I can add Lilly's notes to mine."

"Excellent idea, Delia. Just remember that perfect is the enemy of good enough. Bash needs good enough if he is going to solve this case. And he needs your help. Both of you," Ray said, looking from one woman to the other. Lilly nodded.

"I'll e-mail him my notes today," Delia said. "Should I send you a copy too?"

Ray and Lilly exchanged a look. The only way the case was going to be solved was if Ray, and others, helped Bash. Ray and Lilly both knew that. They'd always worried that Bash would get in over his head someday. Today was the day. Helping Bash was how it needed to be if they were to keep this investigation in Goosebush.

"Sure, send me a copy," Ray said. He got up, squeezed Lilly's shoulder gently, and walked over to the coffee counter.

Though Delia and Lilly had walked to Ernie's store in the morning, they weren't up to the walk home and were grateful when Stan offered to give them a lift. He drove them home in his delivery van, and Delia balanced herself in the back so that Lilly could sit up front. Lilly got out of the van so that Stan and Delia could say their good-byes in private. Lilly put on the teakettle and was spooning some tea into the pot when Delia came in.

"Want some?" Lilly asked.

"Sure," Delia said. "I always thought you were more of a coffee person."

"Roddy bought me a cup of tea today. Milk tea, he called it. It hit the spot. I'd forgotten how comforting tea with milk and sugar could be. I may avail myself of it more often."

"I like both tea and coffee," Delia said. "But I agree about the soothing qualities of tea. I'll go to the store tomorrow and stock up. I have a feeling we're going to need it in the coming days." Delia looked down at the counter and chewed on her bottom lip.

Lilly went over to her and put her arm around her shoulder, giving her a half hug. "Darling Delia, I don't know what I'd do without you. Please be kind to yourself, and take care. Let me know what I can do. You had quite a shock—"

"I'll say," Delia said. "The thing I'm really having trouble wrapping my brain around is who could have done it. I mean, a murderer in Goosebush?"

"Maybe it was someone from out of town," Lilly said.

"Yeah, well, I hope so. I really hope so."

Delia went up to her studio with her tea. Lilly took hers out to the screened-in section of the porch and lay back on the wicker couch. She put the tea beside her and tossed the afghan across her lap. She picked up the biography of Leonardo da Vinci she was working on, but the next thing she knew the book was on the floor, and she heard the front doorbell ringing. She tried to sit up, but advanced middle age, coupled with sleeping in an odd position, made it extra challenging to unfold herself from the couch. By the time she'd shuffled out to the front hall, Delia was already there, letting Bash Haywood in the front door.

"Sorry to intrude. I should've called first," Bash said.

"Never an intrusion," Lilly said. "Come in."

Bash walked into the foyer, and the three of them stood there uncomfortably. That had never happened before, a visit from Bash being awkward. Lilly broke the ice.

"Bash, is this an official visit or a friendly visit? Either is fine, of course. We both understand you have a job to do," Lilly said.

"Personal. I was hoping I could speak with you for a bit, Lilly," Bash said. "Thank you for talking with me earlier, Delia. You have a great eye for detail. There will be some official visits, getting you to sign statements. But that will happen down at the station, not here. Here is not official."

"Good enough," Lilly said. "What can I get you to drink? Delia and I had some tea a couple of hours ago. I can warm up some more. Or, if you're off duty, a beer? Glass of wine? Have you had dinner?"

"I don't know that I'll be officially off duty for a few days, but a beer sure sounds perfect right now. And I'd love to join you for dinner, if it's no trouble, and you have enough."

"It's no trouble," Delia said. "I started a slow-cooker soup this morning; it should be ready in about an hour. I'm in the middle of writing up some notes, but I can—"

"Delia, I'll take care of Bash. You're welcome to join

us, of course. But feel free to go up and finish whatever it is you're working on, and come down to join us for dinner. Or not. Whatever you need to do."

"Bash, I'll be sending you an e-mail in a couple of hours. Keep an eye out." Delia nodded, and turned and went up the stairs toward her rooms.

"I look forward to it," Bash said, watching her go.

Lilly led Bash back to the kitchen. Bash sat in his normal seat at her table, and she went over to the refrigerator to get him a beer. She had his favorite brand on hand, of course. She brought him the bottle and an opener. She knew better than to offer him a glass. They'd dispensed of that routine years ago.

"Is she okay? She had a hell of a shock," Bash said.

"She isn't okay, but she will be. Eventually. I think it's to her credit that she is giving herself time and space to process this. I'd worry more if she acted as if everything was fine." Lilly got herself a beer, and a glass, and put both on the table. She walked over to the cupboard and took out a tin of mixed nuts. She poured some into a bowl and put them in the middle of the table, and then she sat down. Normally, she would have cut up some cheese, chopped up some vegetables, and done more to feed him. But today was not normal.

"So would I," Bash said. "It's been interesting, watching how folks are dealing with this. The gossip has already started." Bash picked up a handful of nuts and tossed them into his mouth. He opened his beer and handed it to Lilly. He picked up hers, opened it, and took a big swig.

"Already? Poor woman hasn't even been dead a day, for heaven's sake."

"Well, it may surprise you to know that Merilee Frank was not the most popular woman in Goosebush," Bash said.

"You don't say?" Lilly said. "I can only imagine you must have a long list of suspects."

"Well—"

"Bash, whatever you say to me stays with me, I promise. Obviously, you don't have to say anything at all. But if I can be of any help—"

"Lilly, you've always been a great sounding board for me. No one was more surprised than me that I ended up wearing this uniform, working here in Goosebush. I like the job well enough, and I love the town. I'd like to think I'm pretty good at it, but you've been a big help over the years helping me sort through things."

"Bash, the town needed you, and you answered the call. You've got an artist's brain, and that works well for a lot of things. My brain works better with numbers and calculations. Together, we've been able to think through a lot of difficult problems over the years."

"Well, never one this difficult. The hardest part for me to wrap my head around is that it must've been somebody she knew. Otherwise, why would she go into the shed to meet with them?"

"That makes sense."

"And if she knew them, chances are good I knew them too."

"You're right, of course," Lilly said. "Goosebush is a small town, and you know most everyone."

"Lilly, I hate to think I know a murderer," Bash said. "The idea of that makes my heart hurt."

"I've always thought that anyone, with enough motivation, is capable of murder," Lilly said. "Now, don't look so surprised. Most people would never do it, thankfully. Otherwise we'd have chaos. But I've seen enough folks in my life teetering on the edge of reason, where one thing could've pushed them over easily."

"What you're saying is, think more about the why, and the who will become clear. That makes sense."

"Yes. Then you have to factor in who had the opportunity. Any idea when it happened?"

"Well, the shed was set up Friday afternoon. Volunteers loaded it up with materials until about seven. Then Ernie locked it for the night."

"He put more tools in at five this morning," Lilly said. "He put the lock back on but didn't latch it."

"Stan got there around seven o'clock, and he thought the shed was locked, but he didn't check. Stan was alone for a while, then Stella delivered food. Other people started showing up around seven-thirty."

"Was the lock closed?"

"Yup."

"Was it forced open?"

"No, but it's a combination lock, and everyone on the Beautification Committee had the combination."

"Not the greatest security measures in the world," Lilly said.

"It's Goosebush. Until today, a good combination lock was enough. After the cleanup, the plan was to make it more secure. But for today, Ernie wanted everyone to have easy access, so they could drop things off."

"So she was killed sometime between five o'clock and seven o'clock this morning?" Lilly said.

"Unless Stan did it—" Bash said.

"Surely you don't think Stan could have—"

"Stan was alone at the site for a while this morning. How do we know he didn't get there earlier?" Bash said.

Lilly shrugged. "What was his motive?"

"According to gossip, he had one. I'd rather not say until I get it confirmed. Once I nail it down, I'll let you know. Anyway, he's not the top suspect."

"Who is?"

"Pete, of course. The husband is always the top suspect," Bash said. "In this case, he may have a motive too."

"Pete? He couldn't . . . he wouldn't . . . I can't imagine . . ."

"Lilly, welcome to my day. I'm writing down the names of folks I've known my whole life and wondering if they could have killed Merilee. It's terrible."

Lilly reached over and put her hand on top of Bash's. She gave it a squeeze. "You've had a bad day, and it isn't going to get easier. Let me know what I can do to help."

"Thank you for saying that, Lilly. I will. In the meantime, this beer is terrific. And that soup smells great. When did Delia say it would be ready?"

CHAPTER 12

"You awake?" Tamara said as soon as Lilly picked up the phone.

"I'm up," Lilly said. "I've been up since six-thirty. Just put the second pot of coffee on. Are you at the office?"

"I am, catching up on paperwork. My Monday morning routine." Lilly had, of course, known that. Tamara was a woman of routine, or as much routine as a real estate agent could have. Running your own agency did give you some leeway, including carving out times to go to your son's games, family dinners on Saturday afternoons, and Tuesday night dinners at Lilly's house, with Ernie and Delia. Lilly also knew Tamara's schedule included laundry on Sundays, yoga on Tuesday and Thursday mornings, getting her hair done on the third Wednesday every month, grocery shopping on Friday nights, and paperwork on Mondays.

"Is Pete there?" Lilly asked. Pete Frank worked in Tamara's real estate office and had since he came back to Goosebush. Pete wasn't great at his job, but he was good at making connections, and for Tamara it was a break-even proposition. Lilly knew that if it were anyone else but Pete, Tamara would have fired him long ago. She had asked Tamara to keep him on, and Tamara had agreed, as much for Lilly's sake as for Pete's. Lilly worried that if Pete didn't have some sort of income, he'd feel compelled to go after PJ for money, and that just wouldn't do. Not after PJ had worked so hard to keep his business afloat.

"No, Pete's not in. But I've spoken to him three times already today."

"Three times? What about?"

"Well, I'm only telling you this. It's a really bad form on Pete's part, and I need to vent."

"Vent away," Lilly said.

"We have an HR consultant who handles our personal and business policies. Pete hasn't been able to get in contact with her, so he's been calling me. He wants to know how fast he can get hold of Merilee's insurance policy payout."

"She only died on Saturday," Lilly said. Tamara was right. It was bad form. "Given everything, I'd imagine things will be tied up, don't you think?"

"You mean because she was murdered?" Tamara asked. "I have no idea, but yes. That must throw things off, especially since nobody has any idea who did it. Yet."

"Bash is working on it," Lilly said.

Bash had come by again on Sunday, to update Lilly and to have a cup of tea. Most of the updates had to do with waiting for lab results and getting people's statements done. Lilly and Delia had both talked him through the timeline they'd created, but nothing new came to light.

"Well, I hope Bash works harder, and faster, though I realize I am likely wishing for the impossible," Tamara said.

"Be nice," Lilly said.

"I strive for kind, but I'm done being nice. Keep helping Bash, Lilly, that's all I ask. I realize people think I only worry about my business, but I'm worried about Goosebush. I feel like we're losing our soul a bit. I told you about what is going on with Mrs. Asher?"

"Portia Asher? Is she still on Boatyard Lane?" Boatyard Lane was smack dab in the middle of the historic district of Goosebush. The entire town was the historic district, sort of. But there was a five-square-mile area in the middle of the town that was deemed the official historic district by the authorities. Parades marched through it, holiday carolers strolled along it, and the Turkey Trot ran through it. Lilly's house was in the middle of the district, as were most of the houses along the coastline. Aside from beautiful vistas, the historic district had a plaque on every house, slightly higher taxes, and several rules that each house had to abide by. Portia Asher lived in a gardener's cottage that had belonged to a large mansion that was torn down a hundred years ago. Lilly had helped her keep up with her gardens in years past but hadn't been over to visit since Alan got sick. She hadn't gone by the house in a year or so.

"Last winter was rough for Portia's house. The heavy snow caved in her porch roof, and her furnace gave out. She's been struggling to get everything repaired, but that isn't enough for some folks."

"Some folks?" Lilly was having trouble keeping

up with Tamara this morning, so she closed her eyes to focus. "What do home repairs have to do with anyone but her?"

"Well, some other things at her house needed repairs as well. A snowplow took out her old mailbox, and apparently her new one isn't up to historical code."

"Not that damned code again," Lilly said. Her house had been grandfathered in so that it didn't need to live up to the town code, but Lilly had still argued against the strict guidelines her friends and neighbors had put in place in the name of preservation.

"Oh, you have no idea. Pat French has been fining the poor woman once a week for the past eight months."

"Fining? For a mailbox?"

"You tried to tell me that the rules were a bad idea, but I didn't listen," Tamara said. "I was trying to protect the district from tacky vinyl siding or fuchsia paint. I had no idea how far Pat would take them. She's come up with standards on picket fences—the size, height, and spacing of the pickets—based on research. Different rules for houses from different eras. Flower boxes must be a certain shape and need to be painted black. Mailboxes, if freestanding, must meet certain height and material requirements—no exceptions. Portia's mailbox is not up to code. Apparently, the base is off, and it's too short and is painted a bright red."

"Red is against the rules?"

"Totally. Cranberry can get a variance, but bright red is out of the question. Anyway, between that and some other issues that Portia has been having, Pat French told her she could put a lien against her house."

"A lien? For a mailbox?"

"Five months of fines, with late fees. Plus, according to Pat, she's behind on her taxes. Anyway, Pat's got it out for her. She brought it up at an emergency board meeting last night."

"You had a board meeting about overdue taxes?"

"We had a board meeting about Merilee's murder," Tamara said. "Bash came in to talk to us. Some folks want to bring in outside help, maybe call in the state police, but Ray Mancini talked them down, got them to give Bash a chance to solve the murder on his own. We want to keep this in the family, so to speak, for as long as possible. As it is, the press is starting to swarm, but so far no one's talking to them."

"Figuring this out could take a while," Lilly said.

"They gave him two days," Tamara said. "Forty-eight hours. That's it. Ray and I tried to get him more time, but we couldn't."

"Well, at least you've tried."

"Yeah, well, I can't help Bash, but I decided to call and let you know about Portia Asher's troubles."

"And you're telling me this because . . . ?"

"Because, like it or not, old friend, you are one of the grand dames of Goosebush—"

"Hardly—"

"You are too."

"Well, if I am, so are you—"

"Fine, fine. We're both grand dames. You're missing the point. I can only push Pat French so far. She can, and has, screwed up many a title search for me in a fit of pique. I can't keep tussling with her. You need to step in."

"Excuse me?"

"Lilly, I don't want Portia to lose her house. Pat is on a rampage. Someone needs to help her. And that someone is you."

Lilly was silent for a few moments. Of course, other people could help. And likely would. But she knew why Tamara had called her. Other people could offer, but perhaps, since Lilly had known Portia Asher her entire life, she could make strides to getting this settled in a way that would let Portia keep her pride but would also get Pat off her back.

"You know, my mother and Portia Asher were friends. I've known her a long time. Thanks for the heads-up. I'll give her a call or stop by. Meanwhile, let me know if you hear from Pete again. Or if you hear anything else. Bash will try to move quickly on this, given the deadline. I hope he moves in the right direction."

"Which direction is that?"

"The direction toward finding out who killed Merilee, not just toward the easy answer."

When Delia came downstairs at eleven o'clock, she found Lilly sitting at the kitchen table, a cold cup of coffee in her hand and the land line sitting on the table in front of her. Lilly was staring at the back wall of the kitchen, as if she had X-ray eyes that could see through her sitting room, past the back porch, and into her gardens. She didn't have X-ray eyes, of course, but still she could see it all in her mind's eye. It calmed her down, and she'd found that she needed calming after her call from Tamara.

"Lilly, are you all right?" Delia asked. She picked

up the phone and put it back in its cradle. She went over to the coffeemaker and turned the machine back on to reheat the almost full pot.

"Tamara called a bit ago. She told me about some town business run amok, asked me to help somebody out."

"So you're sitting here thinking about helping somebody? That's upsetting you?" Delia asked, gently. She'd known her a long time, and though Lilly could be crusty on the outside, Delia knew that she had one of the kindest hearts she'd ever known. Losing Alan had changed Lilly and added another layer of crust. But these last few weeks—Delia had hoped that veneer had finally started breaking apart.

"No, that's not upsetting me. Of course, I'll help however I can. I'm just thinking about everything that's happened in the last couple of days—couple of weeks, really. Plus, these fines. I'm wondering if one thing has to do with another, and how."

"You think somebody was upset with their fines, and so for some reason they killed Merilee? That doesn't make any sense."

"No, I'm think thinking about money, and how the pursuit or lack thereof, can drive people to do things they might not otherwise do. Never mind. I've got thoughts rambling around in my brain, and I'm trying to sort them out. When they come together, I'll let you know and ask for your help in sorting them out."

Lilly looked over at Delia and smiled. "Where are you off to?" Around the house, Delia mostly wore ensembles that featured different shades of black, with an occasional pattern to break them up. But when she was going out, she usually added a splash of color somewhere. Today not only was she wearing a shirt that was mostly purple, but she also had a scarf around her head that was orange and purple. And she had makeup on. Lilly had an idea where she was headed but didn't want to assume.

"I'm heading down to the Star Café. Stan's short on staff and asked me to hostess at the restaurant for the lunch rush. Is that okay? Did you need me for something?"

"No, of course not. Maybe I'll go to the Star and grab lunch."

Delia smiled and did her best not to clap her hands. "That would be great. I'm sure Stan would love to see you. Do you want me wait for you?"

"No, no, you go ahead. I'm going to futz with my hair a bit and try to look a little more presentable. Get that smirk off your face. This is partly your fault; you wanted me to rejoin society. I can't do that looking disheveled."

"No, disheveled isn't your best look," Delia said. "I'll see you later."

Lilly enjoyed walking through Goosebush on her way to the Star Café. One of the best things about the town, and the location of her house, was that she could walk almost anywhere to run her errands. The only time it proved difficult was when she bought more than she intended and ended up having to carry the packages back. She remedied that by always taking a granny cart with her and including a few shopping bags in it. She knew it made her look like a quirky old woman, showing up wheeling a cart, but that was fine with her. She was a quirky old woman. Or a late-middle-aged woman. Whatever. The moment she let her hair go gray she'd become invisible, like many women her age. She decided a long time ago that that just wouldn't do. She owned quirky, but in Lilly style, which meant in good taste and with a bit of an homage to the 1950s, along with current comfort. Her spring and summer fashions included cotton dresses with circle skirts and fun patterns, most of which involved flowers or gardens, as well as cardigans, sneakers, pearls, and a dozen bangle bracelets with charms that had been gifts from Alan. She wore her hair in a short, curly bob that tended toward frizz in the summer, but she didn't care much about that. Her greatest vice was her earring collection—flowers of different shapes and styles. Some of them were costume, some worth a small fortune. Lilly Jayne had always worn flower earrings, and folks had bestowed them on her over the years. In one of her closets, she had a pegboard that took up an entire wall where all her earrings were on display, coded by color. Today's dress was white with blue cabbage roses, with earrings that matched.

Thanks to early town planners who had good common sense, most of Goosebush had sidewalks. Good sidewalks made all the difference. Tree roots had driven them up in a few sections, and Lilly had been doing some research on new sidewalk systems that allowed water to seep through, so that the roots wouldn't feel compelled to break through the concrete for water. They were costly, so Lilly hadn't presented a proposal at a town meeting yet, but that was on her agenda for this fall. Replacing the sidewalks was on the long-term maintenance plan for the town, and Lilly wanted them done right. As far as she was concerned, making them friendlier to plants, and less in need of maintenance over the years, made a lot of sense. Goosebush had been living with austerity measures for quite a while. Lilly had been ignoring them for the most part, but the town meeting last week, coupled with Tamara's call this morning, were part of what was causing the cyclone of thoughts rattling around Lilly's brain.

As Lilly walked, a few cars slowed down to wave, neighbors came out to say hello, and dogs approached with their tails wagging, knowing that Lilly always carried a bag of treats in her pocket. Lilly took a deep breath, savoring the sea air tinged with early spring. Even the faintest hint of low tide over by the bay didn't bother her. Lilly smiled and continued down Washington Street, taking her time.

When Lilly walked into the Star Café, Stan was standing at the coffee bar, wiping down the latte machine. He came around and gestured to her cart.

"I'll put this in the office for you if you'd like," Stan said.

"That's very nice of you. If it's no trouble," Lilly said.

"No trouble at all. I heard you might be joining us for lunch."

"I am, with a dessert of book shopping. I've got a list of mysteries I've been wanting to buy, and I hope I can get them today." Lilly always bought books and then donated them to the mobile library when she was done. The librarian pretended not to notice that more than half of the books hadn't had their spines cracked yet, and several were on the bestseller list.

"Well, anything you can't find I'm happy to order

for you," Stan said. "Though I will say, we've got a strong mystery section. Between Ernie and Delia, they keep a good running list of what I should order."

Lilly looked around at the floor-to-ceiling bookshelves that ran along the wall, along with the free-standing shelves that were on wheels in the middle of the shop. Stan also sold games, stationery, and other sundries, but mostly he sold books. Whenever the library had someone come in to speak, Stan sold that author's books at the event. He also hosted several book clubs every month.

"I can't wait to look around, but now I'm ready for lunch. Any recommendations?"

"Well, even though it's a beautiful spring day, so comfort food isn't necessary, our soups are pretty good."

"Soup sounds perfect," Lilly said. She gave Stan a smile and walked toward the back of the store, where the restaurant doors waited. She caught a glimpse of Delia standing at the front, looking down at the hostess table, scribbling notes. Lilly had to wonder, how busy was the Star Café at lunchtime on a Monday? It was time to find out.

CHAPTER 13

"Lilly, I tried to save you a table. But then a group of eight came in, and I had to put some together. I did save a seat for you at the bar, or you can wait for a table," Delia said.

Lilly looked around the restaurant, which was packed. She saw Tamara sitting in the corner with people she guessed were clients and returned her wave with a smile. "The bar is fine," Lilly said. "Is it always this busy?"

"Yes, usually. If you don't have to shovel lunch at your desk, it's a great place to come and sit and be waited on. Stan's got a limited menu, so the food comes out pretty quickly."

"I hear the soups are pretty good," Lilly said.

"They're great, but honestly, I think you should try one of the salads. Stan's really trying to use fresh, local produce, and he makes interesting combinations, all locally sourced and seasonal."

"Maybe I'll have soup and a salad."

"Wow, Lilly, you're walking on the wild side. Keep this up, and I won't recognize you," Delia said.

Lilly laughed, a sound Delia loved. "I'm going to sit at the bar," she said.

Delia picked up a menu and asked Lilly to follow her. She put the menu down on the counter and nodded to the bartender. "Lilly, you remember Stella, right?"

"Of course I do," Lilly said, settling into her seat. "Good to see you."

"You too," Stella Haywood said, giving Lilly a shy smile. "What can I get you to drink?"

"Iced tea would be terrific," Lilly said.

"Stella makes a ginger sweet tea that's to die for," Delia said. "Later in the afternoon, I might suggest adding bourbon to it, but I think you'll enjoy it for lunch. Have a good one," Delia said, wandering back to the hostess table to wait on the two parties who had just come in.

"I always do what Delia says," Lilly said. "I'll take a ginger sweet tea."

"Coming right up," Stella said. "If you have any questions about the menu, just ask."

"The Lilly Jayne I knew never let people tell her what to do," a disembodied voice from the corner said. Lilly turned to look at the owner of the voice and smiled.

"Cal," Lilly said. "I didn't see you sitting over there in the shadows. The Callisto Pace I knew never sat in the shadows, or in the corner."

"Fair enough," Cal said. "Mind if I come out of the shadows and sit next to you? Fair warning, I might give you a bad reputation by proximity."

"I'll risk it," Lilly said. Cal picked up his pint and slid into the seat next to Lilly. "I take it your art project from the other night hasn't gone over well?"

Stella slid Lilly's tea in front of her, and Lilly nodded thanks.

"You could say that," Cal said. He lifted his glass toward Stella, and she nodded, walking over to pull him another pint. "What did you think of it?"

Lilly looked over at Cal. She'd known him a good many years. Though they weren't close friends, she knew that the question wasn't an idle one. He valued her opinion.

"I thought it was interesting. There are seams in the work that need to be ironed out. Some of the images overpowered the words, which was a shame. Your words are always so spectacular. But I did appreciate that you are trying to incorporate a new level to your poetry. I'm just not sure they worked together. The photographs were stunning, by the way. I don't remember you taking pictures back when our paths crossed more often."

"Photography is a new passion."

"You're good at it," Lilly said. "I noticed the other day that you use your phone. Was that just at the event, or do you use your phone all the time?"

"I use my phone all the time." Cal slid his phone out of his front pocket and laid it on the bar. Lilly picked it up and noticed that it had an attachment on the lens. Cal pointed to it. "That adds depth and allows me to play with my compositions a lot more. If I had to carry a camera with me, I'd never take pictures. But one day last fall, I found myself bored; the words weren't coming, so I took out my phone and started to take pictures of the leaves, hoping the images would inspire the poem. Instead they inspired me to explore the world of images more carefully. I ended up taking an online course. Now I'm obsessed."

Lilly took a long sip of tea. "My, Delia was right. This tea is outstanding. You certainly have an eye for imagery, Cal. A dark, slightly cynical point of view, but anyone who knows your poetry can't be shocked by that."

"You'd be surprised," Cal said. He finished his beer and pulled the new one toward him. "Thanks, Stella."

"Are you ready to order?" Stella asked Lilly.

"I'm afraid I haven't looked at the menu yet," Lilly said. "What do you recommend, Cal?"

"I usually just drink my lunch," Cal said, lifting his glass toward Lilly in a mock toast.

"Oh, for heaven's sake, don't be a stereotype of a drunken poet. That's so boring," Lilly said. She opened the menu, which was blessedly short. She hated having to cruise multiple pages to decide what to eat. Choices of two soups, three sandwiches, and two salads. "We'll take a cup of vegetable soup, a cup of tomato soup, a chicken salad sandwich on two plates, and a house salad split into two bowls. Also, I'll take some more tea. It's delicious. Thank you, Stella."

"Don't break my heart, Lilly, and be like every other woman in my life, trying to redeem me," Cal said, after Stella walked away.

"I'm not trying to redeem you; I'm just trying to feed you." Lilly looked over at Cal. When was the last time she'd seen him? Saturday, at Alden Park, but only from afar. Before then, at his reading last week. What had happened in the past week? He looked exhausted. "Are you all right?"

"It's been a hell of a week, and I'm not as young as I used to be," Cal said.

"None of us are," Lilly said.

"Well, you look terrific. Much better than last time I saw you. You came to that lecture I gave at the Boston Public Library a year or so ago."

"I'm flattered you remembered," Lilly said. She recalled the event well. It was one of the few times she'd ventured out since Alan had died. She'd seen a few of her, or rather Alan's, old friends from academia, most of whom did not know how to react to his still-grieving widow. Cal had not had that problem, giving her a big hug and wondering aloud what Alan would've thought about his ode to a boatyard.

"He would've been flattered," Lilly had said. "You wrote it for him, didn't you?" Lilly remembered the stanzas about the old boat, now in dry dock, the glory of its past sailing expeditions ceased but not forgotten.

"I did," Cal had said. "It was inspired by that boatyard across the street from your house. Also by Alan. Lord, I miss him."

"So do I," Lilly had said. Cal had handed her a copy of his new book, signed. She'd read the poem often over the past two years and had practically committed it to memory. She'd written Cal a note, letting him know how healing she had found his work. He'd never responded, nor had she expected him to. That wasn't Cal's way.

"I'm so glad you're in Goosebush," Lilly said. "I'll try not to be offended that you didn't let me know that you were here."

"Please, don't be upset. Honestly, I did ask about you when I first got here, but someone said they hadn't seen you around, and I assumed you weren't living here. Then these past few weeks have been such a blur, getting ready for the show."

"Ah, the show. Finding models must have taken a lot of time," Lilly said. She was thinking about all the images of the naked women he had included in his slides.

"You have no idea," Cal said. "As I said, I'm getting old. Can't juggle the way I use to."

"Juggle what?"

"Work and life. Work and seeing old friends. Work and women." Cal took another big sip of beer. He reached over and took Lilly's right hand in his left. "Forgive me? I should've been in touch."

"There's nothing to forgive," Lilly said. "Work takes priority, and I know how it takes over your life."

"I wish everyone was as forgiving as you are." Cal and Lilly waited for Stella to unload the dishes of food in front of them. Cal chose the vegetable soup, so Lilly took the tomato. One sip and she was certain she'd gotten the better end of the deal. The two of them ate in silence for a couple of minutes. While Cal had been picking at the food in the beginning, he finished his part of the sandwich with great gusto, so Lilly slid her half over to him.

"About the women, the ones in your art piece," she asked him.

Cal picked up the sandwich and looked at Lilly. "What about them?" he asked.

"Where did you find your models? The photos were fairly intimate in an odd way."

"There's a bit of an artist community here in Goosebush. Stan gives a few of us space to work here and at a warehouse a few miles away. We regularly meet, and I asked for some volunteers. Rest assured, all of the subjects knew these weren't beauty shots."

"Was Merilee Frank one of them?" Lilly asked.

"She was. How could you tell? I tried to keep them anonymous."

"I saw the butterfly tattoo on the back of the shoulder of one of the women. I'd noticed that Merilee had one when she insisted on wearing a strapless dress to the church bazaar last December."

"Can't get much past you, can I?" Cal asked.

Lilly smiled at him. "Are you trying to?"

Cal shook his head. "It's odd to have you back in my life, Lilly. Most everyone else has only known me a few months. You've known me for years. I thought for a while I could reinvent myself, but seeing you, I realized I can't."

"Why would you want to, Cal?" When Cal didn't answer, Lilly reached over and put her hand on his and squeezed it for a moment. "We've known each other for a long time. You and Alan were such great friends. He thought the world of you, did you know that? Despite all your foibles, he thought you were the best of men. I hope you know you never need to get anything past me. I'm here to listen, if you need an ear."

"They say confession is good for the soul," Cal said. He sighed and looked over the bar at the wall of bottles. He didn't look over at Lilly when he answered. "Merilee and I were . . . friends. Good friends, for a while. I'm not proud of that. I usually consider married women off-limits. But there was something about her, at least at the beginning of our relationship. She was a tonic for a man who had been feeling old. She inspired me to try photography. It was great at the beginning."

"How long ago were you seeing each other?" Lilly asked quietly.

"Until about March. Then she broke it off. She wanted to stay friends, but I wasn't terribly interested. I hate to speak ill of the dead, but Merilee was neither the most stable nor the kindest person I ever met. I can handle unstable, and I can handle unkind, but as a package? No thanks."

"Did Pete know?" Lilly asked.

"About our, um, friendship? No, I don't think so. Given the size of Pete, I doubt I'd be sitting here with my face still arranged this way if Pete had known. Merilee often talked about how crazy jealous he was, but how she had him convinced that she was nothing but faithful. I can still hear her cackling about how stupid he was."

"Poor Pete," Lilly said.

"He a friend of yours?" Cal asked, looking over at her curiously.

Lilly took another swig of iced tea. "Pete's my first husband." Now it was her turn to stare straight ahead.

"What? You were married to the oaf?" Cal said.

"He wasn't always an oaf," Lilly said. She was remembering the tanned, trim athlete she'd married. He'd been full of potential back then; at least Lilly had convinced herself of that. In retrospect, had he been? Lilly shook her head and looked over at Cal. "We were married young. Then he left me for someone else—"

"The man's an idiot—" Cal said.

"An act for which I will be forever grateful. It's true. If he hadn't left me, we would have stayed married. And I would've been miserable. I probably would have done my best to make him miserable too."

Cal looked at Lilly long and hard. "Lilly, there are facets of you I obviously know nothing about."

"Well, I should hope so," Lilly said, laughing. "I'd hate to think I was an open book."

"Never an open book. Maybe I should have you pose for me? You could be a hell of a muse," Cal said.

"Thank you, I guess. I'd be happy to pose for you, as long as I can keep my clothes on."

"Well, if you insist," Cal said, smiling.

Lilly blushed. "Tell me, were all of the models in your art piece close personal friends of yours?"

"Well, never let it be said that Lilly Jayne won't ask a direct question. I admire that about you," Cal said. "Some, not all. You know me well, Lilly. Monogamy has never been my strong suit."

Lilly nodded, remembering stories and gossip she'd heard over the years, as well as the never-ending stream of women Cal had brought to faculty dinners and cocktail parties over the years. "I will say that photography is giving me a new way of looking at the world, and that includes women. My interest isn't purely carnal."

"Cal, don't take this the wrong way, but your images aren't the most flattering—"

Cal laughed, and almost choked on a bite of salad. "No, you're right. It must be a phase I'm going through. I try to find the ugly beauty in the everyday. It's harder with people, and I've been determined not to reveal personalities in the pictures so as not to pass judgment. Everyone has a part of them that doesn't flatter but tells their truth. I'm fascinated by that. I tend to use those images and manipulate them to meet my needs."

"Did Merilee mind that?" Lilly asked.

"No, surprisingly, she didn't. She was vain, to be sure, but she liked being an art object. I think she aspired to be an artist herself, but the most she could hope for was being a muse or a model for the work. She talked about opening a gallery at some point."

"That's an interesting facet to Merilee. Sounds like something nice could be said about her."

"Merilee was both self-aware and obtuse. She was also transactional. She knew that the photos weren't about her; they were about my work. She was able to separate our relationship from my work. I wish I could say that about everyone. There's one woman who's gone completely off her nutter, she's so upset by how she was included in the piece. She hasn't spoken to me directly in over a week but is going out of her way to make my life miserable."

"Another good friend?"

"She was," Cal said. "On again, off again. A friend of Merilee's, as it happens. We were seeing each other before I met Merilee; as a matter of fact, that's how we met. Anyway, after Merilee and I stopped seeing each other, Kitty and I picked it back up." Cal looked over at Lilly. "That was terribly indiscreet of me; I don't usually kiss and tell. Anyway, this woman is not happy, and that's been making me think about the art piece I've been working on in general. Honestly, that's made me miserable. If I must choose, do I choose people or my art? I've had to come to terms with the fact that I choose my art. Every time. I'm a terrible human being."

"Maybe not terrible, as long as you're honest from the outset. It seems as if you care more about what Kitty thinks and feels than you anticipated."

"I do. This whole situation has wrecked me in ways you cannot even imagine." Cal stood up and reached into his back pocket for his wallet.

"Put that away," Lilly said. "My treat. You can pick up the next meal."

"Thank you, Lilly, for the meal and for the friendly ear."

"You've always got a friendly ear with me. Don't be a stranger, Cal," Lilly said. Cal leaned over and gave her a kiss on the cheek. He squeezed her shoulder as he walked out of the restaurant. Lilly turned to watch him go and noticed Kitty Bouchard sitting at a corner table, staring at her. Lilly stared right back, didn't bother to smile, and then turned back to her meal. She took a bite of her salad and chewed the combination of nuts, fruit, greens, and a tangy vinaigrette.

"Well, one thing's for sure," Lilly thought to herself. "Cal has complicated taste in women."

CHAPTER 14

Lilly was wandering through the bookstore, a basket full of books at her side. She was reading the dust jacket of the latest Barbara Ross novel and nodded to herself while she tossed it into her shopping basket. She turned, and a gift basket caught her eye. It was one of several, pre-wrapped in cellophane and sitting on a shelf. She picked it up. A small teapot, a mug, a tin of tea, a box of cookies, and three mysteries all displayed on a serving tray.

"Is that a goose on that teapot?"

Lilly started but happily didn't drop the tray. "Roddy, you gave me start. Yes, a goose, and a bush. It's done by a local artist, Caroline Lentz. She makes pots, plates, and mugs, then paints them. This is one of the most popular. The goose and the bush. Goose-bush. Pictorial puns are on her specialties. I hadn't seen this one before, but I really like it."

"It is charming," Roddy said. "I wonder if they have individual mugs? Is this a treat for yourself?"

"No, I'm going to pay a visit to a neighbor, and I

think this may be the perfect thing to take along for her. What brings you here today?" Lilly asked.

"Well, to tell you the truth, I'm here to look for a book on gardening. I was over at Bits, Bolts & Bulbs, and Ernie suggested a title that he said the bookstore carried. My parents were avid gardeners, and I had hoped that it was an inherited gene, but I fear not. I can't tell weeds from plants, and whether the vine I am battling is something I should battle or something I can tame and use for a decorative purpose."

"If it's the vine creeping from under the garden door, the best thing to do is to pull it. It is invasive. It could be put in a container and trained up a trellis, but even that's risky," Lilly said.

"Lilly, I wonder if you would come over to my garden at some point this week and give me some advice? I hate to impose, but you do seem to have a magic touch—"

"Hardly magic—"

"Your reputation precedes you," Roddy said, smiling. "Additionally, I can see your gardens from the second floor of my house. They are magnificent, as lovely from afar as they are up close. I wonder if everyone knows about the intricate patterns that you've laid out with paths, plants, and sculptures? It looks more haphazard on ground level, but from up above I see the pattern. Intersecting circles. Just lovely."

Lilly felt herself blush and smiled. "Of course, I will come over to your house and look at your gardens. I'll bring Delia with me," Lilly said. "You know, back in the day, the gardens of your house were the most magnificent in all of Goosebush. It's true. The original owner laid them out and put in foundational plants and bushes that added weight to the pattern. Each subsequent owner built on but didn't change the core idea, which is a ship's wheel."

"A ship's wheel? Really?" Roddy scrunched up his face, trying to recall what his garden looked like from the upper floors of his house. It looked like a lot of things, but a ship's wheel would not have made Roddy's top hundred guesses.

"Yes, there was a tree in the center—"

"Tree? I had a tree?"

"It was the focal point of the garden. A couple of owners let the gardens go, and the pattern was lost to chaos. Trust me, it will take you very little time to get the garden back in shape. The earth has muscle memory, as do the plants. We, you, just have to help them remember."

"Tell me, do you talk to your plants to help refresh their memories? I found myself swearing at the weeds, and I hope the other plants aren't taking it personally."

Lilly laughed. "I don't think I talk to my plants, but I will confess that gardening puts me in a bit of a trance. I'm not sure if I speak aloud or not."

"So far, I haven't heard anything from over the wall, but it is a wide and thick wall."

"It is, indeed," Lilly said.

"Our wall fascinates me. As you mentioned to me, when the captain and his daughter had a falling out, the wall was built between the houses, with the large, formidable door and an impressive lock. Apparently when he locked the door, he sent the key to his daughter with a note telling her it was hers to open. She sent him back the key."

"How did you hear this story?" Lilly asked. "That's a new one to me."

"Well, I'll confess I went to the Goosebush Library this morning, and visited the Historical Society. I spent a couple of hours reading journals and letters from the captain and his daughter."

"I wonder if the daughter ever regretted sending the key back?"

"I don't know," Roddy said. "It is amazing the lengths that family members can go to hurt one another."

Lilly carefully looked away and let Roddy work through what he was thinking about. It wasn't her place to pry. "Let's find that book for you," she said to Roddy. She put the tea tray in her shopping basket, and then walked over to the gardening section of the bookstore. She picked up the book she was sure Ernie had referred him to, and another one on historic gardens.

"Here, these are both wonderful beginnings," she said.

"Perfect," Roddy said. "I can do more research as well, which I love."

"Let's set up a time for Delia and I to come over and look at your gardens. Delia has made it her mission to do as much historical research on the gardens in Goosebush as she can. I keep telling her she should write a book. Anyway, I know she has pictures of the Winslow gardens. I'll ask her to bring copies over, and we can walk through how to get your garden back."

"The Winslow gardens? Were they the original owners of the house?"

"No, Florence Winslow was the gardener. She was hired by different families in the late-1800s and created wonderful gardens for them. She never got the credit she deserved."

"A function of her being a woman in a man's world?" Roddy asked.

"That, and the fact that she was an African American woman. A distant relative of Tamara's, as a matter fact. Anyway, that's Delia's specialty— uncovering hidden histories and bringing them to light. I know that she'd love the opportunity to see your gardens and will be thrilled that you're willing to bring them back."

"Willing to, yes. Able to? With help, possibly." Roddy smiled, and Lilly smiled back. He handed her a card, which she took. "That's my mobile. Call or text anytime. I'm generally around these days."

"Tell you what, I'll be in touch later this afternoon, after I run my errands."

"And deliver your gift to the lucky recipient?" Roddy asked. Lilly nodded. She hoped that Portia Asher liked tea.

CHAPTER 15

Lilly was going to go home first, but she decided to get it over with. It wasn't in her nature to interfere or to pry. A true New Englander, she felt strongly that it was folks' right to keep their private lives private. But she also knew that pride ran deep, and that people might not ask for help if they needed it. The Asher family had been in Goosebush as long as Lilly's family had. Portia had been a widow for many years, and Lilly suspected that these days she was house rich and cash poor. That was the case for a lot of folks in Goosebush. She knew Portia's children were raising families, and she was on her own. Lilly understood, better now than she ever had, that isolation is a terrible thing, and not good for a person's psyche.

She slowed down as she approached the Asher house and took it in. The house had started off a small gardener's cottage but had been built onto over the years. It crowded the lot it was on, and like Lilly's house, many of the rules that governed the historic district didn't apply. Many, but not all. As

Lilly walked toward the front door; she paused to look at the mailbox. It looked fine to her, but she didn't dally. The curtains in the front of the house were moved aside, and a pale face peered through them. Lilly walked up the front walk, positioned her granny cart off to the side of the front porch, and knocked. She waited patiently and saw the flutter of curtains again, but nobody came to the door. She knocked again and called out. "Mrs. Asher? It's Lilly Jayne. I wanted to stop by and say hello."

After a minute the door opened, and Portia stepped into the doorway, blocking Lilly's path.

"Lilly Jayne, I haven't seen you in years. What brings you here? Are you working for the town these days? Checking up on me?" Portia said.

Lilly was taken aback by the angry look on Portia Asher's face. "I don't work for the town, not at all. I'm behind on visiting old friends, and I'm trying to make up for lost time. The other day, I thought about the visits my mother and I would make here every spring to see your rosebushes, and I wondered if they were still blooming. I can see that they are, which is wonderful. I lost most of my bushes winter before last. I hadn't prepped them well enough, but I had other things on my mind."

Portia's face relaxed. "I lost a few myself that winter. This year, it's my hydrangeas that are giving me a hard time."

"I'm happy to look at them, if you'd like. But first, I wanted to run an idea by you. Do you have a few minutes?"

"Sure, I guess so," Portia said.

"Have you seen these Goosebush mugs, the ones Caroline makes? I was thinking about commissioning some for the next holiday bazaar. You know, as a way to make some extra money for the Beach Conservancy. But I'm not sure. Are they in good taste? I don't want to appear to be making fun of Goosebush. I thought perhaps I should ask someone who cares as much about our town for their opinion. May I come in for minute and show you this?"

Lilly lifted the tray out of her granny cart and tilted it toward Portia. Portia Asher leaned into the doorway and looked at the tray.

"Come in, Lilly, come in. I've seen those down at the Star Café. I hadn't paid much attention to the design. Do you want to bring your cart in or leave it out there?"

"If you can't leave your cart outside in this part of Goosebush, where can you?"

Portia stood back and let Lilly pass in front of her. "Well, sad to say, I don't know as I'd trust it overnight. Even Goosebush has changed, and not for the better. Now, let me look at you, Lilly. Would you like a cup of tea?"

"That sounds wonderful," Lilly said. They went back to Portia's kitchen, and Lilly put the tray on the kitchen table. "Do you have a knife, Mrs. Asher?" Lilly asked. "I want to open this package, so we can take a closer look at the mug. There's a teapot in there too."

"Portia, please. There are some scissors on that block over there."

Lilly used the scissors to pierce the cellophane wrapping, and took out the tea, the cookies, the pot, and the mug and put them on the table. Portia filled the teakettle and put it on the stove. Lilly rinsed out the teapot and the mug. She picked up the mug and showed it to Portia. "What do you think?"

Portia took the mug and held it in her hands. She looked at the design and ran her finger over it. "I like it. Like that the bush has some texture to it too. Shows that this isn't just stamped out on an assembly line. Some real artistry went into it."

"You don't think people would find it in poor taste, making fun of the town name?" Lilly said.

"The folks who would find it in poor taste, those are the folks I don't really care about what they think. You know what I mean?"

"I do, actually. Some people take themselves so seriously."

"Seems like a sense of humor is a rare commodity these days, doesn't it?" Portia said.

"It does. It also feels like it's gotten a lot meaner in the world, especially lately."

"Sure does," Portia said. She opened the top of the teapot and spooned some tea inside. "We'll let that sit for a few minutes. A lovely blend; thank you so much for bringing it. We can also open that shortbread you brought. I do like shortbread. I also have some chocolate chip cookies I made the other day for my grandson."

Portia opened the cookie tin and put some on a plate. Lilly picked one up and nibbled the corner. She took a bigger bite. "You always did make the best chocolate chip cookies," Lilly said.

"Next to your mother's. Rest her soul. I don't suppose you have her recipe?"

"I do, but she must have left something out. Mine don't taste the same. Delia's tried to make them too, and she's a better baker than I am."

"Bring it by, and I'll try to figure out what's missing. The temptation is strong to leave something out, so that the next generation must figure it out themselves, but I'm not going to do it. My grand-son, Chase—do you know Chase? He's a good boy. He comes to visit, bakes with me, helps me around the house. Anyway, I promised Chase I'd give him my recipe with all my tweaks."

"Does he live nearby?"

"He's finishing his last semester at UMass. He has an internship starting in January down the Cape. He's going to move in with me since it's so close."

"That'll be nice," Lilly said. "It will be good to have him around the house this winter, in case we have another snowy one. I don't know about you, but I hate shoveling."

"I hate the fines for not shoveling even more," Portia said. She took out a tea strainer and poured a little bit of tea into her cup. Apparently, she was sat-isfied with the color, because she poured tea into Lilly's cup and then finished filling her own.

"Fines for not shoveling?" Lilly took a sip.

"Or maybe it was a fine for not bringing my garbage pail back to the house within forty-eight hours. Oh, wait, it was the fine for the wrong color mailbox."

"Are you kidding me?" Lilly asked.

"I wish I were," Portia said.

"Who fines you?"

"Pat French and her flunkies. Of course, I think Merilee Frank had put her up to it."

"Merilee? What makes you think Merilee had anything to do with it?"

"Merilee wanted me out of this house. It's next door to a house they put an offer on earlier this spring. She was hell-bent on opening a bed-and-breakfast, and I was putting a stop to it. That's all I need, tourists traipsing in and out all over my front yard. Anyway, Merilee had it out for me. Started making complaints to the town about things around my house, complaining that it wasn't up to code. Pat French latched right on and started writing me up left and right. I hate to speak ill of the dead, but I was hoping that, since Merilee passed, the pressure would be off. But then I got two more notices from Pat this morning. One about the mailbox, one about the recycling bin."

"What about the recycling bin and the mailbox?"

"Well, as you know, the town's got those new recycling bins on wheels. Everyone's supposed to use them. Problem is, mine got stolen. They want me to pay a two-hundred-dollar deposit for a new one. I don't have it right now, so I've been using the old blue bin. Guess that's against some rule or another. Twenty-five dollars a week fine."

"That's ridiculous."

"Course it is. Then there's the mailbox. Chase was so proud of the work he did, getting it installed. But it's not up to code. Those mailbox fines are mounting too. Honestly, at first I was just ignoring them. But now Pat says they can take my house." Portia cleared her throat and swallowed hard.

"Well, that doesn't seem right. Have you talked to the board of selectmen?" Lilly asked gently.

"I called Tamara this morning. I've got a call in to Ray Mancini. Not sure if they can help or not, but I can't lose my house."

"You won't lose your house," Lilly said gently.

"I'm not asking for charity. I don't need charity," Portia said, putting her mug down with a bang.

"I'm thinking that you're doing more of a civic good then accepting charity," Lilly said. "Goosebush can't work like this. Thank you for letting folks know. Let me do some research on this fining business. You can't be the only person affected. Tell you what, I've got a lawyer friend who loves this kind of case. I'll give him a call, get his opinion."

"Well, I'd appreciate that," Portia said. "I hate to burden anyone else with my troubles, but if it can help someone else—"

"I'm sure it can," Lilly said. She drained her mug and put it down on the table. "Well, thank you for the tea. I probably should be getting back home before Delia worries."

"It's nice to have somebody to worry about you coming home, isn't it? That's another reason I'm looking forward to having Chase here. I do have one more favor to ask."

"Yes?"

"It's my hydrangeas. The last couple of years they just haven't been blooming like they used to. I've tried everything, but I'm afraid we may have another bad year. There's still time, so if you don't mind taking a look at them? Nobody knows plants better than you do."

"I'd be happy to," Lilly said.

Lilly offered to help clean up, but Portia shook her off. The two women left the house through the front door and walked over to the side yard, where some pitiful bushes served as a property line. Hydrangeas always looked bad this time of year, but these looked extra peaked. As Portia showed Lilly her hydrangea bushes, Lilly took her phone out and started to snap pictures. She also took clandestine pictures of the offending mailbox. She looked over at Pete Frank's want-to-be house and tried to imagine it as a bed-and-breakfast. How would they get a building permit for that?

Lilly needed to pay more attention to what was going on around Goosebush and ask more questions. It was, she had convinced herself, her duty as a citizen.

CHAPTER 16

"Have you seen this crap?" Delia asked Lilly. Lilly had just gotten home and had come in the side door. Delia was sitting at the kitchen table, on her computer.

"What crap is that, dear?" Lilly asked. She continued to walk out of the kitchen, into the hallway, where she left the cart. She'd take the books upstairs later. Her office/library was next to her bedroom, and she had a shelf dedicated to books to be read. Of course, the books were double-shelved, with others jammed on top. She went through her books every six months, so she had until August 1st to get through these piles. Lilly Jayne was nothing if not precise in her planning and execution. There is a season for everything, and February and August were her decluttering months.

"Come look at this," Delia said to Lilly when she came back into the room. She got up from the table so that Lilly could sit and look at the computer. While Lilly settled in, Delia went over to the sink and got Lilly a glass of water.

"What is this?"

"A blog. It's called Goosebush Gossip," Delia said. On the masthead was a collage of photos, the faces of many Goosebush citizens. Lilly used the mouse and scrolled down. The first blog post was titled "Who's in Charge?" It showed time-stamped pictures of Bash Haywood around Goosebush on Sunday, mostly seeming to visit folks. Lilly noticed that her house was part of the post; a photo showed Bash's car parked in the driveway. Lilly knew that he was likely investigating, but she had to admit the photos appeared damning, considering Bash was eating something in almost every photo.

Lilly kept scrolling and noticed that there were blog posts dating back months. "I've never seen this before," Lilly said.

"Neither had I. Neither had anyone, as far as I know. But since Saturday, whoever writes it has been posting at least twice a day, tagging Goosebush and the murder. A friend of mine posted an entry on Facebook, and I went over to look at it. I think it's gone viral, at least here in town."

"Is that my house?" Lilly asked as she scrolled through posts.

"I hate to say it, but you're a featured player on the blog. Your garden party got a lot of coverage, but mostly from outside the gates, keeping track of who was coming in."

"Who writes it?" Lilly asked.

"That's the question of the hour," Delia said. "There are all kinds of pictures. Most of the gossip is banal. Who was seen eating with whom. Who's building a new addition onto their house, and what it might be worth. Who got drunk last Friday night and passed out in the bushes. That was Pete Frank, by the way. The drunk who passed out in the bushes."

"Friday night?"

"Yup. The night before Merilee was murdered."

"So does that mean he has an alibi?"

"Far from it," Delia said. "Drink your water, Lilly. You need to stay hydrated. Would you like a cup of tea?"

"I'm teaed out," Lilly said. "What time is it? Too early for a glass of wine?"

"Nope, not today," Delia said. She walked over to the wine cooler and took out a bottle of red wine, a mixed blend. She put it on the kitchen table, along with two glasses. The wine had a screw top, which wasn't as "fancy" as opening a cork, but it was still a good bottle of wine. She poured them each a glass and sat down.

Delia pulled her computer toward her. "A post went up a little while ago, but it was taken down. I grabbed a screenshot and saved the photos before it disappeared."

"How did you know to take a screenshot?"

"I wish I could say I was clairvoyant, but I'm not. When the post went live, it had a disclaimer that it would only be up for ten minutes. I happened to be online and had signed up to receive alerts for new posts. Here are the pictures," Delia said. She double clicked on an item on her desktop and turned the computer back toward Lilly.

The picture was taken from a height and showed the corner of Alden Park that was closest to the Wheel. Lilly zoomed in on the two figures in the photo. They were tough to make out, but Lilly recognized them. Merilee and Pete. They appeared to be having an argument.

"Click to the next picture. I made a slideshow of them," Delia said. "There are six altogether that were posted."

"What did the post say?" Lilly asked.

"Just one line: 'Were these Merilee Frank's last words?'"

"That's lovely," Lilly said.

"Isn't it just?" Delia said.

Lilly scrolled through the pictures and saw a fight escalating. In the fourth picture, it looked as if Pete was grabbing Merilee by the shoulders. In the fifth picture, she appeared to be turning away, but he was grabbing her by the upper arm, and it looked like she was twisting to get free. In the sixth photo, a truck blocked the view of the park.

"How are these taken? Where were they taken from?" Lilly asked.

"I've been doing that research, and Ernie asked me to do, you know, the camera research. It's scary. Cameras can be anywhere. They are different sizes, and they all function differently. Sometimes they can be connected to the Internet automatically. Other times the photos need to be downloaded. It could also be a human being who happened to be taking pictures at exactly the right time, but that seems odd. Even if they figure out where this camera was placed, it probably won't be there when they go to look for it. To me, it looks like the camera was on a time-lapse setting and took a picture every few seconds. But I need to look at the time codes more carefully."

"What did the post say again?" Lilly asked.

"The title of the post was 'Prime Suspect.' The only text was 'Were these Merilee Frank's last words?'"

"Bash needs to see this—"

"I'm way ahead of you," Delia said. "I sent him the link to the post as soon as I saw it, and then I sent him the photos. That was the right thing to do, wasn't it? Even though it doesn't look good for Pete."

"That was the right thing to do," Lilly said. "Bash needs all the information that's out there, so he can investigate. Do me a favor; forward the e-mail to me. I want to send it to Ray Mancini."

"I cc'd you on the e-mail," Delia said. "Now I'm sitting here trying to figure out who writes this blog, and why."

"Both good questions," Lilly said, taking a sip of wine. "I'd add one more. What else does this blogger know?"

Lilly went to her library and got her own laptop. Delia started to send Lilly links to her camera research, and Lilly bookmarked it all. She knew that Delia would also provide her a document with condensed information, but the links were helpful to have in the meantime. Lilly also spent some time looking at the Goosebush Gossip site, but not too much time. It made her feel dirty.

"Are you hungry?" Delia asked.

"I am, though after that wonderful lunch at the Star Café, I'm surprised I need to eat again today. How was your shift? Do you do that often?"

"It was really busy, but fine. Stan likes me to come in and help during the lunch rush. I don't get flustered when people are waiting for tables. He says that no one else gets people seated as fast as I do." Delia blushed slightly when she mentioned Stan's praise.

"You have a good mind for organizing and categorizing," Lilly said. "You also have a gift for thinking five steps ahead. All of that probably helps with restaurant hosting duties. I will confess, I was surprised at how busy it was in there."

"Yeah, it is going well, especially lately," Delia said. "Now, unless we want to go back there for dinner, what should we make?"

"Your call," Lilly said. "Surprise me, and tell me how to help."

Within minutes, Delia was doing interesting things with leftover chicken, bacon, and cream. Lilly was chopping up broccoli for the sauce and had just put on the pasta water to boil. Lilly caught Delia up about her visit with Portia Asher.

"What are we going to do to help her?" Delia said.

"Who said we are going to do anything?" Lilly asked.

"Puh-leeze. I've seen that look on your face, but not for a while. Alan used to call it your Fix-It Face. He'd come into the office and say, 'Lilly had her Fix-It Face on this morning, so I may not be able to go to that event tonight.'" Both women worked in silence for a moment, allowing Alan's memory, and presence, to join them.

Lilly finally broke the silence. "Do you think Tamara knows about the Goosebush Gossip site?" she asked Delia.

"I'd think so," Delia said. "Tamara's got her fingers on the pulse of Goosebush. But maybe you'd better call her, just to make sure. You know how upset she'll be if she doesn't hear about it right away."

"True enough," Lilly said. "The water is going to take a while to boil, so let me give her a quick call."

Lilly picked up her wineglass and went out to the back porch. She fished her cell phone out of her pocket and sat down on the wicker rocker. She hit number one on her speed dial, and Tamara picked up right away.

"Tamara, just checking in. I wanted to make sure you've heard about the Goosebush Gossip site—"

"No, hon, I'm still at the office. I'll be here for a while. Pete's here, and we're catching up. It's like old times."

Old times. Not always the best of times for Lilly, and Tamara knew that. "Are you all right? Is he all right?"

"No, not exactly."

"Do you want me to come down?"

"That would be terrific, thanks," Tamara said.

"I'll be right there. Should I call Warwick? Or Bash?"

"No, we're good."

"I'll be there in a few minutes," Lilly said.

Lilly got up from the chair and walked back into the kitchen. "Pete is at the office with Tamara. I'm going to go down there, make sure everything's all right."

"You want me to come with you?"

"No, stay here and finish supper. She mentioned old times, which means he's probably drunk. Tamara and I have dealt with him drunk more times than I can remember. Or choose to remember. I may bring Pete back with me. He could probably use a good dinner."

"Lilly, only you would keep taking care of your ex-husband," Delia said. "I'll make extra sauce and cook more pasta. If you're not back in a half hour, I'm coming after you."

CHAPTER 17

Lilly usually walked to Tamara's office, but tonight she wanted to get there faster. As she left the kitchen, she hit the garage door remote that sat beside the back door. It would take a while for the large wooden door to rise, but Lilly had the timing down. By the time she got to the three-car garage, the door was open, and her bright red Vespa was there, waiting for her. The winter months were tough for Lilly regarding transportation. She could drive, and did, but she preferred walking or, in the summer months, riding around on her Vespa.

Lilly put her helmet on and turned the key. She drove slowly down the driveway, pausing at the end to make sure there was no traffic coming. While she was sitting there, she looked around, trying to see if she could figure out where the camera was that had been taking pictures of her house and driveway. She didn't see anything, but as Delia said, the camera could be anywhere. Lilly hated that idea. She made a mental note to ask Delia how video transmissions could be interrupted. She'd install an electronic fence if it protected her privacy.

Lilly took a right and went down to the Wheel, getting on at six o'clock and driving most of the way around to eight o'clock. Tamara's real estate office was on the right, in a row of very tasteful storefronts. Lilly pulled the Vespa up and parked it at the end of the row. She left her helmet under the front seat and put her key in her pocket. Portia was right; Goosebush had changed. There was a time when Lilly would have felt comfortable leaving the scooter running, but no more. A red Vespa was catnip to folks looking to take a joyride. Lilly took out her cell phone, turned it on, and dialed 9 and 1. She'd dial the other 1 if she needed to, but she'd check out the situation first. The front shade was closed, as was the door shade. Lilly tried the handle, and the door was open. She opened it a crack quietly and peeked into the room. She saw Pete sitting at his desk, his head in his hands. Tamara sat on his desk and had her hand on his shoulder. Lilly opened the door wider, and as she walked in, she heard him weeping.

"Look who's here, Pete," Tamara said quietly. "It's Lilly."

Pete continued to weep and didn't look up. Lilly looked around the office for a box of Kleenex. There was nothing on Pete's desk, nothing, so she looked to the cluttered chaos on Tamara's desk. Sure enough, there was a box of Kleenex sitting on the corner. She walked over and took it, then handed one to Pete.

"What happened?" Lilly asked Tamara.

"Haven't been able to get a straight story," Tamara

said. "Near as I can tell, Pete's been on a bender since Saturday. He tried to go home a little while ago, but there was a police car sitting in his driveway. He freaked out and came here." Lilly raised her eyebrows at Tamara, but Tamara shrugged her shoulders.

"Pete, why didn't you want to talk to the police?" Lilly asked. "I'm sure they wanted to let you know how the case is progressing. Maybe they had some more questions for you."

"They're not looking for Merilee's real killer," Pete said. "They think I did it. But I didn't. You know that, right? Both of you? I could never . . . I mean, she frustrated the hell out of me, but . . . I could never. I loved her."

"I know you did, Pete," Tamara said.

"I did, I really did. Why don't the cops believe me?" Pete said, looking up at both women. Tamara shrugged, but Lilly decided Pete needed to know what he was up against.

"Pete, there's this blog. Delia showed it to me this afternoon. It is a site about Goosebush. Anyway, they posted some pictures of you and Merilee fighting near Alden Park on Saturday. I believe you when you say you didn't kill her. But I've got to say, those photos look pretty damning. They're probably why the police wanted to talk to you."

"There are pictures? Damn it," Pete said. He slammed his closed fist onto his desk, and Tamara jumped up and took a step away.

"What were you fighting about, Pete?" Lilly asked gently. She hadn't had to deal with a drunken Pete for years, but the muscle memory was strong. Keep him talking, distract him, tire him out, get him to go to sleep. There was a couch in the office—that would have to do for tonight.

Pete sat up and blew his nose. He tossed the Kleenex toward the wastebasket and missed. He took another Kleenex out of the box and wiped his eyes. "I wish I could remember. We've been fighting so much lately. We could have been fighting about money, her spending, my son, this town, my job, both of my ex-wives. But I never would have hurt her."

Lilly sat down on one of the office chairs and rolled it over, so she could be eye to eye with Pete. Tamara stepped in to stand beside Lilly.

"Who would have hurt her?" Lilly asked gently. "Because somebody did hurt her, and you should probably help the cops come up with another alternative."

Pete sat back in the chair and took a deep breath. He shook his head and shrugged his shoulders. "Merilee pissed off a lot of people. It was a spectator sport for her. But were folks upset enough to kill her? I just don't see it." Pete's voice faded. "I'm so tired."

"I don't think he's had any sleep," Tamara said. "He's barely coherent."

"We can try to get him to my house, so we can feed him and put him to bed. Or maybe we should put him on the couch?"

"I'd rather he goes to your house, so we can open in the morning," Tamara said. "I'll go get my car—"

The front door opened, and Bash Haywood walked into the office. "No need to take care of him ladies, I'm on it. Peter Frank, you're under arrest for the murder of Merilee Frank—" Bash put his hand under Pete's elbow and cuffed his hands behind his back. He kept talking, glared at both Tamara and Lilly, and guided Pete out the front door.

Tamara and Lilly went down to the police station, but there wasn't much they could do to help Pete.

"We've got to process him, and then question him," Bash said as he and Pete were standing at the front desk and Pete's personal belongings were being processed.

"Pete, don't say anything without talking to a lawyer first. Do you have a lawyer I can call for you?" Tamara asked.

"I don't know. Who was that gal we use in the office, for closings?" Pete asked.

"Mimi. She's the wrong kind of lawyer. Let me make some calls, get somebody down here for you. I'm also going to call PJ—"

"Don't call PJ. He won't want to help his old man. Can't say I blame him," Pete said, starting to weep again.

"Oh? Why is that?" Bash asked.

"Stop talking, Pete," Lilly said. "Tamara's going to find a lawyer, and I'm going to call PJ. Stop. Talking. Say these words: 'I want a lawyer.' " Everyone waited, but Pete didn't seem able, or willing, to say the words. Lilly turned toward Bash. "May I have a moment?"

"I'm busy here, Lilly," Bash said.

"Please," Lilly said in a quiet, firm tone that few ever heard, but none who did disobeyed. Bash and Lilly took a few steps away. Pete was still being processed, and Tamara was standing next to him, ready to steady him if he suddenly keeled over. He looked as though he might.

"Bash, you can't really think that Pete killed his wife?"

"There's a lot of evidence, Lilly. There's this blog. Delia sent me pictures—"

"I saw them. Maybe they had a fight. Don't most married couples fight?"

"Most married couples don't have a knock-down, drag-out fight where he gets locked out of the house and ends up sleeping in the school playground the night before she gets murdered. Most married couples don't have affairs left and right, and then stay married. Most married couples don't do a lot of things Pete and Merilee did. Trust me, there's plenty of evidence."

"Circumstantial. Besides, most of this is old news. Why now?"

"I really shouldn't be—"

"Come on. You know I'm going to find out sooner or later, and for everyone's sake, better it be sooner. For Pete's, so I can get him out of this. And for your sake, so you don't make a career-ending mistake. Tell me what made you arrest Pete tonight. Quickly."

Bash Haywood didn't respect anyone in the world more than he respected Lilly Jayne. She'd been a mentor and a friend for years and had seen him through many dark times. He'd seen many expressions on her face when she looked at him, but never disappointment. Until now. It made Bash flinch, but not doubt himself. He had been wrestling with this decision all day, and he knew he'd made the right call.

Bash looked around. The other officers were still

busy processing Pete, but soon they'd notice that he was talking to Lilly. He already got gentle ribbing about his visits to her house that helped him think through problems. He couldn't let it look like she was telling him what to do.

"You were at the poetry reading last week, right? Merilee was in several of the photographs, naked as a jaybird."

"It was art. There were a lot of naked bodies."

"Well, most of the naked bodies didn't go around bragging about it all week, rubbing her husband's nose in the affair she'd had with the poet. Implying that the relationship was back on."

"But it wasn't—"

"That's not all. Merilee had it in her head to start a B and B."

"I'd heard that. Folks weren't keen on the idea," Lilly said.

"To put it mildly. Anyway, on Friday, the day before she died, they got a definitive no from the board of selectmen about building onto their house. They also got turned down on a mortgage for a new house."

"I'm sure she was disappointed, but still, that's not a reason to—"

"The B and B idea was a Hail Mary pass. Pete and Merilee are not only flat broke, they are hundreds of thousands of dollars in debt. We've only started to look into their finances, but it's a real mess."

Lilly was silent. Pete had always lived on the edge, well above his means. That old saying, "The first generation earns the money, the second generation keeps the money, and the third generation spends it"?—well, Pete was the third generation. Lilly had kept him on a tight leash while they were married, but seeing how he spent money and where was one of the reasons she'd studied finance. She was determined not to be the generation to lose her family fortune, and she wasn't. In fact, she'd grown it tenfold. But that was after her divorce from Pete and the lessons he'd taught her.

"There's one more thing. Merilee had a meeting with a lawyer on Friday. She was planning to file for divorce from Pete on Monday. So there's a pretty good case against him. Even you've got to admit that." Bash looked at Lilly and gently squeezed her left forearm. "I know you care about Pete. And it's a terrible thing to think that somebody you know is capable of murder. But I'm sure, Lilly. He did it."

Bash turned and walked back toward Pete. Tamara was standing off to the side, on the phone. She looked at Lilly and gave her a signal, holding up one finger as if to say, "Give me a minute."

Lilly walked over to Tamara and whispered, "I'll be outside."

She turned toward Pete and put her hand on his shoulder. "Did you tell them you want a lawyer?" she asked.

"I want a lawyer," Pete said.

"Good," Lilly replied. She gave him a smile and touched his forearm gently. "Hang in there," she whispered.

Lilly walked outside and took a deep breath of air. Bash had laid out a pretty good case against Pete. But still, in her gut, she knew he was wrong. Pete had many, many faults. But was he capable of driving a pair of hedge clippers through the heart of his wife? No. She didn't think he had that in him. She had to believe he didn't.

Lilly took out her phone and went through her contacts. She found the number she was looking for and hit DIAL. "Hi, Lilly, how are you?" PJ Frank said. Lilly still wasn't used to the world of mobile phones, where everyone knew who was calling whom if they were in their contact list.

"PJ, I've got some bad news. They've just arrested your father for murdering Merilee. For what it's worth, I don't think he did it. But he is in trouble. I think they've got a pretty good case." Lilly paused. "PJ, are you there?"

"I'm here. I wish I could say I'm surprised, but I'm not. Bash Haywood was by earlier today, asking some specific questions about my relationship with my father. And with Merilee. I got the feeling that Dad was in their sights, Honestly I was relieved that they weren't focusing on me."

"On you? Did you have a reason to want Merilee dead?"

"Oh, let me count the ways. That sounds terrible, doesn't it? I'm just being honest with you, Lilly. I'm not alone on that suspect list though, am I?"

Lilly ignored the question, though she did file it away to ponder later. Who else was on that list? Not just for motive, but also for opportunity. She'd given it some thought, but obviously not enough. She realized PJ had kept talking.

"Sorry, what did you say?"

"I asked if Dad had bail set yet?"

"No, this literally just happened. He's still being processed. Tamara's on the phone, trying to get him a lawyer. They may get him a public defender, if it comes to that."

"If it does to come to that, I'll pay for the lawyer, and put up his bail."

"PJ, I don't want to overstep, but if you need help with either of those things, please let me know."

"Thank you for the offer, Lilly, but it should be okay. Ironic, though, isn't it? You and I conspiring to bail Pete Frank out of a bind? The two people who should be rejoicing at his ill fortune?"

"I stopped being angry at Pete a long, long time ago. I feel sorry for him," Lilly said.

"Well, I feel sorry for him too. I'm still angry at the way he treated my mother, but we've been working hard at getting past that. He's got his faults, God knows, but he's still my father. I'll be right down. Let him know, okay?"

"Yes, I'll let them know. PJ, I'm very serious, if you need my help, please don't hesitate. I've got the money—"

"Lilly, I think the best way you could help my father is to find out who really did this, if you don't believe he did."

"I'll try," Lilly said.

"He's a lucky guy, to have you in his corner," PJ said.

"PJ, I'm in your corner too. You know that, right? Let me know if you need my help, with anything. Anything."

"I will, thanks Lilly. And thanks for letting me know about Dad."

PJ ended the call, and Lilly stood outside the police station for a few more minutes, collecting her thoughts. Her phone vibrated, and she looked down to see a text from Delia.

Where are you? Are you all right?

Lilly texted back: *I'm fine. Sorry, should've checked in. Pete's been arrested, at the station, but coming home soon.*

OMG! Want me to come get you?

No, Vespa at Tamara's. I'm okay to drive. Be home soon. Put the pasta on.

Lilly looked down at her phone and smiled. She'd always prided herself on staying out of people's business. But today, alone, she'd found out about Cal's affairs, gone to see Portia Asher, and now accompanied her ex-husband to the police station while he was being arrested for the murder of his wife. A full day, and one well out of Lilly's comfort zone. She walked back into the police station, to let Tamara know that she was going to head home and that PJ was on his way.

CHAPTER 18

"I'm going to make another pot of coffee. I feel like today is at least a two-pot, maybe even a three-pot day," Delia said.

"Three pots? If I drink my share of three pots of coffee, I won't sleep for a week. Are you that tired?" Lilly asked.

"I'm getting that feeling. We may have a lot of company today, given everything. They'll be in and out all day. It's always more gracious to have the coffee already made so you can say to the person coming in, 'Would you like a cup of coffee? Really, it's no bother. It's already made.' Also, selfishly, if it's already made, I won't miss too much conversation having to tinker in the kitchen."

"What makes you think people will be in and out all day? I have nothing to do with this case—"

"Oh, please, Lilly. Tamara's already called you twice."

"She wanted to let me know the updates on Pete's bail."

"Which are?"

"There's a hearing this morning. Tamara's going to go with PJ. I told her to let me know if they need more cash."

"See? You're involved."

"I'm helping out."

"You're involved. People are going to come by. I feel it in my bones." Delia stood up and rinsed out the coffeepot. A moment later, the front doorbell rang. She turned to Lilly and smiled. "See? It's started already."

"Oh, you." Lilly got up from the table and walked to the front hall. The thing was, very few people who knew Lilly, or Delia, came in the front door. Most came in the side door, by the kitchen. So Lilly already knew that it wasn't a friend ringing the bell. She took a deep breath and hoped it wasn't a foe. She was tempted to look out the side windows but decided that would be rude. Better to face folks head-on. She unlocked the door and swung it open.

Roddy was standing there, the garden book she'd recommended in his right hand, with a notebook on top. The garden book had Post-its sticking out at the top and on the side, with scribbled notes everywhere.

"Very sorry, but you didn't call me, so I don't have your number," Roddy said. "I desperately need your advice. I hope I'm not intruding."

"No, please come in. I'm sorry; it has been a bit chaotic around here. I hope you'd like some coffee. Delia just put on a fresh pot. Come back to the kitchen."

Roddy followed Lilly back to the kitchen, a couple of steps behind her. He tried to not be too obvious as he looked around. Every nook, every cranny, every doorway showed personality, good taste, and some beautiful artwork. He hoped he'd be able to spend some more time in this house, exploring its wonders and getting to know its owner a bit better.

"Delia, Roddy stopped by for some gardening advice. I mentioned to him yesterday that you've been doing some work on the Winslow gardens and may have some insights to share with him. I assume that's why you're here?" Lilly asked Roddy.

"Are you going to restore the garden? That would be so wonderful," Delia said. "Florence Winslow and her gardens deserve much more recognition than they've gotten over the years. It would be wonderful to be able to showcase her work," Delia said.

"Honestly, after some homework last night and two hours wrestling weeds this morning, I'm beginning to think I should just pave the backyard. Ah, ladies, you should see your faces. I'm just joking. I would never do that. My sainted mother would haunt me forever. But I'm having trouble getting my bearings and understanding where to even begin. I was using a rake, and it broke in half. That's why I decided to come over and throw myself at your mercy. I need a complete list of where to start, and how."

Delia poured the coffee into three mugs and put them on the table. "Milk? Sugar?"

"Black is fine, thank you." Roddy took a sip. Lilly got up from the table and went over to the cupboard and got three tins of baked goods.

"I hope you're hungry," Lilly said.

"Did you bake all these?" Roddy asked Lilly, who was removing the lids of the tins. He looked into the tins and took out a lemon scone. Delia set some plates on the table, and he used one of them. "This is delicious."

"I like to bake," Delia said. "But these actually

came from the Star Café. Sometimes Stan gives me the leftovers at the end of the day. I bring them here and redistribute them."

"Redistribute them?" Roddy said, peering into each tin.

"Ernie and Tamara have breakfast here several times a week. Sometimes Warwick comes by before he goes to school. Bash Haywood shows up a couple of times a week. Then there's Ray Mancini . . ."

"So, it sounds as if the town of Goosebush stops by for breakfast," Roddy said.

"Not the entire town," Lilly said. "But, yes, come to think of it, we have a few regular visitors. It's a good thing that Delia is dating someone who runs a café. Saves on my grocery bill."

Delia shot Lilly a look, but Lilly ignored her.

"So you broke a rake?" Lilly asked, taking a maple walnut scone and putting it on a plate. She'd already had breakfast but couldn't pass this up. It was one of her favorite flavor combinations, in scones and in ice cream.

"Well, to be honest, it was probably not the best implement to use for the particular job, but it's all I had. I have to buy some tools, but I wasn't sure which ones I need." He opened the book in front of him and turned the page of garden implements toward Delia and Lilly. "I suppose I could buy them all, but I want to be practical about this. Which ones do I need? What type of hoe? Is there a rake you suggest?"

Delia laughed, and Lilly joined her. "Roddy, after you finish your coffee, let me take you out to the shed in the greenhouse," Lilly said. "Buying garden tools is one of my vices. Any new gadget, handle, angle, and I must have it. We are a bit oversupplied, aren't we, Delia?"

"A bit, but it does come in handy when we get volunteers together to work on projects."

"What kind of projects?" Roddy asked.

Lilly paused. What kinds of projects? "Ten years ago, it was this and that, a bit of everything. Lately, it's mostly been working on the boatyard, helping them keep their bushes at bay. Some beach projects. We all donate our Christmas trees to help save the dunes, and a few of us take care of the grasses obsessively. No huge garden projects in the past few years, though I'm hoping we can get the Alden Park project back on track."

"It's still a crime scene, so we can't restart the project for a while. But I've been thinking about those pictures, the ones the poet took," Delia said. "The ones of the flagpole area, through the weeds, with the trash. Pitiful. I say we tackle that. Get rid of the weeds, make the flagpole a centerpiece, not an eyesore. I talked to Ernie yesterday, and he's got some flats of flowers that need to get into the ground."

"This is a little bit out of the blue, isn't it?" Lilly asked.

"Sort of, I guess. It's just that . . . well, I was looking forward to getting Alden Park fixed up. That being on hold, then seeing the town through that poet's eyes—that all made me take a closer look. Goosebush needs a refresher. You've always said gardens, and flowers, reflect the soul of the gardener. I think that's true for the town too; its soul needs some saving," Delia said.

"You know, there's a fine line between being

charmingly authentic and becoming a clichéd small New England town," Lilly said. "We don't want to overdo things like flagpole gardens. That could tip us into cliché."

"Hello? How well do you know me? Do you think I would take part in anything that had cloying charm? Please. I'm talking about a rustic garden, not something that belongs on a postcard. I'll come up with a historically accurate sketch to put before the next town meeting for a vote."

Lilly smiled. "You're right. That would be a great project," Lilly said.

"Besides, it will give folks in this town something else to talk about. Get the spotlight away from Pete's troubles," Delia said. She looked at Roddy. "Pete Frank was arrested last night—"

"Oh, I've heard. It's all over that dreadful blog," Roddy said.

"You read the Goosebush Gossip site?" Lilly asked.

"My daughter sent me the link yesterday. Apparently, it had shown up on her Facebook feed and made her think of me. Ah, well, I should be grateful she reached out, I suppose. It also made the papers today." Roddy took a muffin out of the third tin and split it in half, putting half on his plate.

"For what it's worth, Lilly doesn't think Pete did it," Delia said.

Roddy looked at Lilly. "Any particular reason?" he asked.

"My gut. I just don't think Pete could have done it."

Roddy nodded. "Any idea who could have?"

"I'm thinking about that," Lilly said. "Maybe I can think more while I'm planning the flagpole garden with Delia." Lilly regarded Delia for moment. She was always impressed by Delia's thoughtfulness, the way her mind worked. She was right, of course. The project would only take a couple of hours, and it really did need to be done.

"Tell you what, Roddy," Lilly said. "Come back to the shed, and I'll lend you a couple of tools and a miracle rototiller. How about if Delia and I come over this morning, look around, mark off what you should get rid of, and what you should cut back and try to save? That'll keep you busy for a few days, and I bet it will give you some ideas about how you want it to look. Delia can also grab some photos and get you photos of other Winslow gardens for comparison. How does that sound?"

"That sounds good to me," Roddy said. "Do I have time for another cup of coffee?"

"I'd imagine so," Lilly said, standing up to get the pot, and pouring both herself and Roddy another cup. Delia waved her off. "Delia and I need to talk about the flagpole plans. Unless you've already got that mapped out?" Lilly asked Delia.

Delia went over to the bench and picked up her notebook. "As a matter fact, I've made a couple of sketches. Ernie told me what he had on hand, and I figured we'd use those. Plus, you've got a ton of those grasses in the greenhouse. They're taking over. They will be nice accent pieces."

"We'll need to get approval, of course," Lilly said.

Delia shrugged her shoulder as if she was resigned to that fact. She wasn't, of course. She'd just wait until Roddy was gone to help Lilly understand that at times it was better to ask forgiveness than permission. This may be one of those times.

Roddy watched as Delia and Lilly poured over Delia's drawings, making some changes and then compiling a list of what they needed to get the work done. Part of him wanted to volunteer to go with them, but this was their project. He didn't want to impose. He'd give them support at the town meeting, if they needed it. In the meantime, he was happy to come over for coffee and hoped he could invite himself back again soon, if not for the scones, then for the company.

"You really do have a bevy of gardening instruments to choose from, don't you?" Roddy asked.

"Lilly's never met a hedge clipper she didn't like," Delia said.

"Well, that's not exactly true. The reason I have so many hedge clippers is that I met several I don't like, but I always keep them hoping that the garden fairies will come in and make them better. That said, it's time to get rid of some of these." Lilly looked around and found a couple of five-gallon buckets. She consolidated their contents into one and handed Delia the empty one. "Delia, let's get Roddy set up. He's going to need some of those claws, you know the ones, to help him weed. How are your knees, Roddy? If they're like mine, we'll need to get you longer handles so you don't have to squat. You need a decent rake. Garden shears. Hedge clippers. Do we have extra gloves?"

"You don't have to do all of this," Roddy said.

"Please, don't stop her," Delia said. "I've been trying to get her to clean this place out for months. This stuff is just a drop in the bucket. The garage is overflowing."

Lilly laughed. "What?" Delia asked.

"Drop in the bucket. You're carrying a bucket. And putting stuff in it," Lilly said. She turned toward Roddy. "Delia doesn't have the best sense of humor."

"I don't have the best sense of humor? I have an excellent sense of humor," Delia said. "I just don't think wordplays are terribly funny."

"Well, to each his own, I suppose. There's just something about it. You *are* holding a bucket . . . it just tickled me."

"It was nice to hear you laugh, even if it was at my expense," Delia smiled. "Do you have gardening gloves, Roddy? We have an extra pair we could loan you."

"I could go and buy myself some—"

"Roddy, if you go down to Ernie's, you may as well kiss the rest of the day good good-bye," Delia said. "Here's what I think the plan for today should be. You borrow this stuff, test it out. Let's go over and look at what you've got to do, and you can get to it. Then, tomorrow, when your arms and legs are so sore you can barely move, going to Bits, Bolts & Bulbs and buying supplies will be your excuse for not doing more weeding."

"I think that's how we end up with so much stuff," Lilly said. "Procrastinating by going to Triple B."

"It's gotten so bad Ernie tries to talk us out of buying things," Delia said. "But we persist. As a matter of fact, we have a shopping list. We should head down there later. But first, how about we go over to your house and separate the weeds from the plants?"

"That sounds terrific," Roddy said. "If only we could get through the garden gate—"

"The key's been gone for years. Truthfully, I've never had much cause to look for it. Never been so fond of my neighbors that I wanted to use a short-cut," Lilly said.

Roddy pondered a quick retort but thought better of it. He didn't want to push it with Lilly, or with Delia. Besides, he was a man who liked his own privacy. He couldn't blame others for liking theirs. He picked up the bucket and turned toward them both. "I appreciate your advice, ladies. My garden appreciates your help."

Lilly reached over and grabbed her gardening gloves, and Delia's. "Let's go," she said.

CHAPTER 19

Getting from the back of Lilly's house to the front yard was not a simple feat. That was on purpose. Though the house itself was situated on a double lot, Lilly had used up every square inch. Standing in the backyard, to the left were the garage and the driveway. The garage was at the end of a large retaining wall that didn't have any steps up to the backyard. The side of the garage had a door that led into the gardens, with steps down to the garage itself. Thanks to some engineering and a few well-placed drains, the garage never got flooded, even though it sat at the bottom of the driveway. Because of the angle, it had a second floor of storage. Back in the day it had been the chauffeur's apartment.

To the right of the house was Lilly's greenhouse. The greenhouse butted up against the garden wall on one side and Lilly's house on the other. Again, it blocked the entrance to the back. This back garden had been the pride and joy of generations of the

Jayne family. It was her private sanctuary, open to the public once or twice a year during garden tours and to friends and family more often. But usually it was just her private place, and Delia's.

"Let's walk through the garage," Lilly said. "It's easier than traipsing through the house." She opened the back door of the garage and stepped aside to let Roddy in. She reached to the right and flipped on the light. Though she knew the space so well she could have walked through it in the dark, she also knew that it could be a minefield for the uninitiated.

Roddy stopped, gobsmacked. The garage was huge, and there were two cars, with room for a third. Two Vespas were parked toward the front. There were hooks, shelves, and pulley systems on all three walls, with detritus everywhere. Roddy wondered if there was order in this madness. If there was, it wasn't clear. But still, it was a marvelous cacophony of color and texture and unexpected bibs and bobs. There were outdoor decorations for different seasons, large gardening implements, ladders, step stools, a snowblower, and more tools that he could not fathom the purpose of but that seemed well used.

"This is marvelous," he said, and he meant it. Roddy had lived a very ordered, compartmentalized life. He aspired to have meaningful chaos. Perhaps he could spend time sitting in Lilly's garage for inspiration.

"Don't look too closely, Roddy," Delia said. "This place has magical powers. A few weeks ago, I came in here looking for a shovel, and the next thing you know I found a box with nothing but hinges from a hundred years ago, with little tags attached to each one indicating exactly where it came from. That box of hinges, and those notes, have become an obsession of mine."

"Anything that has to do with history, or research, becomes an obsession of Delia's," Lilly said. She walked toward the front of the garage and hit a button on the side. The large wooden door slowly started to roll up. "This place is a graveyard of old things, that's for sure. I can never bear to throw anything out. Nor could any of my forbearers. See that lineup of teakettles? They're all burned out, waiting for a tinsmith to come by and fix them. I'm trying to figure out how to use them as planters."

"Most folks would throw them out," Roddy said.

"Not the Jayne way," Delia said. "Besides, you'll never know what you'll find. A box, a packet of letters partially eaten by mice, a musty board game, dozens of odds and ends that derail you for hours."

"Then there is the occasional surprise of finding your ex-husband standing in your driveway," Lilly said.

Delia stepped forward and saw what Lilly was talking about. Pete Frank had parked at the edge of the driveway and was walking toward the side kitchen door. When he saw Lilly, he stopped, paused, and then walked toward her a bit more slowly.

"I didn't do it," Pete said.

Lilly turned toward Roddy and Delia. "You go on over without me. I'll be over shortly."

"Come on in, Pete," Lilly said. "There's probably some more coffee. You look like you could use a cup."

"I didn't do it," Pete said again.

Lilly poured him a cup of coffee and put it in the

microwave for a few seconds. She didn't say anything, but when she turned back toward the table, she realized Pete was waiting for a response from her.

"I believe you," she said. Lilly did have to wonder. Did she believe him because she actually believed he didn't kill his wife, or did she believe him because she couldn't fathom the idea that someone she was once married to could murder somebody? He did cheat on her and spend her money as if it was water, so he wasn't without character flaws. But murder? Pete had easier ways to get rid of Merilee, didn't he?

"Do you have any idea who might've done it?" Lilly asked.

"That's one thing I've always loved about you, Lilly," Pete said. "You never sugarcoat things, never beat around the bush. No tea and sympathy from you."

"Pete, I'm sorry for your loss. But even you must admit, a tea and sympathy response from me would ring false. We're well past that, don't you think?"

"Fair enough," Pete said. "I really treated you like crap when we were married. I've always been surprised you're even willing to talk to me again after the way I—"

"Water under the bridge. Goosebush is a small town. It makes no sense for me to have enemies here, when I'm going to run into them every day at the post office or the grocery store. Not that I'm very likely to run into you in a grocery store."

"Yeah, you're right. I eat most meals out, at the Star Café. Those days are over now too, I'm afraid. For a lot of reasons," Pete said. "I've got to live on a budget. Long past time for that. But when Merilee was around, magical thinking kept that at bay. Believe it or not, she was worse than I ever was about budgets."

"That's hard to believe," Lilly teased him.

"But true. We always lived beyond our means, but it had gotten really bad these last couple of years. I thought moving back to Goosebush would make things easier, but instead she felt obliged to compete with my past, my ex-wives, and what I used to have when I lived here."

"Surely she understood that when you moved away and stepped away from the business, your father had no choice but to leave the business to your son. He helped run it all those years."

"Moved? That's a nice way to put it. My old man felt I abandoned him, and I suppose I did. But PJ didn't, and he inherited the business and the house, fair and square. I understood that. I understood my failings as both a father and a son. But Merilee? I think she assumed PJ would step aside and give us the house. We had bought a smaller house, one of the beach cottages, but she hated it out there. When he didn't give up his own house, she felt obliged to find us a house as big, and as grand."

"I'll never forget her asking me if I ever thought about selling this place," Lilly said.

"When did she ask you that?" Pete asked.

"At Alan's funeral." Lilly looked right at Pete, and to his credit, he tried to meet her gaze but eventually looked away.

"God help me, I loved her," Pete said. "She was like a drug I couldn't get enough of. But this past year or so? I've come to realize she really was a terrible person. For a long time, she was able to mask her terribleness. She could really be fun to be around. But these last few months, the mask slipped. Even I saw the truth. I was probably the last one to realize it."

"Why didn't you leave her?" Lilly asked softly.

"Like I had every other wife?" Pete said. "I've thought about that a lot these last few days. It was partly that I need to be married. I like having a wife, and I never left one without somebody else in the wings. I'm too old, and too tired, to have somebody waiting."

Lilly felt her breath leave her lungs and had difficulty taking in another. This level of self-reflection and honesty from Pete? She didn't expect it, and she wasn't sure how to proceed with the conversation. Fortunately for her, she didn't have to. Pete was on a roll.

"Sorry, Lil, I forgot for a minute you are my first victim," Pete said. "There's another reason I didn't leave Merilee. And this one . . . this one doesn't help foster my case of innocence at all." Pete picked up the cup of coffee with a shaky hand and took a deep sip. He closed his eyes and took a breath. When he opened them, Lilly noticed that they were glistening with unshed tears.

"Merilee had me sign a lot of paperwork before we were married. Because of my track record, the fact that she was my third wife . . . she told me she felt that she needed protection." Pete snorted a short, mirthless laugh. More of a bark, actually. "I was so in love with her, she was so young and beautiful . . . It didn't take much to convince me. Honestly, I thought she was going to be my last wife. While we were married, I assumed all our debts. When we were first married, she had a career as a marketing executive. She worked for a huge firm and pulled in a great salary. But then we moved to Goosebush. She decided to go out on her own and be a consultant. Problem was, she didn't have a lot of clients. She did have a lot of business expenses, though. I was always good at spending money I didn't necessarily have, but I knew when to stop. Merilee was a bottomless pit, and we're deep in the hole."

"You've got your house—"

"Mortgaged to the hilt. Our cars are leased. I'm a lousy real estate agent. Surely Tamara's mentioned that."

"Tamara's mentioned nothing of the kind," Lilly said. She wasn't going to let Pete bask in self-pity that wouldn't do him any good. Besides, her patience for self-pity was limited.

"I may be able to pull that one out. I like real estate and can probably make a go of it if I apply myself. If I'm given the opportunity to apply myself. Plus, and I realize this is another point against me, there's a life insurance policy."

"Most couples have life insurance," Lilly said.

"Well, we had quite the policy. Merilee was banking on me dying first and wanted to set herself up to be a wealthy widow. Our agent insisted it be reciprocal."

"So you'll be a wealthy widower?" Lilly asked.

Again, Pete barked out a laugh. "More like I'll be out of debt. But I'll take it. Course, if I'm convicted of her murder, I won't get anything." Pete took another sip of coffee and drained the cup. "Earlier, you asked me who else might have had a motive to kill her. The list is long. I did love her, believe me I did, but the list is long. Plus there's that damn video of me fighting with her that morning."

"Video? I thought it was pictures?"

"Apparently, it's a video, and the pictures are screen shots. Someone realized that the timing was too staggered to be time-lapse pictures."

"What else is in the video?"

"What isn't in the video is me leaving her on the corner. I went down the back alley and into the office to cool off. No one was there. The alarms had already been turned off for the day, so even that can't help me with an alibi."

"Do you know who took the video, where it was from?" Lilly asked.

"Bash is trying to figure that out, but you won't be surprised to know he's not sharing his findings with me. Besides, I barely remember the fight."

"Really?" Lilly asked. She thought back to the video and the heated argument. In her short marriage to Pete, she'd never fought that hard with him. In all her years of marriage to Alan, she'd never had a knock-down, drag-out fight. Arguments, yes. But raised voices, never.

"We had two modes of conversation, fighting and loving. Usually we kept the fighting to private spaces." Pete looked right at Lilly and shook his head. "I just lied to you, Lilly. I do remember what the fight was about. She'd just seen that poet guy at the Star Café and fawned all over him. She asked when she was going to get to pose for him again. You're going to think I'm an idiot, but it never occurred to me . . . You remember that show he did, with the pictures of all the naked women? Turns out my wife was one of them. A willing model, and more."

"More?"

"They had an affair," Pete said. "I'd suspected, but she always denied it, and I believed her. I chose to believe her. Suddenly, in the Star that morning, I felt like an old fool. I realized I was the butt of jokes. I confronted her, but you know what she did? She just laughed at me. Laughed. 'You really are an idiot. Do you know that?' Those might have been the last words she said to me. I grabbed her by her upper arm, but she got away. A truck drove up and honked. It was like I was woken up from a dream. She walked away from me, into Alden Park. Like I said, I snuck into the office. That was the last time I ever saw her, but she was alive. I swear, Lilly, she was alive. At that moment, I could've killed her, but I didn't."

"Maybe they could find the truck driver?" Lilly said.

"No one's going to believe me," he said. "Hell, I wouldn't believe me. But you must. Someone else did this, and you need to help me find out who it was."

CHAPTER 20

"Do you believe him?" Ernie asked. Ernie, Delia, and Lilly were in the back of Bits, Bolts, & Bulbs with a large sheet of graph paper lying on a worktable in front of them. Delia had sketched a diagram of the flagpole and was looking at images on her phone to make sure she got the dimensions right. Lilly never had made it over to Roddy's house, and she was looking at the pictures Delia had taken of it. They were very Deliaesque, which meant that they focused in on details, but there weren't many pictures of the garden itself. Delia had also taken some pictures of the garden door from Roddy's side of the wall, including close-ups of the lock. There were boxes of keys all over Lilly's house, and Delia planned to look through them all.

Delia had an encyclopedic mind, one that searched for answers and made connective clues come together like few others could. Though Lilly would have been fine plotting the flagpole makeover with a simple drawing, she knew Delia's work habits well enough to know that she required precision and a depth of detail on every drawing before she was comfortable. Her working habits gave Ernie and Lilly time to catch up.

"I do," Lilly said. "I also believe that Bash thinks he has his man, and for good reason. Pete makes the most sense."

"Are you going to help Pete?" Delia asked. She looked up from her drawing, right at Lilly.

"I'm not sure what I can do," Lilly said.

"You're the only person who thinks he's innocent," Delia said. She went back to her drawing, pulling out a colored pencil to add depth to the edging around the flagpole in the center of the Wheel.

"Am I really the only one?" Lilly looked at Ernie.

"Pretty much," Ernie said. "I could be convinced he didn't do it, but I could be as easily convinced he did. Also, for what it's worth? I think he's right about the suspects. The list is pretty long."

"What are people saying?" Lilly asked Ernie. Ernie always knew what was going on around Goosebush and was a great source of gossip. Lilly pretended she was above it, but Ernie always shared it with her anyway. He did it as a public service, convinced that the more Lilly knew, the better off the citizens of Goosebush would be.

"Well, it's only been a couple of days. People are still in the 'poor, poor Merilee' phase, though no one has said that with a lot of real emotion. Come to think of it, I think Pete is the only person who's sad that she's gone. Doesn't mean he didn't kill her," he said.

"What you need to look for is opportunity," Delia

said. "Who could have killed her and put her in the shed? I mean physically killed her, not wanted her dead."

"I wonder if there's any more video from the gossip site," Lilly said.

"The truck that blocked the view didn't move until after her body was found," Delia said.

"How do you know that?" Ernie asked.

"I've been asking around. Remember when you asked me to look into cameras? Turns out, my paranoia was for good reason. There are cameras everywhere. Can we finish this first? I can only focus on one thing at a time." Delia gestured to the garden plot in front of her.

Lilly took a deep breath and counted to four. Patience was a virtue, one that was not inherent in Lilly's nature. But while dealing with Delia, patience was often required.

"Of course," Lilly said. "Show us what you're thinking."

"I'm thinking three things," Delia said. "First, that we need to keep it simple, something that looks good in all four seasons and requires minimal upkeep. Maybe in the summer we add some annuals for spots of color, but otherwise I'm thinking grasses, some more cobblestones, a bit more of a hardscape. The grasses also need to be short, so that folks can see over the tops. That seems like a safety issue to me." While she'd been talking, she continued to draw, and Ernie and Lilly quickly got an idea of what she was talking about. Ernie made some suggestions about the materials to be used, and Lilly recommended substituting a few plants. The discussion didn't take long. The three of them had talked about gardens so often they had shorthand ways of communicating and had developed a common vocabulary.

"What's the second thing you're thinking about?" Ernie asked Delia. Like Lilly, he knew that when Delia started a list, she needed to go all the way through it before her attention could be diverted elsewhere. Unlike Lilly, Ernie had a never-ending wealth of patience; it was one of his greatest attributes.

"How was this allowed to get so bad?" Delia asked. She looked at both Ernie and Lilly, and then pulled out another colored pencil to work on the drawing while she talked. "Alden Park, I guess I can see letting that get overgrown. But the flagpole, in the center of town, in the center of the Wheel? Sorry, you know I'm not one for monuments necessarily, but that shouldn't look like crap. And it does. You know that square piece of granite on one side of the monument? Did you know that on the side there's a brass plate, and on it is listed all the folks from Goosebush who died in World War II? Seems to me something like that should be polished, and a feature, not an overgrown afterthought. I've gone to enough of these town meetings over the years to know that there should be a fund to keep public spaces looking decent, but there never seems to be any money to actually do the work."

"I've offered to round up volunteers, but Pat French says there's no budget for the work," Ernie said. "I've also offered to contribute the plants, but then Pat says there are liability issues with that."

"That's ridiculous," Lilly said. "How has she been allowed to get away with this? I write a check every year to contribute to the Goosebush Beautification Fund."

"The funds have been diverted to things like roadwork," Ernie said.

"You haven't been paying close attention these last couple years," Delia said. "We've told you about all this, but I don't think you've heard us."

"Well, I'm hearing you now," Lilly said. She took a notebook out of her purse and jotted down a few thoughts. One of them was to call Pat French and set up a meeting.

Delia nodded, secure knowing that Lilly would take it from here. Delia couldn't do much on her own, but Lilly could. Especially with Delia and Ernie backing her up.

"Third thing," Delia said. "I'm sick of asking for permission. Let's just do this. Clean up the flagpole. Polish that brass plate."

"Just walk into the middle of the Wheel and start planting?" Ernie said. "Pat is such a stickler for rules, I half expect she'd have Bash come over and arrest us."

"That's why I say we do it in the middle the night."

"In the middle the night?" Lilly asked. "Like thieves, under cover of darkness?"

"No, more like garden vigilantes, fixing things. If we get caught, we'll confess. But if we don't get caught, Goosebush will just wake up to a neater, prettier flagpole. With the three of us working on this—"

"Four," Lilly said. "Tamara. Don't forget her."

"Right, Tamara. She'd be really ticked if we didn't at least tell her," Ernie said. "She's been worried about these issues and the fines that Pat's been charging people in the historical district when things are not to code."

"I've heard a little bit about this," Lilly said,

thinking of Portia. "They seem harsh, harsher than the folks who came up with the rules intended."

"They are," Ernie said. "Rather than an act of preservation, they become a weapon."

"But Ernie's on it," Delia said.

"What does she mean by that?" Lilly asked Ernie.

"Well, this was Delia's idea too. I'm going to start stocking historically accurate pieces, built to Goosebush historic preservation specifications. PJ Frank has a couple of people in the lumberyard doing the work. We're doing what we can to keep the costs down. We'll build fence posts and pickets, exactly the right size. Mailboxes to spec, that meet the parameters set out. Window boxes that are preapproved. PJ is going to start building historically accurate doors, and he's working with a glassblower to make them look authentic. We're pricing these things on sliding scales. Folks who can afford to pay full freight will. But there are a lot of people who are house poor in this town, so we're here to help. We're going to roll it out officially around the Fourth of July, but we're already taking orders."

"That sounds wonderful," Lilly said. "I'm happy to help if—"

"Lilly, the reason we waited to tell you is that I didn't want you to have to come in and save the day. Again. You do that a lot in this town; don't think I don't notice. PJ and I are working on a business model that makes sense. Neither of us will make a lot of money, at least not at first. But PJ wonders if there will be a demand from other people with historic houses in other parts of the state. Delia's been compiling tons of historical information for PJ to work with. PJ loves the idea, and it's allowing him to keep a couple of craftsmen employed full-time, which is good if business picks up for him. I think it will."

Lilly smiled at her friends. Though not born here, they both loved Goosebush as much as she did. "The gardening in the dead of night is not my idea of a good time, necessarily, but I'm in. When do we want to do this flagpole project?" She gestured toward the drawing, which Delia had kept working on. Lilly noticed that she had made the granite monument more of a feature and taken her advice on the plantings. Lilly made herself another note in her notebook, to pot up some of her special grasses, the ones that took on a purple hue in the twilight while remaining a vibrant green during the day.

"Ernie, do you have what we need?" Delia asked.

Ernie turned the drawing toward him and made some notes in the corner. "Sure do," he said. "I'll pull some of the materials I was donating to the Alden Park project and replenish them with my next order. Assuming you have the plants?" he asked Lilly.

"Enough to get us started," Lilly said. "Listen, Roddy was with us when we started to talk about the project. Should we tell him what we're up to?"

"He won't tell anyone," Delia said. "I mentioned that garden fairies may start taking on projects in town, and that he should act surprised. He said he would, and I believed him. There's something about him that I trust, and I don't usually say that about handsome strangers."

"He could charm the paint off a fence, that's for sure," Ernie said. "I'm with Delia. He won't tell anyone. So when should we do this?"

"Well, no time like the present. Any of you have plans for tonight?" Delia asked.

"None that can't be changed," Ernie said. He took his phone out of his pocket and hit a button. "Hello, Tamara? Guess what you're doing tonight?" Ernie winked at Lilly, who couldn't help but break into a broad smile.

CHAPTER 21

Deciding to do something arguably illegal that evening created a flurry of work that needed to be done in short order. Lilly went home to get the plants ready. Delia and Ernie waited at the store for Tamara to drive her truck over. It didn't take much convincing to get Tamara on board, but getting her to volunteer her truck took a little more doing. Ernie's pickup had his store logo on the side and was bright yellow. Delia drove a small car. Lilly's car was a Jeep, a very old Jeep, that she only used to drive around town. Tamara's car was a black, nondescript SUV that seated seven comfortably and could haul a lot.

Lilly enjoyed the walk back to her house. It was familiar, comforting, and lovely on a spring day. As she approached the Wheel, there were a couple of ways to go. If she went to the right, she only needed to cross two streets to get to hers. If she went to the left, she needed to cross five streets, all of which had heavier traffic. Nonetheless, she chose the left, using the time to take a good look at the flagpole and snap some pictures. She barely made out, through the underbrush, the gray monument Delia had told her about. She couldn't believe she'd forgotten it was there. She looked around, trying to think about where they could park the truck. They planned to do the deed well after closing time for the Star. There were a couple of spots in front that would work.

As Lilly walked by the Star and that row of stores, she looked to her right toward Alden Park. Where had the camera been? Darn it all, she hadn't asked Delia for more details on that. Lilly looked around but didn't spot anything. Wait, what was that? On top of the light pole? Was that a camera? She took another sweep of the landscape. This time she found a couple more possible camera locations. Delia was right, camera spotting could make you paranoid if you let it.

As she walked home, Lilly thought about her mother. What would her mother think about Pete's predicament and the goings-on in Goosebush? Not much, of that Lilly was sure. Her mother had been fond of Pete, until he left Lilly. After that, he was dead to her. She never said the name Pete Frank again. If he entered a same room where she was, she'd leave.

Her father had, upon hearing of Lilly's engagement, said to his daughter, "You, my darling, you can do better than Pete Frank." That had given Lilly pause, but she hadn't been sure he was right. And besides, Pete was a good guy. They'd make a good life together. A good life was all that Lilly expected. Great was for others. Good was enough. It wasn't until later, much later, that Lilly admitted aloud that she should have listened to her father.

As to the goings-on and this gardening dilemma? Lilly knew her mother would have been more than up for gardening around the flagpole, but she would never have done it in the dark of night. She would've parked in the middle of the Wheel, taken out her garden caddy, and gone to work. If anyone had tried to stop her, she would have stared them down. Lilly had to admit, there was a part of her that wanted to do the same. But there was another part that was intrigued by fixing this one thing in Goosebush under dark of night. If they could pull this one off . . .

Lilly let herself in the front door and walked toward the back of the house. She went into the library and pulled her chair over to the shelves along the side of the wall. There was a cabinet in the middle of one of the shelves with a closed door. Lilly opened it and pulled out the desk that was hidden behind the doors. She pulled the tablet she left charging in there toward her and turned it on. She had a more formal office upstairs, off her bedroom. She used this space to write notes, print things out quickly, and make lists. She pulled her notebook out and turned to the page where she'd been scribbling earlier. She transcribed the notes in the appropriate places. Unlike Delia's amazing abilities to provide information so that anyone could access it, Lilly's organizational systems only made sense to her. She had come to rely on virtual Post-it notes that she moved around and kept track of on all her devices. She'd also come to realize that she needed to write everything down these days; otherwise she'd forget them. That didn't used to be the case, but age had caught up with Lilly in unexpected ways. Unless she jotted down things like passwords, locations of files, planting schedules, and perfected plant food concoctions, she'd forget them. Rather than fight it, she kept her notes in a dozen different places so that she could always access them.

After Lilly was finished typing her notes, she sat back in her chair and took a deep breath. She closed her eyes and spent a moment clearing her mind. Inhale one two three . . . exhale one two three . . . inhale one two three . . . exhale one two three. That always made her feel better, though she decided she would need to take a nap before this evening's activity. Lilly opened her eyes and looked around at her collection of memories. That always calmed her. Her life with Alan had been, indeed, great. Lilly had placed certain mementos so when she sat in this spot, she could look up and remember Alan and their trips together. Her eyes swept to the right, then to the left. She stopped for a moment. Something was wrong, was missing. What was it? She closed her eyes and pictured the shelf as it should be, and then reopened her eyes. Where was that clay bowl? The one Alan had bought her in Greece? It was worth a small fortune but was even more precious because of the memories it contained of that magical trip to celebrate their tenth anniversary. She stood up and took a closer look. The bowl was missing. When was the last time she'd seen it?

She thought back to Merilee looking at her depression glass the day of the garden party. Had it been there then? Or had Merilee stolen from her?

"You're in here," Delia said. She finally found Lilly in the greenhouse, cleaning out pots, banging things about with more force than was her usual nature. "I guess you didn't hear me call your name."

"No, sorry. Lost in my own thoughts." Lilly turned toward Delia and put her hands on her hips. "I hate to speak ill of the dead, but you remember that Greek bowl, the one from Alexandria? It was in the library."

"The one on the third shelf from the top, in the second bookcase along the wall?"

"That's the one. It's not there."

"When did you see it last?"

"The last time I clearly remember seeing it was before the garden party. The day of the party I caught Merilee Frank in there."

"Stella Haywood was in there too, wasn't she?"

"Are you suggesting Stella may have stolen the bowl?" Lilly asked.

"No, I don't think Stella did it. But she may know if anyone else was in the room. She was on guard, remember? It would be worth asking her before you speak ill of the dead."

Lilly sighed. She'd jumped to conclusions, something that was not normally in her nature. "Yes, of course. You're right."

"I'll ask Stella next time I see her, if you'd like," Delia said. "She works several shifts at the Star Café. I'll probably see her tomorrow."

"Thank you," Lilly said. "Where are Ernie and Tamara?"

"Both back at work," Delia said. "It's only four o'clock. We loaded up Tamara's truck. She'll be by to get us around midnight."

"Midnight?"

"The Star closes tonight at ten, so we should be okay. Honestly? With the four of us working? It won't take that long to get this done. It doesn't have to be perfect, for now. It just has to be better."

"I agree. I'm still going to need a nap. I thought I'd make some soup—"

"I've got dinner ready to go," Delia said. "I'm defrosting some sauce and got some fresh ravioli. Salad, bread. Basic, but filling."

"Sounds perfect," Lilly said. Lilly had many skills and could cook when it was called for, but she did not enjoy it. Delia did and was good at it.

"Go ahead up and take a nap if you want," Delia said. "I'm going to work on this for a while." Delia reached into her bag and pulled out a black plastic box the size of a deck of cards.

"What's that?" Lilly asked.

"A portable hard drive. These are recordings from some of the cameras around Alden Park. They're from the day before and the day of Merilee's murder."

"How did you get them?"

"Well, I may or may not have put out an open call for any footage people may have. And people may or may not have been sending me things the last couple of days, which I may or may not have compiled onto a hard drive."

"Bash Haywood should have access to those files," Lilly said.

"He does. I gave him a copy. He's the one who asked for my help in gathering them. Ernie told him I'd been doing research, so he called me to talk about the best way to find as much footage as he could. We agreed that if I asked for it and compiled it, he wouldn't need a warrant, so I did it. Though I don't think I'll do it again, even for Bash. The invasion of privacy freaks me out."

"Does he know you have a copy as well?"

"I didn't tell him I did, if that's what you're asking. But there was something about the way he asked me for help—when I took the hard drive over to him. He asked if you knew I was helping him. When I said no, he told me I should tell you. So I'm doing that. Give me a chance to go through the files, and I'll let you know what I find out. Okay?"

"Okay," Lilly said. Frustrating as it was, Lilly had to leave Delia to her systems and let her go through the data on her own. In the meanwhile, Lilly was going do some more thinking about who else had a motive to kill Merilee Frank.

CHAPTER 22

Lilly couldn't quite decide what to wear for midnight gardening at the flagpole, but she finally settled on black yoga pants, black boots, and a black fleece. She went downstairs and found Delia in the kitchen making a cup of tea. Delia's ensemble was similar to Lilly's, but wearing shades of black was Delia's norm.

"I'm nervous," Lilly said. "Is that ridiculous?"

"Adrenaline is good for you. It will help you focus," Delia said. "I pulled out some tools that we can take with us. I figured we'd drive your car down and park behind the Star Café."

"No one down there knows what we're doing, do they?"

"No, I did what you told me to do. I'm keeping Stan out of it, but if he asks me point-blank, you know I'm going to have to tell him the truth."

"Knowledge after the fact is different than before the fact. Honestly, I don't see how we could get into trouble for this, but I would like to keep a lid on it."

"You got it, boss," Delia said, giving Lilly one of her rare smiles. "Proud to be part of your Garden Squad, on our first adventure."

"Garden Squad? First adventure? What are you talking about? You watch too many of those action movies."

"You watch them with me, Lilly. An unlikely group of friends, coming together with a common goal—"

"To replace weeds with plants whenever possible," Lilly said.

"To restore order from chaos," Delia said. "Grab your water bottle, let's go."

"You know, I never realized how dead Goosebush nightlife was until tonight. Not one car has come around the Wheel, and we've been here an hour already," Ernie still whispered, but he was right. It was quiet.

"It's a school night. Most of the businesses around here close by nine o'clock, especially on a Tuesday night," Tamara said. "Still, I'm glad this isn't taking as long as I thought it might. When I saw the plans you three had made, I thought it would be three- or four-hour job easily."

"Many hands make light work," Lilly said. "You're a quick weeder, by the way."

"Years of practice. I can't tell you how many open houses I've held, and I walk up the front walkway and I notice weeds. They spring up last minute and spoil a look," Tamara said. "I've taken to showing up a bit earlier, putting on my gloves, and getting it done. I don't dally when it comes to weeds."

"What's next?" Delia asked. They had put all the weeds into a composting bag, and she'd put them aside to load into the back of Lilly's car, along with two bags of trash they'd collected.

"I've dug the four holes for the grasses," Ernie said. "Lilly, why don't you get those in and work your magic so that they'll grow. Delia, I know you want to get that brass plaque polished, so get to it. Tamara, you and I are going to rearrange a couple of these rocks and put out a couple more. Then we'll spread the mulch, and we're done."

It didn't take long to get the work finished. The four friends spent another half hour around the flagpole, cleaning things up. They gathered up the extra materials, the composting bag, and the trash, and walked behind the Star to put them in Lilly's truck. Lilly threw a tarp over everything and closed the back hatch. She turned toward the three of them and smiled.

"Phew," she said, taking off her gardening gloves and shoving them into the front pouch of her fleece. She wiped her sweaty hands down the front of her yoga pants. "What time is it?"

"Almost two," Tamara said, having pulled out her cell phone.

"I'm wide awake," Ernie said.

"Me too," Lilly said. "I'd love to suggest we all go back to my house and have a glass of wine to celebrate. But I don't have to go to work in the morning."

"Nice thing about being the boss, I can be a little late," Tamara said. "My first appointment isn't until eleven."

"I asked Jackie to open for me," Ernie said. "I wasn't sure how long this would take."

"Well, then, let's reconvene at my house. I'll leave the driveway gate open."

Delia got behind the wheel to drive them home and decided to take the long way, down the back alley to a side street that fed onto the Wheel, so they could drive past their handiwork. As they got near the flagpole, Delia slowed to a crawl. They looked out to the left and took a long glance.

"It doesn't look that much different, does it," Delia said.

"I think it looks a lot different," Lilly said. "Much neater. All that trash that was collected there? Gone. The monument stands out now. We didn't want it to look so different, just spiffed up. We reached our goal."

"How hard is it to make these figs with blue cheese?" Ernie asked Delia. The four friends were sitting around the kitchen table, with an assortment of leftovers, cheeses, crackers, nuts, and chocolates laid out in front of them.

"Not hard at all," Delia said. "I know you love them, so I had a batch ready to go in case you came by."

"You're a good woman," Ernie said. He popped another fig into his mouth and then reached over to grab some pepperoni and cheese. "This is a delightful repast. Well done, Delia."

"I'm sorry to say I finished off your ravioli," Tamara said. "I hope you weren't planning on leftovers."

"I have three more batches of sauce ready to be defrosted in the freezer," Delia said. "And more pasta, if you're still hungry."

"No, this is enough. I was nervous before we got

there, so I didn't eat dinner." Tamara took a piece of bread and soaked up the rest of the sauce.

"I was a wreck too," Ernie said. "But you know what? This was great. We'll be sore and a little tired tomorrow. But we fixed the eyesore in the center of town, together."

"Order out of chaos," Delia said.

"What did you say?" Tamara asked.

"Delia thinks we're some sort of garden avengers," Lilly said.

"A Garden Squad, more like. We don't have superpowers," Delia said, standing up and taking Tamara's plate from her, putting it in the sink. She got a clean plate from the cupboard and handed it to Tamara. Then she went over and took out four cookie tins and put them on the table.

Ernie pulled one of the tins toward him and took off the lid. "Seriously, how can you two not weigh four hundred pounds each?" He took a cookie out and nibbled the edge. "What, pray tell, is this nirvana?"

Delia blushed, pleased as always that Ernie appreciated her baking. Delia baked a lot, working hard to be as good a baker as she was a cook. She mostly gave her cookies and cakes away to the nursing home down the street, the folks who worked at the boatyard, Bash Haywood and the rest of the people at the police station, Tamara's office, and Ernie's store.

"A new recipe. New to me, anyway. It's one of Lilly's mother's. Oatmeal and coconut. You melt the butter and barely bake them, which is why they're so flat and chewy."

Tamara picked up one of the cookies and took a

bite. "Oh, I remember these. I loved when she made them. She'd always send me home with a bagful."

"Somehow, Delia has inherited my mother's baking gene. She's going through her old recipes and organizing them for us."

"Well, these taste exactly the way she made them, which is great. I swear, half the recipes my grandmother left my mother never tasted the same," Tamara said.

"Oh, I've got a couple of those," Lilly said. "I'm trying to figure them out."

"Lilly's mother made notes on her recipes, talking about the tweaks she made. It's fun looking at them. It helps me imagine what she must've been like by seeing what she cooked and baked."

"Well, Delia, if you ever want to know anything about Viola, you can ask me," Tamara said. "I knew her practically my whole life, loved her like a second mother. I know she would be pleased you are making her cookies and taking care of Lilly."

"Someone has to take care of Lilly," Ernie said. "She takes care of the rest of us."

"We take care of each other," Lilly said. Her voice was husky, and she took a sip of wine to clear it.

"And tonight we took care of Goosebush," Tamara said. "Lilly, I hear you stopped by to visit Portia Asher."

"Is there anything you don't know?" Lilly asked.

"A few things, like who killed Merilee Frank, but that's for another time. How did the visit go?"

"Ernie, you said that you are going to have historically approved mailboxes for sale at the store soon. How soon?" Lilly asked.

"I have a couple of prototypes in the store now,"

he said. "PJ has a few done in his shop. Tell you what, it would be great to see how hard they are to put in. If only we knew someone who needed a new mailbox . . ."

With that, Ernie raised his glass toward the women sitting around the table. Each looked at him and raised her glass in turn. The four clanked and took sips. Portia was going to get a new mailbox. Lilly had already ordered her a new recycling barrel that was being delivered before the next pickup day.

"As for Merilee?" Delia said. "I'm going through some video recordings—"

"How did you get recordings?" Tamara asked.

"Don't ask," Lilly said. "Plausible deniability."

"I didn't do anything illegal, mostly," Delia said.

"Lilly's right, I don't want to know."

"Once I go through them, I'll have a better sense of who went into Alden Park after Pete and Merilee's fight, but before we got there. So far, it looks like Pete, PJ Frank, Cal—"

"Cal?" Ernie asked.

"The poet," Tamara said.

"Pat French, Ernie—"

"Ernie? You have Ernie on the suspect list?" Tamara said.

"She's talking about opportunity, not who did it," Lilly said.

"And Stan," Delia said. She looked truly miserable naming that last suspect.

"Stan was setting up food tables," Lilly said. "He had a reason to be there."

"Well, if you look at this with the clinical eye, Stan had motive. Merilee made every effort to make his life miserable, and she succeeded. I'm not sure why;

Stan never told me. But I guess, if you make a list, he has to be on it," Delia said.

"Delia, I commend your objectivity, and thank you for telling us. We need to know all the facts if we're going to help Pete or anyone else who may get on Bash's list. Now we've got to talk to all those folks," Lilly said.

"I didn't do it, for the record. But one of the others is probably a murderer," Ernie said. "What a terrible thought."

CHAPTER 23

The party broke up soon after the suspect list was made. Before he left, Ernie suggested that Lilly go over to the Frank Lumberyard and talk to PJ about the mailbox stand he was putting together, so she could get a sense of what it would take to make it work. Lilly agreed, chiefly so that Ernie wouldn't jeopardize a business relationship by accusing someone of possibly being a murderer. Besides, Lilly had known PJ almost his entire life. One of the perils of living in a small town was that you couldn't help but know your ex-husband's new wife and family. Over the years, Lilly and PJ had forged their own relationship. She always used him as a source for lumber and custom-made cabinetry. He appreciated her business and took good care of her.

Lilly took a chance and drove over to the lumberyard around nine o'clock. Sure enough, PJ had inherited his grandfather's work ethic and had obviously already been at his desk for a while.

"Hey, Lilly, to what do I owe the pleasure?" He

got up and walked around his desk and shook Lilly's hand. He also leaned over to kiss her on the cheek.

"Good to see you, PJ. I hope you don't mind me just dropping by, but I had something I want to talk to you about." Lilly saw a flicker cross PJ's face, but he recovered quickly. He waved her to a seat and went back behind his desk to sit in his chair. PJ looked a lot like his father but had a great deal of his mother in him too. He was handsome and, from everything Lilly knew, a good man.

"Ernie and I were talking last night. I understand you are helping him provide some historically accurate materials for folks," Lilly said. PJ sighed, and a real smile broke out across his face once again.

"Oh that? Yes, it was Ernie's idea. People kept coming in and asking him if he carried the specific picket sizes and end caps that the historic district required. He decided he should start stocking them and came to me to see if I could manufacture them. Once he told me why he wanted them, I was in. Those rules are a killer. Besides, I appreciate the business, and the thought."

"It's good to keep things local," Lilly said.

"You've lived by that creed, which my grandfather appreciated. You always gave work to our lumberyard, despite everything."

"Your grandfather was a good man. I never had a beef with him," Lilly said.

"Well, he thought the world of you, that's for sure. Anyway, this project is turning out to be interesting. We're working on making pieces at different price points, so it is a lot more affordable for folks."

"How about mailboxes? Honestly, I had no idea until recently that there were mailbox rules."

"We've got those too," PJ said. He reached for a

file and flipped it open, turning it toward Lilly. "A little more complicated. I doubt there's another town in all of America that is as fussy about mailboxes as Goosebush is. I swear, there are more rules about them than there are about breaking and entering."

"I've got to admit, I feel a little guilty about all this. I was on the historic commission for years and came up with some of those rules. Though I don't ever remember talking about mailboxes."

"The rules only became enforceable with fines a couple years ago," PJ said. "Someone tried to use plastic fencing, and half the town lost their minds. So Pat French came up with a solution. Stricter rules and bigger fines. It made sense to me for a long time."

"Is this trickier than a regular mailbox to install?" Lilly asked, pointing to one of the prototypes. It looked very similar to the mailbox Portia's grandson had installed. Similar, but not exact. Obviously, he had tried to follow the rules. That made Lilly angrier on Portia's behalf.

"No, if anything, it's easier. We have a metal rod going up the center with a four-tined prong on the bottom to give it stability while it's being installed. The hole needs to be a bit wider, but it won't move."

"I'd like to buy one. With a red mailbox—historically accurate, of course."

"I can put that together for you today. Is this for you?"

"No, a friend. A surprise."

"A friend who's getting fined?" PJ asked.

Lilly nodded. "By the way, PJ, if you ever run across people who can't quite pay the entire bill, reach out to me, all right?"

"Will do," PJ said. "Another Lilly Jayne charity project?"

"Not charity. I just don't like the idea of my neighbors being fined to the poor house, you know?" Lilly said.

"I do, and I agree. I try to help folks when I can. I've been thinking that we should have some sort of formalized process to help folks out. Maybe a grant folks can apply for."

"That's a great idea," Lilly said. "I know a few folks who may be interested in helping out. Maybe we can combine this with the work the Beautification Committee is fundraising for." She took out her phone and texted herself a note.

"Say, Lilly, have you seen the flagpole today?" PJ asked, looking right at her.

Lilly flinched but took pains to make sure her face stayed impassive when she looked back up at PJ. "Flagpole? Which flagpole?"

That was a fair question, since Goosebush had several flagpoles around town. One at the police station, one at each school, one at the library, one at the center of every rotary, and several at private houses. Patriotism ran deep in Goosebush.

"The one at the Wheel. Something magical happened there last night. It's been cleaned up. Looks great."

"Maybe Pat French found some funds," Lilly said.

PJ stared at Lilly for a moment more, then gave in. If she had anything to do with it, she wasn't going to let on. "Well, whoever did it did the town a service. I drove by today and went around a second time. I never realized how much a cleanup like that matters until it happens."

"It's a shame the Alden Park project has been derailed, at least for a bit. Oh my, how insensitive of me," Lilly said. "I should be thinking about poor Merilee, not a park project, at a time like this."

"It's okay to think of both," PJ said. "Though the Merilee situation hits close to home, what with Dad being arrested and all."

"Well, it was awfully decent of you to help put up bail money for your father. Is he staying with you?"

"No, my mother's in town; she's been staying with me for a while. They can't both be under the same roof. The perils of divorce."

"Rhonda's in town? I thought I saw her the other day, but I couldn't be sure," Lilly said.

"She goes to great lengths to avoid seeing you," PJ said. "Cards on the table, Lilly, you should know she always felt really bad about what happened with her and my Dad; she never meant to hurt you."

When an odd conversation to be having with somebody, Lilly thought. The son of her first husband and his mistress. A good man, and someone who became a friend to Lilly on her own, despite the name he shared with his father. "PJ, the past is the past. Your mother doesn't need to avoid me. I doubt we'll ever be close friends again, but she's not my enemy. This is going to sound terrible, but your father leaving me to be with your mother was a gift. If I'd stayed married to Pete, I never would've married Alan. And he is, was, the best thing that ever happened to me."

"You're quite a lady, Lilly," PJ said. "I don't know if I'd be as gracious in similar circumstances. I'm pretty sure I wouldn't be. My folks are complicated. When Dad had an affair on Mom, she kicked him out, but he was leaving anyway. Merilee had gotten her claws into him. I'm not sure she ever recovered. Then there's the house situation."

"House situation?"

"Yeah, Merilee tried to sue me for partial ownership of the house. When Dad found out, he made her drop it, but it caused a rift. Mildly put."

"She really was a piece of work, wasn't she?" Lilly said.

"She really was," PJ said. "Dad tells me you don't think he did it."

"No, I don't. Do you?"

"This is going to sound terrible, but I'm not sure. My mother keeps insisting he didn't, couldn't, have done it. I told her there's probably another list out there that has my name on it too."

"It does seem like there's a list of suspects," Lilly said. "Has Bash spoken with you?"

"Yup, a couple times. I don't deny it: I had motive. Fortunately, I also had an alibi. There's less than an hour window when it happened. I was at the park, sure, but I was with somebody. That gave me an alibi."

"Well, that's good."

"It's someone I've been dating," PJ said. "That may make his alibi questionable, but fortunately a couple of other people saw us."

"I'm glad you've been seeing somebody, PJ," Lilly said. "You deserve to be happy. I hope I get to meet him at some point."

PJ smiled at Lilly. "Lilly, you're the best. Nothing fazes you, does it? The answer is yes, you'll meet him. And the other answer is, no, I didn't kill Merilee. There are times I could've, but I didn't. Now, do you want that mailbox delivered, or do you want to pick it up?"

CHAPTER 24

As Lilly walked up to Tamara's side door, Warwick was coming out, almost colliding with her. "Whoa, sorry, Lilly," he said. "Bit of a late start this morning. I'm used to Tamara driving the morning schedule, and she slept in today. I got out the door in time but realized I forgot my phone, so I came back between classes. Amazing how tied I am to this thing."

"I resisted a smartphone for so long, but Delia finally wore me down. What a difference it makes," Lilly said. "Remember last winter when we went up to Vermont for an overnight and couldn't get cell service? The three of us showed signs of complete addiction that weekend."

"I'll tell you what, Vermont went off my 'maybe we'll retire there' list that weekend. I used to think I could unplug, but no longer. Plus, hourly texts from Tamara are my touch points throughout the day. Tell me, are you part of the reason my wife didn't get home until almost four o'clock in the morning?"

"Part of the reason," Lilly said. She wondered how much Warwick knew. She doubted Tamara kept much, if anything, from him. She'd need to confirm with Tamara first, but he should be brought into the loop. If nothing else, he could post bail if they all got arrested.

Warwick looked down at his phone and smiled at Lilly. "Great to see you, but I've got to run. My students await." He gave Lilly a dazzling smile and jogged out to the front of the house, where he had parked his car at the side of the street.

Lilly tapped on the side door and got no response. She opened it and walked in. She called out for Tamara. No response. She walked into the foyer and stopped at the bottom of the stairs. "Tamara, it's Lilly. I'm down in the kitchen."

"Great, thanks for letting me know. If there's coffee, have some. If there isn't, could you make some? There can't be enough coffee this morning."

"Will do," Lilly said. Lilly walked over to the coffee maker and was pleased that Tamara had finally upgraded their machine. For the last year or so, the warmer plate on their old coffee maker had barely functioned, and nothing but brown water ever came through the filter. Tamara had always argued that since she so rarely drank coffee at home, it was fine. But Lilly had always noticed that when Tamara came to her house, she asked for and got a cup of coffee and savored it. It didn't help that Warwick didn't drink coffee. He was a caffeine-free guy, something that Lilly could never fathom.

Lilly made the coffee the way she liked it; two extra scoops guaranteed it would be so dark you couldn't see the bottom of the mug. While it was perking, she went to the refrigerator and pulled out some cream for Tamara. Cream was one of Tamara's few indulgences.

Lilly was pouring two cups when Tamara walked

in. "Sorry for the delay. I'm a wreck today," Tamara said.

Lilly looked at her friend. Tamara looked put together, as always. Perhaps a little more concealer under her eyes, but otherwise polished, professional, and lovely. Lilly smiled. Whereas she had softened a bit through the middle over the years, had creaky knees that required flat shoes, and had long ago let her hair go gray, Tamara if anything looked better now in her early sixties than she had as a younger woman. And despite having had four children, she was fit. Tamara's mother had been a beautiful woman, so Tamara had good genes. But Lilly gave Warwick a lot of the credit for the fact that Tamara was aging with a joyful grace. He made her very happy and kept her on her toes.

"I went to see PJ this morning and thought I'd stop by on my way home," Lilly said. She sat down and took a sip of her coffee. Tamara walked over to a cabinet and opened it, searching for something. She finally found a box of breakfast bars and took one out. She lifted the box toward Lilly, who declined the offer. Breakfast bars were perhaps healthier, but Lilly had scones at home. It wasn't even a question of where her calories were going to come from today.

"Aren't you the early bird?" Tamara said. "Warwick had to drag me out of bed this morning. But being tired was worth it. I feel good about what we did last night. It was kind of fun."

"PJ mentioned it, the flagpole being spiffed up. He asked if I knew anything about it. I gave him a non-denial denial," Lilly said.

"I was checking the Goosebush Gossip site a few minutes ago. There's mention of the flagpole getting a face-lift, but the site says there was no idea about who had done the work," Tamara said as she sat down at the table and picked up her phone, clicking a few buttons and then handing it to Lilly. Sure enough, the flagpole was a feature story on the site. Lilly read the story quickly.

"Interesting shot, don't you think?" Tamara said. Lilly scrolled back up and saw exactly what Tamara was talking about. Wherever the camera was, it had a perfect vantage point over the flagpole from a higher level. There were very few structures in that area where the camera could be placed that would give it that vantage point.

"I wonder if whoever writes the site has some pictures of us doing the work?" Lilly said.

"I wonder too. Could be, if they have a camera going all the time. Maybe that's the next story?"

"Delia's been doing some research on cameras. I'll talk to her, see if she has any ideas about what kind of camera this might've been and where it was located. Maybe it's a traffic camera, and Goosebush Gossip was able to tap in."

"Surveillance cameras are all the rage. I can't tell you how many clients I have who list a high-tech security system as a must-have. I guess it's a good idea, but wow. Makes me paranoid to go out and get my paper in the morning in my bathrobe."

"I hear you. Does one of your neighbors have a camera fetish?" Lilly asked.

"Not that I know of, but now I can't be sure. At the last board of selectmen meeting, we were talking about surveillance cameras. It can't surprise you that Pat French is a big fan. I wouldn't be surprised if she has cameras everywhere. I've never met anyone so inclined to getting into people's business, and I've been alive a long time."

"We both have," Lilly said.

"I keep thinking about who Pat is like, but she's unique. She knows everything about everybody or tries to. Acts like that's her job."

"It really hasn't been that long, but you and I aren't good judges of time. We've been here all our lives. She moved here, what? Five, six years ago?"

"More like ten; she moved in to live with her cousin and take care of her. Edith passed away six years ago," Tamara said.

"I still can't believe she left Pat the house. All that talk, all those years, of leaving it in a trust to the Historical Society."

"Edith didn't know Pat was out there when she was making that decision. Anyway, maybe that's why Pat's become her own preservation society, much to the detriment of everyone else in town."

"Maybe," Lilly said. "Oh, by the way, I ordered a mailbox from PJ for Portia. He's going to deliver it to my house this afternoon. We need to figure out when to install it."

"I'm in," Tamara said. "Maybe a night off though?"

"Yes, I think a night off would be good. But we'll need to do it at night. I'm really hoping we can do this so that no one notices, including Portia or her grandson. Though she did ask me to look at her hydrangea bushes, so that might be a good excuse for me to go over again and take some measurements if we need them."

"I've been thinking about some of the houses in town, and the history. We've got the four-hundredth anniversary coming up, and folks like Portia Asher carry a lot of that history inside them. Do you think Delia would be willing to take on the project of doing some research on the old houses and tracing back the owners?" Tamara asked.

"I'm sure she would, but isn't that what the Registry of Deeds is for?"

Tamara paused for a minute, playing with her coffee mug and running a fingernail down the side. Finally, she looked up. "Lilly, being on the board of selectmen has been interesting. Mildly put. So much of what we think is based on what we've been told. I think it would be helpful to know that what we've been told is the truth. Get some facts to back up the stories. You're lucky; your relatives built your house. I'm lucky, we can trace this house back to when it was first built. But it's not just the houses; it's the land—who owns what, where the boundaries are. I've been trying to get the town to consider resurveying the public lots, and I'm running up against a lot of opposition to the idea. I have to ask why."

"Well, you don't actually *have* to ask why, but you wouldn't be Tamara if you didn't."

"Don't you give me that, Lilly Jayne," Tamara said. "I see your brain whirring from over here."

"You do," Lilly said. "Let's figure out a time for you to come over and talk to Delia, and I want to be in the room. See if I can help. I can see the can of worms a survey might open. Does Pat French think it's a good idea?"

"She tells me she thinks it's a good idea," Tamara said. "She probably sees dollar signs flying at her as property values can also be reassessed. But she isn't a voting member of the board."

"How long have you been thinking about this?" Lilly said.

"That last town meeting put a bee in my bonnet. Warwick and I've been talking about it. He hears a lot from the parents of the students on his team. I'm hearing from people trying to sell property that there are holdups."

"Do you think any of this has to do with Merilee's death?" Lilly asked.

"No, probably not. Merilee was trying to get her hands on PJ's house—"

"PJ mentioned that," Lilly said.

"But a real estate mogul she was not."

"How about Pete? Do you think he's been paying attention to survey boundaries and property taxes?"

"That's a good question," Tamara said. "I've tried to talk to him about it a couple of times, but he's like us. His family has lived here for so long that he doesn't question the status quo."

"I always thought I liked the status quo, but now I'm realizing that not questioning it wasn't a good practice. It worked for me, but not for everybody," Lilly said.

"I hear you," Tamara said. "I'm finding as I get older, I'm more willing to question, to risk something not being in my own self-interest."

"There is power in being a middle-aged woman, for sure," Lilly said.

"Especially one with a best friend. Listen, Lil, I've got to get to work. Text me later, and let me know if you and Delia have some time to talk. Maybe we can all have dinner together tonight? Delia can defrost some more of that sauce?"

"Sounds like a plan," Lilly said. "I'm going to try and talk to Pat French at some point today, so I'll have that to report back."

"Gird your loins, girlfriend. Pat French under the best of circumstances is trying, and with the flagpole that got fixed? She's probably in a state," Tamara said.

CHAPTER 25

Lilly went out to her Vespa and put her helmet on. She loved the freedom of riding her Vespa around town, though it was hard to be incognito while traveling. She had taken to wearing leggings under her cotton dresses, a lesson learned after a few gusts of wind created a balloon effect that did nothing to support Lilly's modest nature. Before she turned the scooter on, she took out her phone and checked her messages. There was a text from Ernie:

Can you come by? Delia's here. Talking cameras.

Fortuitous timing, thought Lilly. She engaged the engine and pushed out into the street, after having checked both ways several times. Lilly had all sorts of mirrors attached to her Vespa and to her helmet, to help her with blind spots and navigation. She also drove very slowly, which was more the norm in Goosebush anyway. Years of winter, salting, plowing, summer heat, and wear and tear had rendered most of the roads in Goosebush a challenge of potholes, bumps, and missing bits of pavement that brought up the original cobblestones. Like many of the residents on the main roads in town, Lilly didn't mind the potholes since they slowed people down considerably.

Tamara's house was out toward the lumberyard, so Lilly made her way back, circling around the first rotary without having any cars to navigate around. She drove down the main drag, Washington Street, and glanced over at her house, on the right, as she drove past. On her scooter, she couldn't see over the garden wall, which was just as she liked it. You really couldn't see Lilly's house unless you were in the boatyard, looking across the street, since the house was set so far back and raised up on a hill. Lilly's father used to joke that most of the building restrictions happened because of their house and how much the neighbors hated it. It was a big, over-built Victorian in a town that favored more Federal-style homes.

Lilly continued down Washington Street, eyes on the road. She sensed a car behind her but stayed in the middle of her lane. She was going the speed limit.

As she approached the Wheel, there was an up-tick in traffic. She tried to keep the scooter moving, but eventually had to put her feet down because traffic had slowed to a crawl. Lilly hated going around rotaries in the best of times, and this wasn't it. She looked to her right and left, and put on her blinker to the left. As soon as people got off the Wheel, they moved forward at a quicker pace, so it was hard for her to find a time to be able to merge, but finally someone made room. She drove up behind the Star Café and parked the Vespa. She locked her helmet under the seat and took her bag out of the basket on the back. She made a motion to fix her hair but knew it was a lost cause.

She walked back to the right and to the corner of the stores on this part of the Wheel. She noted that people slowed down going around the flagpole, and that there were clusters of cars coming in from all directions. More than one person was leaning out, taking a picture of the flagpole. She paused to take a good look at their handiwork. In daylight, she could see places where they'd missed with the mulch, and she recognized that they needed to pay attention to a bit more than just the grasses and the corners. But the granite monument looked good, and Delia had done a great job polishing the brass, which shone in the sunlight.

"Looks great, doesn't it?" a male voice said. Lilly turned and noticed that Ray Mancini had come up to her left. "I didn't realize how bad it looked until I saw it this morning. Wonder who could have done it?"

"A concerned citizen, or two, most likely," Lilly said. "The shame of it is that not much was done. A bit of cleanup, some new plants, that's it."

"Well, if you talk to Pat French, it's hardly a small amount done. She's acting like there was an infiltration of saboteurs overnight."

"Pat French is on the wrong side of progress this time," Lilly said. "When's the next town meeting? I want to make sure that Alden Park stays on the front burner, and that we get the work done as soon as possible."

"We'll get that done. Hopefully by the time the next town meeting comes along this Merilee Frank business will hopefully be well behind us by then."

"They've already arrested Pete Frank," Lilly said.

"Bash has his heart set on Pete Frank as the killer," Ray said. "I understand the desire to have a closed case as soon as possible."

"I can imagine the pressure is enormous, but I don't think Pete did it, for what it's worth."

"It's worth a lot," Ray said. "I don't disagree with you, but I'm focused on making sure the case is handled with every legal precaution."

"Making sure Bash looks good," Lilly said. "You take good care of him."

"This case could make or break a career. But if you think he's on the wrong path, you should probably invite Bash over for a cup of coffee soon. Have a conversation with him, let him in on your thinking as long as you've got some facts to back it up."

"I've got to visit a few more people first. I want to have something to talk to him about," Lilly said.

"You watch your back, Lilly," Ray said. "Whoever killed Merilee has some rage issues. They think they're safe. You're wrestling with a hornet's nest. You know you can call me anytime, day or night, right?"

"Keep your phone on, Ray," Lilly said. "I may just take you up on that sooner than you think."

It took Lilly a while to walk around the Wheel and cross all the streets until she could get to the other side, to Bits, Bolts & Bulbs. When she walked into the Triple B, the clerk in the front gave her a wave and mouthed "in the back" while flipping her thumb toward the office.

Lilly walked in and found Ernie and Delia sitting on the same side of the worktable, looking at a computer. Spread out on the table were several cameras.

"Sorry it took so long," Lilly said. "Getting through town there was quite a traffic jam. People were stopping to look at the flagpole. I had to park behind the *Star*."

"It's the talk of the town," Ernie said. He got up, crossed over to the office door, and closed it. He gestured for Lilly to sit on his abandoned seat and pulled another stool over to the table. "Lilly, you should know, you're the one everyone thinks did the work. You and Delia. A few folks have asked me if I thought you two were responsible."

"What have you told them?"

"I've told them that I was grateful to whoever was responsible," Ernie said.

"I obfuscated the same way with Ray Mancini just now," Lilly said. "He said that Pat French didn't take it well."

"What does Pat French take well?" Ernie said.

"Ernie, look at this," Delia said.

Ernie got up and moved behind Delia, and Lilly leaned in.

"What have you two been up to?" Lilly asked.

"I was up most of the night, looking over the video recordings," Delia said. "Some of them were from traffic cameras; some came from stores. For a couple, I can't identify where the shots were taken. Someone may have a drone. Anyway, the more I look, the more I see how people could have gotten into Alden Park, and no one could've seen them. We always think of the road being the only point of egress, but there isn't a fence around the park. If we get in the park, we can take some pictures that may help me know where else to look for cameras. Does that make sense? I'm a little tired."

"You must be. You didn't drive, did you?" Lilly asked.

"I walked," Delia said. "Wanted to clear my head a little and check out some of the camera positions."

"So we're back to motive, and then we need to figure out opportunity?" Lilly asked.

"Yeah, I think so," Delia said. "Of course, this had to happen on the day when half the town showed up to help clear the park."

"I've been thinking about that," Ernie said. "That makes me think that this wasn't premeditated. More like a crime of opportunity."

"Explain," Delia said. She looked up from her computer and focused on Ernie.

"Since they can pinpoint when the murder occurred within such a short period of time, whoever did it took a huge chance of being seen. There were lots of suspects, but also lots of possible witnesses. So unless they are an adrenaline junkie, they probably seized an opportunity."

"You're right, Ernie. I wonder if Merilee had planned on meeting whoever killed her in the shed? Was there an e-mail or a text?" Delia said. "I wonder if they found her phone?"

"If she set up a meeting in the shed on her phone, the case would have been easier to solve. I wonder if the shed was a last-minute decision, an opportunistic place to meet? Folks started showing up early. Maybe Merilee saw someone, forced the meeting, they went into the shed, and she upset the person in such a way that they lashed out. Grabbed whatever was close by—"

"Hedge clippers," Delia shuddered. "Whoever did it had to be strong too."

"Not necessarily," Lilly said. "If the person was angry, adrenaline may have kicked in. Which means that it would have drained out of them later." She paused to think back to their time at the Star Café after the murder. She'd need to go home and look at her notes, but no one person seemed more out of sorts than anyone else. Everyone had been pretty shaken up.

"Well, not to get too graphic, but whoever did this also would have had to change clothes, right?" Ernie said.

"Good point," Lilly said.

"So while the videos themselves are useless," Delia said, "maybe we can see if anyone changed."

"Or didn't come to the Star Café. Maybe this person committed the crime and left?" Ernie said.

"The worst thing we can do is to limit our way of thinking. We need to hold onto the idea that anything is possible. Who knows what could have triggered someone to kill Merilee." Delia said.

"But one thing we do know, it wasn't an accident. Someone had to get pretty close to her," Ernie said.

"So we think she met someone in the shed, rather than her being killed somewhere else and moved?" Lilly said.

"There was a lot of blood in the shed," Delia said. "Like all over the place. If she'd been killed outside and moved, there would have been blood outside too."

"Once the town releases the shed back to my custody, I'm going to have it destroyed," Ernie said. "Delia, sweetie, I'm so sorry you had to see that."

"Thanks, Ernie. I'm not getting a lot of sleep

these days, but trying to figure stuff out helps. So I'm going to leave it to the two of you to keep talking to people. That's not my forte. What I'll do is keep looking at video recordings, doing some research, gathering data. Bring me back any facts you need verified. Don't assume anyone's telling the truth. I'm going to work on a timeline, with more information about what we found out so far."

"We're probably following the path that the police have already been down," Ernie said.

"I'm not so sure of that," Lilly said. "It's something Ray said to me earlier. They think they've got their person. They'll leave it up to the prosecutor's office to decide if they can make their case or not."

"Which could mean that if Pete did do it and they can't make their case, he'll get off scot-free. Or, if he didn't do it, someone else won't get charged if they've stopped looking," Ernie said.

"Even if Pete doesn't get convicted, this is a hell of a cloud to have hanging over his head," Lilly said. "Something PJ said to me this morning bothered me. He bailed his father out, but he's not sure he's innocent. Pete's made a lot of mistakes, but he doesn't deserve his son thinking that he's a killer."

"So on top of being clandestine gardeners, we're going to keep seeking out the truth, is that right?" Delia said.

"That's right," Lilly said.

"Cool," Delia said, going back to her computer.

CHAPTER 26

Lilly walked back toward the Star Café, this time walking the other way around the Wheel. Crossing the streets was still dicey, but she took her time. She was amazed at how many people were stopping to look at the flagpole. She paused for a moment and took out her phone to take a picture.

"This is your doing, isn't it?" Lilly turned toward the woman shouting at her, but she knew the voice. She took a deep breath, counted to ten, and let it go. She fixed a smile on her face and turned toward Pat French.

"Good morning, Pat, or is it afternoon? I've lost track of time today. Busy day, tough to get around here."

"You did this, didn't you? Don't act all innocent. You know what I'm talking about. You cleaned up the Wheel."

"Is that why all this traffic is here? A war monument that's been cleaned up?"

"See! I knew you had something to do with this.

How did you know there was a war monument near the flagpole?"

"You forget, Pat, that I've lived here my whole life. I've forgotten more than you know about this town." Lilly's smile had faded, and she stared right at Pat. To Pat's credit, she didn't look away, but she did seem to grow in fury.

"Oh, you'd be surprised at what I know. Troublemaker, that's what you are. Cleaning up—"

"That's another thing," Lilly said. "How is cleaning something up causing trouble? Have you gotten a bill for materials or time? Did whoever did this somehow desecrate the monument? Honestly, Pat, rather than be upset at the person who did this, you should take out a full-page ad on the Goosebush Gossip site and thank them for doing your job."

"You can't talk to me like that," Pat fumed.

"Like what? Tell you what, Pat, as a citizen of Goosebush, I will call your office later this afternoon and set up an appointment to come down and look at these rules and regulations you've set up. That this flagpole has not been tended to on a regular basis is an atrocity. An atrocity, I'll admit, I hadn't noticed until somebody cleaned it up and I see how much better it looks. I pay taxes, Pat, a lot of them. Looks like I'm going to need to get some accounting for where they go. Because it isn't the public gardens, and it isn't the roads. Where's the money, Pat?"

"Are you accusing me—"

"No, I'm not accusing you of anything," Lilly said quietly. "What I'm saying is if there isn't enough money to do the work that needs to be done, we need to find more. And it can't be on the backs of folks who can't get their fence fixed."

"Well, you'd have more authority to check on all this if you were on the board of selectmen, which you aren't," Pat said.

"True," Lilly said. "Is there still an empty seat? Maybe I need to run again. I've been on and off the board for years. I'm rested and ready to go. It would be a lot of fun to work with you, Pat. See that? You've given me an idea."

"I'm going to find out who did this," Pat said, gesturing to the flagpole. "And they'll pay. There are permits for this sort of thing. Rules. If we let people just do what they want willy-nilly, this town will go to hell in a handbasket faster than I can say do-re-mi. You may not care about that, but I do. Tell your little friends that."

Lilly watched Pat walk past her and toward Ernie's store. She took out her phone and texted him. *Pat French is en route. On her broomstick.*

Ernie sent a text back. *Thanks for the heads-up. I'll get my bucket of water ready just in case.*

Lilly was hungry and decided to stop by the Star Café before she got back on her Vespa to go home. She walked in and was confronted by a small line at the coffee bar, and a longer line at the restaurant. Lilly didn't like lines. She turned to go back out the door, but Stan called to her.

"Ms. Jayne, can I buy you a cup of coffee?" Stan asked from behind the bar. "That table over there is just opening up."

"Any chance you might be able to join me?" Lilly asked.

"That would be great. I could use a break. Give me two minutes."

Lilly went over to the now-empty table and wiped it off with a napkin. She sat down and opened her phone, jotting some thoughts from today on a new page. Then she looked back at her other notes about the case, putting facts back in her brain so she could reconsider information.

"Hmmm, I'd forgotten about that..." She thought to herself. She pulled out her phone and texted Ernie.

Remember the chemicals in Alden Park? Did you ever figure out what that was?

Ernie texted back in a minute. *Pat French just flew out. Some sort of salt mixture. Not terribly hazardous to people, but lousy for plants. Wonder if it has anything to do with anything?*

Who knows? She texted back. *Maybe Merilee found someone dumping the salt water and accused them? Just another factoid to keep in the mix.*

Delia and I were talking, I'm coming over for dinner tonight, so we can assess where we are.

Great, see you then.

Stan came up to the table just then with a tray, complete with two cups of steaming coffee and a small dish of assorted pastries. "Sorry, I don't want to interrupt—"

"You're not interrupting, I'm just texting with Ernie. I'll talk to him later today."

"Planning new adventures?"

"Adventures?" Lilly asked. Stan just smiled at her, but Lilly didn't blink. She was getting good at that.

"Who knew some weeding and some nice plants would cause a traffic jam in downtown Goosebush today?" Stan said. He took a sip of his coffee.

"Who indeed?" Lilly asked. "That wasn't what we were texting about. This is going to sound ridiculous, but Ernie and I are trying to figure out what happened to Merilee Frank."

Stan's eyebrows raised, and Lilly noticed his hand shake as he put his coffee down. "Don't you mean who happened to Merilee Frank? Didn't they arrest her husband?"

"Well, I don't think her husband did it, so I'm sticking my nose in where it doesn't belong to see if there's a way I can help him out."

"That's nice of you, considering. Isn't he your ex-husband?"

"We were married years ago, when the earth was young. I owe him one for divorcing me."

"Plus, he was married to Merilee, which is enough suffering for one man in a life," Stan said. Lilly didn't know Stan well, but she'd never heard him use that tone before.

"You weren't a fan of Merilee's?" she asked.

"She came this close to putting me out of business last year," Stan said.

"Mind if I ask what happened?"

"No, as a matter fact, I'd appreciate you listening to the story. I keep thinking somebody needs to know what she was like. I'm not a huge fan of Pete Frank either, but she was the worst. Last year we had just opened. It was chaos. One day it was raining, and the floors were slick. I had gone back to get the mop and the yellow warning signs, but then Stella came rushing back to tell me that Merilee had slipped and fallen. She threatened to sue, showed me a doctor's X-ray detailing her injuries. Between the money and the publicity, I would have gone out of business before we even officially opened. I didn't know what to do, but she offered me a deal."

"A deal?"

"A deal. I'd feed them for year. Merilee and Frank. More than once I thought the lawsuit would've cost me less. Their bar bill alone was staggering. But the year was almost up."

"When?"

"Next week," Stan said. "I was planning a party and was intending to bar them from the store."

"Is that possible?" Lilly asked.

"Probably not, but I was going to try. Merilee kept joking around, pretending she was going to fall, so they could get another year out of me."

"That must have been very trying," Lilly said. And, she thought, a pretty good motive for murder. As if reading her thoughts, Stan continued with his confession.

"Pete's not that bad, though the man can drink. She is a horror. Was. I didn't kill her, in case you've got a question about that. Not that I didn't fantasize about it every day. But my fantasies were about poisoning her meal. Slow-acting poison that would kill her when she was back home, not in my restaurant."

At that, Lilly did register surprise. "Sorry, Ms. Jayne. I swear, I only killed her in my imagination. And on the page. I write short stories. I may have killed her once or twice there, but I would never do it in real life. I'm a lover, not a killer."

"Why are you telling me all this?" Lilly asked.

"You know that Delia and I are friends. She told me you're trying to figure out what happened to Merilee. She may have mentioned that I was on the list—"

"That must've been quite the conversation."

"You know how Delia is. If you don't want to know what she's thinking, don't ask her. Anyway, she told me you would find out sooner than later, and I should tell you my story. She suggested that maybe I wasn't the only person in Goosebush being forced to support Merilee and Pete's lifestyle."

"Do you think they were blackmailing other people?"

"Blackmailing. That's a helluva term."

"That's what she was doing," Lilly said. "I believe you when you say you didn't kill her, but surely you can see—"

"That someone else might have been driven over the edge? Yeah, I guess I do. I'll tell you the same thing I told Delia; if I hear anything I'll let you know. I promise. As I said, Pete's not my favorite guy, but he shouldn't go to trial if he didn't do it."

Stan had to leave Lilly then, to help deal with the long coffee line. Perhaps confession was good for the soul, because he seemed lighter having told her his story. Much more for Lilly to think about. Merilee blackmailed Stan for food. His question was a good one. Who else was under Merilee Frank's thumb? Might they have been driven to murder?

CHAPTER 27

Stan wouldn't let Lilly pay for her coffee, and she didn't push it. She was glad she had stopped, as much to get insight from Stan as to have some food before she made her way back home. She was tempted to buy a large puzzle that featured vintage postcards, since working on puzzles quieted her mind, but then remembered her Vespa and imagined how hard it would be to navigate getting into traffic while riding on the little scooter and holding a puzzle. She made a mental note to come back and get it when she was walking and had her cart.

Lilly went out the front door, turned to her right, and went to the end of the block. Another right, then another right to get her scooter from behind the Star Café. She started to unlock the Vespa and extract her helmet from under the seat. After a moment, she felt that she was being watched. She looked around and saw Kitty Bouchard sitting on the back stairs of the Star Café, smoking a cigarette.

"Kitty," Lilly said. She nodded her head and turned back toward the Vespa.

"Lilly, good to see you," Kitty said.

Lilly ignored her and put her purse under the seat. She sat on the Vespa and put the key in the ignition. She was about to put her helmet on when Kitty suddenly appeared and stood in front of the scooter.

"What the—" Lilly said.

"You have a minute?" Kitty said.

"Kitty, we have nothing—" she said.

"Listen, Lilly, I know I'm not one of your favorite people. I've always been sad about that, believe it or not. I've made some terrible choices in my life, and they cost me."

"They cost a lot of people," Lilly said.

"Fair enough," Kitty said, taking another drag off her cigarette. She turned her head and blew the smoke away from Lilly. "There's a rumor going around town that you don't think Pete killed Merilee."

"Not a rumor, a fact. I don't think he did it," Lilly said.

"If Pete didn't do it, who do you think did?" Kitty asked.

"Coming up with a list isn't my job, it's the police's."

"But we both know Bash Haywood thinks he has his man, as it were."

"Kitty, why do you care? Last time I saw you and Merilee together, you were shooting daggers at her with your eyes."

"See, that's what I'm talking about. If I'm not on a list, your list, I'm going to be. I had a million reasons to kill Merilee Frank. And, heaven help me, I'm not sorry she's dead. But I didn't kill her. I need you to believe that."

"You said you had a million reasons? You want to give me one or two?"

"So that you can build a case against me?"

"Kitty, I don't have time for this nonsense. I still have no idea why you're talking to me. If you had a million reasons to kill Merilee, come up with an alibi for when she was killed, in case somebody asks."

"That's a problem," Kitty said. "I don't have an alibi. I went to the park early, left for a minute to go over to PJ Frank's house, but he wasn't there. So I went back to the park, and I was there until after they found her body."

"No one saw you?" Kitty shook her head and looked down. "Then you are in a pickle," Lilly said. "You mind moving out of the way? I need to get home."

Kitty didn't move. Lilly was tempted to run her over, or try to, but instead she took a deep breath. Kitty wanted Lilly to know something, but Lilly wasn't going to feed into her drama. Instead, Lilly thought back to the last time she'd seen Kitty, before the day of the murder. Was it at Cal's poetry reading? Yes, that was it. Lilly closed her eyes and thought of that night. Yes, Kitty Bouchard was definitely there. And very, very unhappy. Next Lilly thought about Cal's photos, the slideshow. She opened her eyes again and looked at Kitty. The color of Kitty's hair, a bad dye job trying to look trendy, and her overgrown cut. Lilly glanced down at Kitty's forearm, which was visible below her pushed-up sweatshirt-clad sleeves. Was that a moon and a sun tattoo? Why did that look familiar?

"Were you one of the women in Cal's photos?" Lilly asked her. She saw the color rise in Kitty's face and watched as the younger woman looked down at her sneakers.

"I was," Kitty said. "I was given to think I was going to be the only model in Cal's show. I was wrong, of course. I never should've thought—someone like Cal—guys like that don't go for women like me. Not long-term."

"I've known Cal for years," Lilly said, "and he doesn't go for anyone long-term. Never has. Maybe he will one day when his own mortality finally hits him. But he's what my mother used to call a rake. Hits on anything that moves but has the requisite charm to pull it off."

"Did he ever hit on you?"

Lilly laughed. "No, I was the wife of his friend, and became his friend. Truthfully, Kitty, I'm not the sort of woman men hit on."

"You're formidable and have gravitas. I'm not and don't. Never have. You know, you make aging look so easy. But it's a nightmare for women like me. I'm not used to men like Cal losing interest in me before I lose interest in them. I don't like the feeling. Especially when I lose their affection because they start to have an affair with a friend of mine. I caught them in his apartment one day. She was barely dressed."

"Maybe she was just posing for him?" Lilly asked. She had heard a lot of the story from Cal, but it occurred to her that even Cal might have his reasons for telling his own version of the truth.

"She gave me the definite impression that it was more than just posing."

"Do you think Pete knew about that?"

"I have no doubt he did, since I told him. At least, I e-mailed him."

"Really? When? That seems—"

"Extreme. I've been losing it a bit lately. I've got it bad for a poet. Such a freaking cliché. Merilee knew all about it. I told her from the very beginning. She knew what he meant to me. And then she . . . What kind of person does that? To a friend? Adding salt to the wound, she started teasing me about it. All the time."

Lilly tumbled what Kitty had told her around in her brain.

"When did you tell Pete?" Lilly asked.

"That night, before he killed Merilee," Kitty said. "I found out she'd been leaving notes for Cal, pretending they were from me."

"He mentioned that he was having stalking issues. Garbage outside his door—"

"His studio door, yes. Merilee did it but made sure I'd get the blame."

"Why?"

"Why not? Merilee lived to make other people miserable, especially me."

"Kitty, I'm not sure what you want, but thank you for telling me that you had motive and opportunity for killing Merilee."

"I also told you I didn't do it," Kitty said.

"Fair enough, you did. Tell me, what are you doing back here anyway?"

"Smoking a cigarette. I rent a studio from Stan on the top floor of the building. He doesn't let me smoke inside, so I come back here."

"You rent an apartment from Stan?"

"An artist studio, not a living studio. He rents out four different spaces—one to me, there's a water-color artist next door, the sculptor next door to her, and then Cal rents the fourth studio. That's how we met."

"If you don't mind me asking, what's your art?"

"I write and paint a little bit. It's an indulgence, but I share an apartment with two other people and need a quiet space to work."

"What side of the building is your studio on?"

Kitty looked perplexed but answered the question. "I'm on the front of the building, looking over the Wheel."

Lilly and Kitty looked at each other for a moment. Kitty's studio was in the front of the building? Lilly thought about the angle, the view from that place.

"What do you write?" Lilly asked.

"This and that. Articles for magazines. I write romance novels under a couple of different pseudonyms. That's mainly how I pay my bills."

"Interesting," Lilly said. "You've got a bird's-eye view on the heart of Goosebush from up there."

"I do, but Stan makes us leave before he closes up downstairs. Maybe, if I had been around last night, I could've seen who did the work on the Wheel. But, alas, I wasn't there, so I didn't see anything."

This time it was Lilly's turn to feel her color rise.

"Kitty, keep thinking about who might have seen you on Saturday. Make a map; trace your steps. Lots of people were taking pictures that morning; you might have been caught in some of them, and they might give you an alibi. I know you and Merilee were friends at one point, so on some level this must be very difficult for you. For that I'm sorry. In the meantime, if you think of anything else I should know, let me know. Now, I really do need to get home."

Kitty stepped aside and didn't say anything more to Lilly. What more was there to say? Lilly put her helmet on and turned on the Vespa. She pushed off and made her way to the end of the alley. She looked at her rearview mirror and saw that Kitty was still standing there, watching her go. She didn't look back, but she did raise her hand in a salute and then drove onto the Wheel to head home.

CHAPTER 28

As Lilly drove toward home, she slowed down to look at Roddy's house. From the street, on a Vespa, it was hard to see what his yard looked like, though his house was set much closer to the street than hers. Much more like the norm of the rest of Goosebush, the norm that the people who had built Lilly's house had eschewed. The front hedges looked more tamed, and the grass had been mowed and seemed greener. "Good for him," thought Lilly. "He's cleaning up."

She had pulled over to the side of the road while contemplating Roddy's house, and at that moment, he came around the front. He was carrying two brown paper bags, likely full of weeds. He looked up and saw her, and waved. She waved back and then engaged the Vespa and moved it into her driveway. Rather than going all the way to the garage, she parked it at the top of the driveway and got off. She walked over toward Roddy.

"If you put those bags out, Pat French will fine you faster than you can say do-re-mi," Lilly said. She realized that she still had her helmet on and took it off.

"I don't think I've ever said do-re-mi in my entire life," Roddy said, a smile pulling at the edges of his mouth as he watched Lilly pat her hair, but accomplishing nothing toward getting rid of the helmet head her ride had caused.

"I've never said it either, but Pat said it to me a while ago, and that must have put it in my head. In any event, lawn refuse pickup is on the third Thursday of every month. Tomorrow is only the second Thursday. Having garbage cans, or lawn refuse, out for more than twenty-four hours can get you a fine. It can also get you raccoons, but that's another story."

Roddy looked at the lineup of refuse bags that he had brought out. Four of them. Dammit. He had felt so accomplished, getting rid of all the weeds, but now he had to take them back inside.

"I'll help you carry them back down your driveway," Lilly said.

"You don't have to do that—" he said.

"No bother," Lilly said. "Happy to help. And I'm going to butt into your gardening business for a moment."

"Oh yes?" Roddy asked.

"Yes. I wanted to point out that the ivy out here is choking your stone wall."

"Perhaps the healthiest plant in my entire yard, that ivy?" Roddy asked.

"The very same," Lilly said. "Problem is, it burrows between the stones and eats away at the mortar. If it climbs up the side of your house, it can get under the siding. Whenever I see an ivy-covered house, I think less of charm and more of the damage it is doing."

"So I should pull it?" Roddy asked. He sighed, fatigued at the thought.

"You should pull it," Lilly said. "It can wait for a while; Delia and I will come over and help you in a few days. But it should be done," she said, flashing him a brief smile and then turning to walk back toward her Vespa to put her helmet on her seat. She walked back over and picked up a bag of weeds. They weren't too heavy, so she grabbed a second bag as well. Roddy picked up the other two, and they headed back down his driveway.

"Since you're here, dispensing advice, can I ask you a question? A gardening question about my backyard?"

"Of course," she said. They walked down the driveway in silence. She'd been wrong; the bag was heavy, but the driveway wasn't long. Lilly looked around. When was the last time she'd walked along this driveway? It had been years. She'd never been particularly close to her neighbors, and the previous owners of this house had gone out of their way to annoy Lilly. The last time she'd walked down this driveway must have been when she trick-or-treated as a young girl. Was that possible?

It took a moment to realize that Roddy had been talking as they walked. He paused, waiting for a response.

"I'm sorry," she said. "I'm afraid I was walking down memory lane, trying to remember the last time I walked down this driveway. When I was a little girl, the owners had a haunted house in their garage every year, so that must have been it. It's been years. Whenever I came to visit, I'd use the front path, but even that was years ago."

"Years? The more I talk to people around Goosebush, the more I realize that previous owners of this house didn't travel in very social circles here in town."

"No, you're right. They kept to themselves mostly. They had an apartment in Boston and only came here on weekends, and not every weekend. The people before them? Also, not very social. Maybe it's something to do with the house; people who live here tend to remove themselves from the town itself."

"Well, that streak is about to be broken. At least, I'm going to do my best." They put the bags down and walked around to the back of his house. Lilly stopped at the corner and took it in. It was a nice, big backyard. And at one point, the gardens must've been lovely. But now it was a mess. Lilly could see the work that Roddy had already done, but there was so much more to do. Roddy led her toward the center of the yard.

"Delia went through what I should pull and what I should leave and just cut back. I've been pulling this, but then I happened to smell my hand afterward and realized it was mint. I'm fond of mint, and I wondered if I should keep it?"

"I like having mint available too, but the only way to grow it is if you put it in a pot. It's an invasive plant and takes over."

"In other words, keep pulling."

"Keep pulling," Lilly said. She walked over to the garden wall and pointed out the ivy that was climbing over it. "That's like the plants up front. Pull it. And that stuff, growing under the door? Pull it."

"Pull it. I thought I was in pretty good shape, but I'm feeling as if my arms are going to fall off. Look at this place; it's a mess. Pull it, indeed. That alone will likely take me the rest of the summer."

"It will take a while, but not that long. Destruction takes so much less time than construction. It looks like you've already made some progress," Lilly said.

"Not much, I'm afraid. My daughter tells me that this house will teach me patience. I've never been a terribly patient man, so I hope that's true. Truthfully, I don't think she believes I'm going to stick with this and get this garden going again. I'm sufficiently stubborn that that's enough to push me forward, egg me on."

"There's nothing like family to push buttons," Lilly said.

"My daughter and I have a very odd relationship, one I'm trying to mend. I'd be delighted if I thought she was trying to push my buttons, because that shows a level of caring about me that I don't think she has."

"Oh, I'm sure that's not true—" Lilly said.

"Please, I like that you're very forthright in your opinions. Don't change that now, just to make me feel better."

Lilly laughed. "All right, I wish for you that your daughter cares enough to get annoyed with you soon. Maybe you can talk her into coming down and helping you. Did you say she lived in Boston?"

"She does, with her husband and their daughter. My granddaughter. I'm hoping they'll come down this summer to visit."

"Visiting Goosebush in the summer seems like a pretty good bet," Lilly said. "Make sure you get a beach sticker, so you can take them over the bridge to the Goosebush beach. It really is lovely. The bay side is perfect for family and for dangling a baby's feet in the water. In the meantime, let me talk to Ernie. Maybe he has an idea of an implement you can buy or rent to help you, or somebody who needs to earn some extra cash and can come over and help you pull some weeds.

"There are a lot of teenagers looking for work, and some older folks looking for extra cash. Ernie keeps a running list in his head, and he can give you some names. It might be the fastest way to get this done."

"I wonder if he hired people to do the area around the flagpole last night?" Roddy said, winking.

"Maybe," Lilly said, shrugging her shoulders. "I just got back from driving to the Wheel. With all the traffic, you'd think nobody had ever seen a little mulch and some landscaping before."

"Sprucing up always makes people take note," Roddy said. "That's why so many people came to Alden Park that day, to help clean it up. Taming the wild. It's human nature to try. That can mean anything from a garden to a person."

"It's human nature to try to tame?" Lilly said. She thought of Merilee and the energy she gave off. She made people behave badly, behave wildly. Who decided to tame her, and why? She didn't have long to ponder that. She and Roddy had made their way to the front of the house again. Lilly saw that the truck from the Frank Lumberyard had tried to pull into her driveway, but it was blocked by the Vespa. "I'll see you later, Roddy," Lilly said over her shoulder as she moved quickly toward her house. "I have to take that delivery."

CHAPTER 29

"I thought we were doing this later this week," Tamara hissed.

"Portia Asher called me just as the mailbox was being delivered and told me she'd gotten another fine, this time with late fees that she just couldn't fathom. Apparently, there was also a more formal letter, threatening a lien on her house. I told her I'd take care of it, and not to worry about it. Was I wrong?" Lilly said. She put her shovel down and turned to look at Tamara. "Weren't you the one who asked me to help her?"

"Well, I didn't think it would mean me sneaking out two nights in a row, gardening by moonlight. Tonight there's not even moonlight. There's barely streetlight. Why can't we hire somebody?"

"Because she's a proud, stubborn, difficult old woman who doesn't want to seem like she's giving Pat French or anyone else in the Goosebush town hall the time of day, much less admitting she's wrong. This just needs to happen."

"In other words, she's another cranky Yankee.

Just like the two of you," Ernie said. He stood up
and stretched his back. "Stop your bellyaching. This
could be a lot worse, a lot worse. I'm glad her grandson didn't decide to use cement footings on this. Of
course, he overbuilt it. This thing's going to weigh a
ton. But if we can get some leverage, it's not going
to be hard to get it out of the ground. Delia's gone
to get water, right? We're almost ready to mix the
cement."

Lilly was tired, very tired. Tamara had a right to
be upset. Lilly would not have gotten everyone into
gear but for the phone call from Portia. She sounded
so desperate. Lilly had promised she'd take care of
it. Take care of it all. And so the Garden Squad had
their second job of the week.

"Here's the water," Delia said. She put the five-
gallon pail down along the curb. "Should I move
Ernie's truck closer, so we can put the old mailbox
in it?"

"Yes, that would be great," Ernie said. "Tamara
and Lilly are getting cranky, so we've got to get a
move on."

"Shut up, Ernie," Tamara said. "Let's get this
baby out of the ground and into the truck."

True to Ernie's prediction, the mailbox weighed
a ton. It took them a few minutes to wrestle it from
the ground, but wrestle it they did. They put it in
the back of Ernie's truck. He'd take it to the dump
in the morning.

"Well, he dug quite a hole, so we don't have to
redo that. Let's see how far down this new mailbox
goes; we might even have to raise it up a bit. It's supposed to be a certain height—Tamara, do you have
those stats?" Ernie asked.

"I have them," Delia said. She took her smart-phone out of her back pocket and turned it on. She scrolled through and read some numbers to Ernie. The four of them lifted the new mailbox into the hole, and, sure enough, it needed to be raised about six inches.

"Let's remember to tell people about the depth of the hole and the height the mailbox needs to be," Ernie said to himself.

"Ernie, I'll send you an e-mail right now and re-mind you to do that," Delia said. "I could make up an installation guide if that would be helpful."

"Thank you, Delia. I don't know what I'd do with-out you," Ernie said. "Now we're on to the mixing and holding portion of the evening. Let's put the cement into the hole, with the pole. Make sure everything's all level and facing the right direc-tion." Ernie measured the height one more time. "Perfect. Delia, can you put in the rest of the ce-ment? I'll help hold it straight. Then I think we should stay here, make sure it sets."

"Oh, good, we get to wait for cement to dry. What do you propose we do to fill in the time?" Tamara asked.

"Why don't we tell everyone about our day?" Lilly said. "I'll start." And start she did. She told every-one about her meeting with Stan and her unex-pected encounter with Kitty. She also told them about her conversation with Roddy, even though it had nothing to do with the case.

"So Kitty's our best suspect now?" Delia asked. She shoveled the last of the concrete into the hole, and Lilly and Tamara held the mailbox while Ernie held levels to different sides and pushed the pole in different directions to make sure everything was straight. He took one last measurement, and everything seemed to be in good shape.

"Just hold it there, ladies, that's great." Ernie said. "What else did you want us to do, Lilly?" he asked.

"See her hydrangeas, over there? I brought some fertilizer for them. There's a jar in my bag—the old Fluff jar with the red lid. Use that, sprinkle it all around the roots. They'll be so grateful. The soil balance is off. Also, put some of those nails into the ground so they turn a better color for her. They'll turn around quickly." Ernie gave Lilly a mock salute and found the jar in her bag. He was tempted to take it and have it analyzed. The secret of Lilly's concoctions was something he was forever seeking.

"Are you okay holding the mailbox?" Delia asked. "Because if you are, I'll finish putting the dirt in the hole and get the flowers around the base. Do you want to use the grasses as well, or were they left over from last night?"

"I brought them for Portia. Around the mailbox sounds perfect."

"The same grasses we used around the flagpole?" Tamara asked. "What's this, our signature? Like the Scarlet Pimpernel, our sign that we were here?"

"I sure hope so," Ernie said. "I love the idea of leaving our mark. While I'm planting nails, let's get back to Kitty. So she was having an affair with the poet. And Merilee broke them up . . ."

"Or, rather, diverted his attention for a while. I haven't seen Cal for years, but he's not a one-woman man. Never was," Lilly said.

"I wonder if that was the first time Merilee had an affair," Tamara mused. "Or, if Kitty did tell Pete like she said she did, was this the first affair Pete had found out about? If you ask me, that gives Pete another motive. Seems like we're adding suspects rather than eliminating any."

"Has anyone been able to confirm PJ's alibi?" Lilly asked.

"I did," Ernie said. "He was with his friend."

"What about Stan's alibi?" Lilly asked.

"I'm still looking at the digital recordings, from the cameras I could get my hands on. It's hard to give anyone an alibi. You can't see anyone going into the shed. Besides, like we said, people could be coming into the park from all different angles. The photos we have been able to find so far only come from the Wheel, Ernie's shop, places like that."

"Speaking of which," Lilly said, "Kitty Bouchard has an artist studio overlooking the Wheel. I wonder what her angle would be from there, and what a photo would look like."

"You think she took pictures?" Delia asked.

"Apparently she's a writer and uses it as her office. She says she writes romances under different names."

"I can check into that—" Delia said.

"I can't help but wonder, what else is she writing? Kitty Bouchard has always struck me as a most unpleasant woman with a moral ambiguity that I do not hold in high regard. And now I find out she's a writer, with a bird's-eye view of what goes on in the busiest part of Goosebush."

"You think she's the Goosebush Gossip," Delia said. She looked up at Lilly from where she had been planting flowers around the base of the mailbox. Lilly and Tamara were still holding the post steady, but Delia and Ernie were busy getting the rest of the gardening done.

Tamara looked down at Delia and then up at her

friend. "You two are scary," Tamara said. "Is that what you are trying to say, Lilly?"

"I think it was," Lilly said. "The ideas were just starting to form. Delia, do you think there's any way we could confirm that?"

"I'm not sure," Delia said. She stopped planting and sat back on her heels, still squatting on the ground. Lilly shook her head. Even at her youngest, and most nimble, she could never sit like that. Nowadays, her knees could barely tolerate her sitting down on a stool and standing back up. How she longed for her younger knees.

"Maybe I could send Kitty an e-mail and try to figure out the IP address her reply was from." Delia twisted her lips around and chewed the inside of her cheek. "Let me think about this. I'm sure there's something I can figure out."

"After a good night's sleep," Lilly said. "Ernie, how much longer should we hold this?"

"Tamara, let go of your side. Let's see if it moves at all. Lilly, take your hands off, but not far in case you need to grab it again." Lilly did as she was told, and the mailbox stayed put.

"Well, at least something worked out the way it was supposed to today," Tamara said. "We're no closer to finding out who killed Merilee Frank, but the mailbox situation is under control."

"No closer? I couldn't disagree more. Just a few more bits of information, and I think we'll know who did it. Yes, it was a good day all around," Lilly said. She reached into the bag of supplies she'd put by the curb and took out a jar of her special nourishment for new plants. She sprinkled it around the mailbox and then screwed the lid on and put it back in her bag.

CHAPTER 30

"You're getting a late start, aren't you?" Delia asked, as Lilly dragged herself and an armful of books into the kitchen at ten o'clock.

"I've been up since six," Lilly said. "I went to bed thinking about Roddy's garden, and Alden Park, and historical accuracy, all that stuff. I had the oddest dreams. Then I remembered the family archives."

"Family archives? Beyond what's in the library?"

"Sort of. Have I shown you the safe in my closet?"

"The one with your documents?" Delia asked. She didn't react to the idea of a safe she hadn't seen before. Nooks and crannies were part of the undiscovered country Lilly's house offered her.

"The one along the back wall of the cedar closet, behind where we keep the coats?"

"No, you haven't shown me that safe."

"Really? I thought I had. I don't go into that closet much. The safe is climate-controlled, if you can believe it. It was my father's pride and joy. Fireproof, hidden away. My folks, and now I, keep all our precious bits and bobs in there. Of course, what my parents considered precious, what I consider precious, may not be precious to most people. A family Bible, photos, old letters. You'd find it very interesting; I'll have to show it to you. Anyway, one of the things my father kept in the safe was this book."

Lilly put the piles of books down gently on the table and picked up the top one. It was very large, ledger sized. She set it beside the others, so she could open it and protect the binding. Delia noticed that Lilly had archive gloves on and was wearing a smock over her pajamas. Lilly gingerly opened the book, and Delia leaned forward to look at one of the drawings. It was old, very old. Delia recognized it from a lithograph framed on the wall of the historic section of the library.

"That's an excellent replica," Delia said.

"This is the original," Lilly said. She was focused on the book and missed the look that went across Delia's face. It was a look of horror and fascination. Lilly finally looked up at the other woman and smiled.

"Local history has been a family hobby for years and years. It may surprise you to hear that a stubborn streak a mile wide has also been part of the family history. Add to that a strong need to ensure that facts were accurately recorded, as well as the stories of the different people who used those facts and how they used them."

"What do you mean?" Delia said. She stood up and got a cup of coffee for Lilly. She put it far away from the book but pointed to it so that Lilly knew it was there.

"Thanks for the coffee. I could use some," Lilly said, but she didn't make a move. Instead she turned a page in the book, and Delia leaned over her shoulder to see what it was. Another drawing, this time of what looked like Alden Park. Delia noticed the date in the corner, 1857.

"What do I mean?" Lilly said. "I wish you had known my parents, Delia; you would have liked them. They were both what many considered eccentric. That, also, is a family trait inherited across generations."

"I've never thought of you as eccentric, Lilly," Delia said.

"You don't? Well, I suspect we're kindred spirits, and that is keeping you from being objective about that. Anyway, you know as well as anyone that those in power decide what is historical fact. Nuances, other people's stories, often get lost in the records. Going back for as long as my family's been in Goosebush, our family journals tell the stories about the town."

"There are copies in the library. I've read some of them," Delia said.

"Well, we haven't donated them all to the Historical Society. Or rather, I should say, there have been people in town who didn't want all the stories in the Jayne Chronicles, as they're called, to come to light. Often the family scribblings, were not friendly to the common beliefs the town history is built on. They exposed some inconvenient truths about people who were railroaded out of property, about the Native Americans who lost their land, or people who were forced out of town, in some cases."

"Truth telling the Jayne way," Delia said. "Plain, simple, and direct with a strong moral compass. Sounds right."

"Lest you think my family were beneficent do-

gooders, you should know that everything was written down partly to blackmail folks into doing the
right thing when necessary."

"Blackmail? What you mean?"

"Well, for instance, it has been said that my great-
great-grandfather knew that somebody in town had
had an illegitimate child with one of his servants,
who was then cast out of the family employ. This
was, unfortunately, not uncommon. But it was often
unrecorded. Except by my great-great-grandfather,
who not only recorded it but also had some of the
people involved write letters supporting the story,
which he kept. Two generations later, when the
maid's grandson claimed a parcel of land to build a
house on in Goosebush as his inheritance, there was
pushback. Claims that the man had no right to the
land. But the Jayne family records proved that wrong,
that the man did have a claim. The records righted
a wrong."

"That's great," Delia said.

"Yes, but that's where the editing of what got donated for the town historical records comes into
play. In other hands, the information could be wea-
ponized."

"I see. So they didn't donate everything."

"Again, it's more complicated than that. My parents archived all the family records. Instead of giving the Historical Society originals, they started to
give them copies. Good copies, but you can see on
some of the records a little 'VLJ' worked into a
drawing, or on the corner of a document. That
stood for Viola Leigh Jayne, my mother. She was an
excellent, excellent copyist. The originals are upstairs in the closet, and a few of them are in a vault
at a small museum."

"Aren't some of these official town records? Aren't decisions based on those town records sometimes? Like property lines, that sort of thing?"

"Yes," Lilly said. She'd always hated that part of her family tree felt so superior that it held the secrets of Goosebush, to be disbursed when necessary. The original Goosebush gossips, but serving a higher purpose. But really, who decided what was a higher purpose, after all? The Jayne family? That was quite the burden, one Lilly had never embraced.

"Is that even legal?" Delia asked. "Shouldn't town records be complete, and somewhere the town can access them?"

"They are someplace where the town can access them—in my closet," Lilly said. "As I said, there are copies of most everything in the library. If the Historical Society ever gets their own space, they'll go there. But there was a time, when I was a girl, when things started to get hairy around here. Who owned the public lands, who oversaw them, what development could happen? That sort of thing. There were a few people in town who thought that a large commercial settlement would be good for Goosebush. You know, razing all the buildings on the Wheel and creating a multi-level commercial storefront, something more modern."

"This was what, fifty years ago? So modern would've been the 1960s? Yikes, that would've been terrible. I'm glad that cooler heads prevailed and the town charm held on."

"Well, it was thanks to my parents and a few other folks that the town charm did prevail. But with that came some complicated tax codes and a few land-lease deals. I don't know what made me think of them, honestly. Maybe my ancestors were knocking on my subconscious while I was sleeping. Nobody's talked about them, but they should."

"Lilly, take a sip of coffee, and start from the beginning. What are you thinking about?"

"You remember that town meeting, right before we started the work on Alden Park?" Lilly asked. Delia nodded. "They showed a map, with some of the boundaries around the park. It seemed off to me, but the park is so overgrown I wasn't making the connection. But here, look at this picture. You see where these borders are? See that huge bolder there? If I'm remembering correctly, the map they showed at the town meeting showed that as the outer edge of the park."

"But on this drawing, there are hundreds of feet beyond the bold line on both sides."

"Yes, there was a much larger boundary around the park. Now, it is entirely possible that those boundaries shifted over time, but how and to benefit whom?"

"Well, that corner near the boulder, that's where they built that row of town houses."

"Awful things," Lilly said.

"But part of the future of Goosebush, so Pat French always says. A new tax base."

"Look at this one," Lilly said. She carefully opened the book to another page, which showed the area near the Frank Lumberyard. Again, Delia looked over her shoulder. According to the drawing, the Frank property lines went all the way back to the edge of the marsh. "And look at this," Lilly said, holding up her phone for Delia to look at. There was a map of Goosebush that showed a road along the marsh, and a few houses on what seemed to be Frank land.

"Maybe the Franks sold some land," Delia said.

"Possible, but see those footnote references, written near the marsh? Here are the notes. According to them, in 1900 it was decided that nothing could be built within three hundred yards of the marsh. Those houses are a lot closer than three hundred yards."

"There must've been a variance filed," Delia said.

"Of course, but who made that decision, and when? Did it go through the proper channels? I'm not even sure why I'm thinking about this. I suppose our nocturnal visits have gotten me thinking about planning gardens, and the way things used to be around here. When the public lands were spruced up. When gossip was done in the grocery store, not online and anonymously. When neighbors looked out for one another, instead of fining them."

"Or killing them."

"There's that too."

"Do you think one has anything to do with the other?" Delia asked Lilly.

"I do, but I couldn't tell you how or why. It's a gut feeling I have," Lilly said.

"Time for me to get to work then," Delia said. "I'll do more research, try to find out what the official documents look like and, if they were changed, when that happened. What are you up to?"

"I am going to go out and do some weeding and clear my head. Then I think I need to go and visit Pete," Lilly said. "If anyone sold the lumberyard land, it would have been Pete. I can't imagine PJ or his grandfather doing it, even if they needed the money. The Frank family was behind a lot of the town ordinances to preserve and protect."

"Maybe Merilee sold the land or talked Pete into it." Delia said. "That road and those houses are only a couple of years old."

"See what you can find out about that land sale," Lilly said. "But don't let anyone know you're looking."

"My specialty," Delia said.

CHAPTER 31

Lilly went out to her back garden, thinking about how best to approach Pete. What was she going to ask him? She hoped he knew that she was on his side, and she was. But, and this was a big but, if he was guilty, she wasn't going to help him not go to jail. The uncertainty of even asking that question tickled at the back of Lilly's mind. She went into the side of the garage and took out her gardening belt and a pair of gloves. She also picked up a bucket. Weeding and pruning always helped Lilly think. The necessity of weeding was obvious, though Lilly's gardens never looked overgrown or in desperate need of attention, at least these days. It was true that the year Alan got sick, the gardens suffered from neglect, but Delia had stepped in and done her best. Tamara and Warwick helped as well, though neither of them had thriving green thumbs. Tamara had connected Ernie to Delia so that he could help. And a friendship was born.

Pruning, proper pruning, was an undervalued gardener's art. Left to its own devices, many a bush or plant would happily overtake the rest of the garden. For some folks, pruning seemed harsh since it called for cutting back and trimming healthy growth. But plants thrived when they were taken care of properly. Still, Lilly used a lighter hand than others might have. She wasn't fond of perfectly manicured gardens, but she did like everything to look maintained. And thus, the pruning. Get rid of dead branches in the fall so that new growth could come in in the spring. In some cases, pruning meant cutting back flowers so that there would continue to be blooms. Lilly planted enough flowers that she could always have fresh ones and take them to friends all summer long. It was still very early in the season, but between the greenery and a few flowers, today's pruning expedition helped her make a small bouquet.

Lilly paid attention, but it was mindless attention created by years of practice and expertise. Solving a murder? Not her area of expertise, but she needed to learn. Not just for Pete's sake. She worried about Bash. He'd come to it in a circuitous way, but she knew that he liked being the police chief of Goosebush. And he was good at it, though his mind did not tend toward complex conspiracies and murder plots. Nor did it need to, usually, in her small town. But now it did. If Bash failed at his task or didn't handle it well, she worried that he would lose his job. Since Bash helped support the rest of his family, Lilly had to help him stay employed. She couldn't imagine what else he could do as well as keeping the peace in Goosebush.

As Lilly pruned and weeded, she thought back on the last couple of weeks. She didn't, and wouldn't, ask Delia how she was going to do her research. Better she not know. But she had no doubt Delia would provide her with the information she sought, one way or the other.

Cal's performance-art piece also skittered across the memory slideshow Lilly was pondering as she wrestled with some errant mint that must've popped under the garden door from Roddy's house. She went back to the garage to pull a couple of pots and transplanted some of the mint while she was thinking about that night at the theater. Most of her attention had been on the lens of the neglected areas of Goosebush and how terrible they looked. She hadn't paid much attention to the bodies artfully photographed in varying modes of undress. She pulled off the glove on her right hand and took out her phone. She made herself a note to go by Cal's studio and see all the pictures. Had she not paid enough attention to the role those pictures might have played in Merilee's death? Aside from giving Pete motive and upsetting Kitty, what other actions might that performance piece have spurred?

She thought about the mailbox and the flagpole, but didn't ponder them long. Those were more civic actions and had less to do with Merilee's death. Thinking about them gave her pleasure, but she didn't allow herself to dwell. There was too much work to be done to pat herself on the back. Besides, they were such small gestures in the grand scheme of the work that needed to be done.

Lilly continued to wander through her garden, though finding things to prune was getting more difficult, since she kept at it regularly. There was something very satisfying about the clipping and clearing action that she needed to do right now. She felt her phone vibrate in the pocket of her apron and then heard the "ta dah!" sound. A text from Delia. She took both gloves off and sat on a bench.

Look at the Goosebush Gossip site, the text read. Lilly opened a browser and did as she was told. "SAFETY INSPECTION THREATENS FUTURE OF THE STAR CAFÉ," the headline read. Lilly scrolled down. The story was about the artist studios on the fourth floor of the building and whether it was a code violation for them to be there. Ray Mancini was quoted as saying he hadn't known that they existed, and he wasn't sure that they should. The story made it sound as if Stan had been trying to get away with something, though Lilly couldn't imagine what. How much rent could he be getting from the four artists on that floor? Not much, but probably money he needed, perhaps to keep the building operating.

Lilly sighed. This was officially none of her business, but she was going to make it her business. She texted Ray Mancini and asked to see him. While she waited for a text back, she scrolled through the Goosebush Gossip site. In the past, before the murder, there had been at least one post a day. Lilly noted that most of the images of people on the site were not posed but were rather candid shots. These days, with the capabilities of people's phone cameras, you could have your picture taken anywhere and not know it. Whoever took these pictures was good at doing it clandestinely. Lilly scrolled more quickly now, looking at the pictures from upper angles like the ones that had been on the site from the day of the murder. There weren't many, just a few, mostly of people arguing on the street. Lilly went back and read a few more entries. She didn't recognize the voice of the writer, but she did know one thing. The one person never featured on the Goosebush Gossip site was Kitty Bouchard. Lilly did a search of the site to confirm that. The three times Kitty had been mentioned were in conjunction with attendees at events, not as a focus of gossip. Lilly put her own name into the site's search engine and was surprised to find a few dozen mentions. The site had gone up right after Alan got sick, and to her chagrin, his illness was mentioned a few times. There was a picture of her at the funeral, and a mention of the reclusive Lilly Jayne, questioning when she would come back into Goosebush society.

Lilly hated that she'd been mentioned and that her personal business had been a story. She looked down at the phone in her hand and thought. If this benign series of stories angered her, how would a more personal attack feel?

Lilly spent a few more minutes looking at the gossip site, doing searches on the different people who were part of this investigation. It would've been easier on a computer, but that would have meant leaving her garden, and she didn't want to do that. She looked up PJ Frank. The only stories about him were in conjunction with his father and stepmother. There were dozens and dozens of entries about Merilee. None about Pete unless Merilee was included. Lilly put Pat French's name into the search bar. Four stories came up, all with pictures. None of the pictures were flattering. Apparently, Pat's nickname on the site was "Penal Pat, the Permit Denying Prude." Lilly fought the smile that tugged at the outer corners of her lips.

A text came in. It was from Ray Mancini.

Going to Pete's. There's a situation. Need your advice. Can you come over to his place around noon?

I'll be there, Lilly texted back. She stood up, giving her knees a moment to settle in. Just enough time for a shower to wake her up, but not much else. She'd have to learn more about the adventures of Penal Pat later. She made a note on her phone to remind herself and bookmarked the link to the search page.

CHAPTER 32

Lilly rode her Vespa over to Pete's house. Well, she would always think of PJ's house as Pete's house. But this was the house that Pete and Merilee had bought when they moved back to town. Lilly hadn't been over there in years. The house was one of three built in the mid-1960s, right near the beach. They were originally built as cottages, for seasonal use only. They were set side by side, with backyards that went up into the conservation lands and looked out into the bay, with the ocean in the distance. Two of the houses remained seasonal, but Pete and Merilee's house had obviously been winterized. As Lilly walked up to the front porch, she noted a building permit on the side window. She leaned over to read it. It was for a remodel of the house, adding a second floor and creating a bigger footprint. The permit said that there was a hearing scheduled about the building next week. Lilly didn't remember hearing about this project. She really needed to pay more attention to what was going on in Goosebush.

She knocked on the door, and Pete answered it. He looked like five miles of bad road, with bloodshot eyes, an untucked shirt that had stains down the front, and a days-old growth of beard. His hair shot up in clumps around his head, as if he'd been pulling it from his scalp.

"Lilly, what are you doing here?"

"I asked her to come over," Ray said from down the hall. "Let her in."

Pete did as he was told but didn't look happy about it. Lilly followed him down the hall as he shuffled toward the rear of the house. The rear of the house, counterintuitively, had the views. When she got into the back room, she looked out the windows and noticed stakes with orange plastic tied to them that reached to the edge of the conservation land. There were sliding-glass doors all along the back and a deck with a grill on it.

Ray stood up and gave Lilly a kiss on her cheek. He offered her a cup of coffee, which she accepted. As Ray walked toward the left of the house and the galley kitchen, Lilly took the opportunity to look around. She'd come to visit somebody in one of these cottages when she was a young girl, and again when she was a teenager. She remembered her mother telling her something about the cottages, but she couldn't remember what. Her hands itched to make a note on her phone, but she didn't do it. She'd need to remember.

"Are you undergoing renovations?" Lilly asked. It was a fair question, given the disarray of this front room that took up half the house. There were building samples strewn about, plans tacked up on one of the sliding-glass doors, and boxes everywhere. Lilly looked into the kitchen and realized another reason that Merilee and Pete had eaten at the Star Café every day for the past year. They couldn't possibly cook in that kitchen. There wasn't a stove, for one thing. Lilly looked at the overflowing garbage pail in the middle of the kitchen. It was full of empty boxes of frozen food. A sweep of the room showed a large microwave sitting on the dining room table. Obviously, that was put to good use.

"We'd planned on—" Pete said.

"All plans for any renovations are on hold," Ray said. "Don't look at me like that, Pete. You knew I was against them from the beginning, but Merilee wouldn't hear the word no. Looks like you wasted a lot of time and money on architectural drawings that aren't going to happen."

"Nothing is a done deal until the entire board of selectmen votes," Pete said. "These three houses, they're gold mines. If the town doesn't recognize what they—"

"Pete, these houses were built on leased land. Folks own the houses, not the land. Plan was to tear them down after thirty years, but they keep getting renewed. Probably should've gone with the original plan, so that folks didn't get thoughts in their minds about McMansions right on the ocean."

"I remember my mother telling me about the leased-land plan, but I don't remember the details," Lilly said.

"Back fifty some odd years ago, some landlocked rich folks in Goosebush wanted an ocean view in the summer. They made a deal with the town to lease the land and build cottages that could be only used during the summer months. Everyone agreed on modest homes, and the result was these three cottages. The idea was that the leases would be up in thirty years, but as I said, they kept getting renewed. The town made some good money on the leases, and there were restrictions on who could buy the cottages. When Pete moved back, he and Merilee were able to buy this one, mostly because of Pete's family connections."

"Merilee always thought, and so did I, I guess, that once my dad died I would get the family home. But then he left that, and the business, to PJ. So we were stuck here."

Lilly turned and looked at the ocean. "Hardly stuck," Lilly said. "That view is a tonic."

"You can see the water from the second floor of your house. You can see everything from your house," Pete said. "You're lucky that the house stayed in the family and that you don't have kids to get in the way of your inheritance."

"You're lucky that you have a son who took care of his grandfather and cared enough about the family business to make a go of it," Ray said. "If it had been up to you and Merilee, you would've lost it all years ago. Lilly's family is lucky that she's got a mind for business. That wasn't always the Jayne family trait, if I remember correctly. This mess is of your own making, Pete, and insulting Lilly won't help you get out of it."

Pete clenched his fist, opened it, and closed it again. He took a step toward Ray, but Ray continued to calmly pour three mugs of coffee. Lilly turned away, embarrassed for Pete. She looked around. This wasn't a home; it was a storage unit with a microwave. She walked over toward the coffee table, which was covered in boxes. There were piles of shipping labels, Bubble Wrap, flattened boxes, packing tape. She saw one box that was partially open, with a Bubble-Wrapped item that didn't quite fit sticking out of the end. There was something about the color that looked familiar. She took a deep breath and bent over to pick it up.

"This is my bowl," Lilly whispered. She turned toward Pete, who looked away, color rising in his cheeks. "This is my bowl." Her hand shook, and she put the bowl back down on the table. She picked up the box and saw that it was addressed to someone in Kansas City. She pulled a piece of paper from the box and noted that the item had been sold via an auction site for a thousand dollars. They'd gotten it cheap. It was worth ten times that, easily.

Ray came over and put his coffee and Lilly's down on the coffee table. She handed him the packing slip, and he read it.

"Were you sending this out?" Ray said.

"Merilee had a few orders outstanding when she passed. I had no idea—"

"Pete, man, I really wish I could believe that, but I don't. I can't believe one of my oldest friends was a crook, is a crook," Ray said.

"It wasn't me, it was Merilee. You have to believe me. I knew she was selling off family heirlooms to raise some money for us. But she'd run out of that months ago. Boxes kept going out, and I had no idea where she was getting the stuff she was sending."

"Well, obviously, she was stealing some of it," Lilly said. "She stole that from me, the day of my open house."

"You can't prove that—" Pete said.

"No, I can't. I *can* prove that this is my bowl and will do so. Let's call Bash, shall we, so we can get this all on the record."

"No, please, don't do that. He's already got it out for me—" Pete said. He turned and walked toward the sliding-glass door and pounded his fist against the window. The door shook in its frame but did not break, thankfully.

"Lilly, why don't we go out to the deck, and we can talk. Pete, bring your coffee and come out with us."

Ray slid the door open, and the three of them filed out to the deck. There were three plastic Adirondack chairs lined up facing the view, and each of them sat down, studiously not looking at one another. Lilly took some deep breaths and exhaled slowly. She needed to calm down and listen to why Ray wanted her to come over.

"Did you know that Merilee was selling stolen goods?" she asked Ray. "Is that why you asked me to come over? To help figure out what to do? Seems like you need a lawyer, not a businesswoman, to help with that."

"Well, aside from your bowl, I'm not sure the goods were stolen," Ray said. "Seems like most folks gave Merilee things, and then she sold them."

"What do you mean gave?" Lilly asked Ray. She turned toward Pete and asked him the same question.

"I don't know," Pete said quietly. "I honestly don't. I knew she had some side businesses, her consulting business, other things that helped bring in money. I was doing okay selling real estate, not great, but it was getting better. For most people, we had enough money. But Merilee wasn't most people. These last couple of days, I've been going through things in the house, looking at old records. The police have copies of everything and went through everything themselves. She had this calendar, with notations about meetings, and dollar signs beside the meetings. Some of the meetings were in the future. I have no idea what they were. I noticed a couple with the initials PF and remembered one of those days was when she had lunch with PJ, trying to get him to give us the house."

Pete stopped talking, and tears started to roll down his cheeks. Lilly looked over at Ray. "What's he talking about?" she asked him.

"Well, it seems like Merilee may have been blackmailing a few folks."

"Including PJ?" Lilly asked.

"Looks like, maybe. Pete wanted me to look into it, especially now," Ray said.

"Now that Merilee's gone," Lilly said.

"I'm in an awkward position, Lilly," Ray said. "I'm no longer on the force, but an officer of the law is always an officer of the law, even when he's retired. I get a bad feeling about all of this. If I keep digging, I'm just going to find out more dirt about Merilee. Question is, to what end? Does the dirt just help make sure that Pete's convicted of her murder?"

"I didn't—" Pete screamed.

"I believe you, Pete. About that, I do believe you," Ray said. "But you've got to admit, this doesn't look good. Especially now, when Lilly recognizes something that was stolen from her. Have you mailed anything else since Merilee died?"

"No, I haven't," Pete said. "I told you that when I asked you to come over and help. People started to complain, and I need some help figuring out what to do."

"Don't do anything right now," Ray said. "Nothing. As a matter fact, you're not even going to stay here. You're coming home with me, staying in the guest room so you can dry out and start to think straight. Lilly, I asked you to come over because I was worried about the business implications for Pete, since it looks like Merilee made a tidy sum on these auction sites and hadn't paid taxes. Folks may not have paid attention to that sort of thing while she was alive, but now that she's dead? Now it looks like there are a lot more than business issues at stake."

"Sure looks like it," Lilly said. "Pete, do you have records of all of that?"

"Given everything that's going on, I wonder if we should just let this be for the moment. Seems like it's just more ammunition for Bash's case against Pete," Ray said.

"Ray, if Merilee was stealing from other people, or blackmailing them, it also seems like this could help find other suspects."

"It could, but I'm afraid we're going to need to leave that to the authorities." Ray got up and walked back into the house and returned carrying a black notebook. "This is Merilee's planner, where she kept the cryptic notes. I'm going to take this over to Bash. But first, Pete and I are going to go and pack him some things. Keep an eye on this, won't you, Lilly? We'll be back in twenty minutes or so. Come on, Pete. Let pack."

Lilly had the good grace to wait until Ray and Pete had stepped over the threshold back into the house before she opened the notebook. She took out her phone and started taking pictures of every page. She wasn't sure how much help this would be. There were only initials and different icons next to them, mostly dollar signs. She flipped through the book. Merilee hadn't put a key to the code in the book. Lilly hoped Delia would be able to figure it out. She was grateful that Delia had insisted she upgrade the memory on her phone. She was able to take pictures of all fifty-two pages before Pete and Ray came back.

Ray suggested that he take Lilly's bowl with him when he left a few minutes later. He promised to process it as soon as he could and to get it back to Lilly. Lilly left Ray with a receipt for it, along with the sales receipt and the box that Merilee had presumably been working on shipping. What had happened at the cottage was swirling around in Lilly's mind, but she forced it out for a ride on her Vespa. One of the reasons Lilly loved getting around Goosebush on her scooter was that it forced her to pay attention, notice the roads, look at the houses, really see what was going on. If anything, the last few weeks had taught Lilly she hadn't been paying close enough attention. She was determined to stop that now.

She drove over to Alden Park and pulled the Vespa up on the sidewalk near the park itself. She walked in and did her best to walk the perimeter. She carried her notebook with her and made some sketches. She found the boulder in the corner and noted that the fence for the town houses was just feet away. The grasses in the corner were all yellowed. That is where the chemicals, or salt, had been poured. She took pictures of that and did her best to take a panoramic shot from the center of the park to the edges. She stood in the middle of the area and shook her head. Perhaps there had been a variance, or land had been sold by the town and she hadn't known about it. It all could be innocent. But something had encroached on Alden Park and taken away some of the public lands. That would not happen without her knowledge ever again. She was also more determined than ever that the park would be cleared soon and made into a usable open space for the community. Lilly forced herself through the underbrush and walked along the edge of the park. A path had been cleared along the edge, and she noted a lot of dog debris along the path. She did her best to sidestep it but did stop and make a note in her book that that was another element that needed to be cleared out, cleaned up, and dealt with. Dogs should be able to walk in the park, obviously. But owners needed to pay attention.

There were no fences along the back edge that ran parallel to the road, but there were some thorny bushes that Lilly did remember from the past. She already knew the houses behind the bushes, mostly PJ Frank's house. Had he planted the bushes? For that matter, had his grandfather? Why? She looked down and around and noticed a wall of poison ivy along the edge of the Frank property line as well. Wild or planted? Between the thorns, and the poisonous plants, this was definitely a barricade so that the public wouldn't use their land. Not very neighborly of them, for sure. Lilly walked around the final edge as she headed back toward the street. Again, a tall fence blocked the back alley behind the stores that were on the Wheel. Lilly heard some rustling over on the corner, and a rat darted in front of her. She held back a scream, but just barely. She hated rats. There shouldn't be rats near Alden Park. Again, something else that needed to be addressed. She walked back out into the street, but instead of going to her Vespa, she took a left to look down the alleyway. Sure enough, overflowing dumpsters with more garbage than the stores on that part of the Wheel could possibly have generated. That, that deserves to be fined, she thought. Not old ladies' mailboxes. She took some more pictures with her phone.

Maybe garbage was out of Pat French's purview, she thought. Doubtful, but worth a check. She hesitated for a moment but went back to her Vespa. Time to pay Bash a visit.

CHAPTER 33

Lilly walked into the police station, which was very quiet on this Friday afternoon. She asked if Bash was in and was sent back to his office. When he saw her in the doorway, he stood up, came over, and gave her a kiss on the cheek. He noted the light scratches on her legs and her arms, and the leaves on her dress. Rather than ask, he'd wait for her to tell him what had happened, if anything. Maybe she had been gardening.

"I've been over to Alden Park," Lilly said. "When can we get back to that job, and get the park cleared?"

"How about if I release the site on Monday? We've taken the shed off-site."

"Good enough. We can set up something for next weekend. So you've got all the evidence you need from the park?"

"Now, Lilly, you know I can't get into—"

"Bash Haywood, what do you take me for? I'm just a concerned citizen, asking if I can continue a civic-pride community cleanup that is desperately needed. Have you seen the dumpsters that run alongside the park, behind the fence? I think there is a rats' nest that lives off the overflow of those dumpsters. It doesn't look like they've been picked up for weeks. The dumpsters, not the rats. Who's in charge of that?"

"Well, the dumpsters are privately owned. The businesses make arrangements for pickup, but they should be kept up. Are they really that bad?"

"I would say so; they're probably a health concern." Bash laughed at Lilly, but then he noted her face. She wasn't joking. She took her phone out and flipped to the pictures of the alley, choosing the best one. She handed it to Bash, who looked properly shocked.

"When did you take this?" he asked.

"Not even an hour ago," she said.

"That's odd," Bash said. "I drove by there early this morning, and the dumpsters were all empty, or looked it."

"Why were you driving by the dumpsters?"

"Well, this is more of a Goosebush sort of crime, but a few folks have started to complain about some illegal trash dumping."

"Illegal trash dumping?"

"As you know, everyone in Goosebush was given two barrels late last year. One for recycling, one for trash." Lilly nodded. The barrels had wheels on them, as well as covers. They were able to be hooked to the side of the garbage and recycling trucks, which made it easier for the trash men. Every family, every house was given one of each. Each barrel had been marked with an identification number and the address. There had been a few instances of stolen recycling bins or trash barrels that had risen to the top of the crime blotter in town, but usually it all got sorted out.

"If you lose your barrel, you have to buy a new one. If you want a second barrel, you have to buy it. Between that and the town dump no longer being open to residents without a sticker except for every third Saturday, some folks in town have taken to dumping their trash in dumpsters, rather than paying for overflow. The businesses have been complaining, but it's hard to track who does the dumping when."

"Is that a good use of police time?" Lilly asked.

"Another good question," Bash said. "Not necessarily, but given what happened to Merilee, I've been paying more attention, wondering if folks are trying to get rid of evidence and in ways that I wouldn't anticipate otherwise."

"Have you been dumpster diving for bloodied clothes?" Lilly asked.

"No, not me," he said. "But others have been. Haven't found anything yet, but that's not surprising. There are a million and one ways to get rid of evidence in a town like Goosebush. This case is a tough one. Not a lot of clues to go on."

"It sounds as if you're still investigating. I thought you were convinced that Pete had done it."

"I am convinced Pete did it," he said. "But a part of me still can't believe it. Besides, I have you and Ray haunting my dreams, whispering in my ear, asking if I've considered every single suspect and eliminated them. Problem is, the more I consider Merilee's life, the more suspects there are. No lack of motive."

Lilly nodded. They'd come to the same conclusion, though she didn't tell Bash that.

"Anyway, enough about that," he said. "I'll let Pat French know we're reopening the park for cleanup next week."

"Why do you need to let Pat French know?"

"She claims that the plans for the park overstep the property line. She's working on re-surveying the land."

"Maybe I should talk to Pat directly, because I think she's wrong. If anything, I think the other uses of the land have encroached on the park. I'm checking on that."

"I asked her for a map of the park right after Merilee was killed, and she didn't have one ready to go. Ray went down to the town archives and pulled this one. You want a copy? I've marked it up a bit—"

Lilly looked at the sheet of paper Bash had pulled out. He had marked it up; the shed where Merilee had been found was indicated, along with some points of egress to the park, complete with arrows. Lilly had been wrong. She'd missed some gaps in fences and other places where people could have snuck into the park. She'd need to go home and compare this drawing to the pictures she had just taken.

"A copy would be great," Lilly said. "If we're using older drawings, then we need to make adjustments. This will help. More than you know."

As Lilly left the police station, she almost ran into Stella Haywood. "Just the woman I want to see," Lilly said.

Stella looked shaken. "Me? Why? What did I do?"

"You didn't do anything," Lilly said. That I know of, she thought. Interesting reaction. "Do you remember the day of my open house, when you were in my front sitting room watching over things?"

"I do," Stella said carefully.

"Remember when Merilee was picking things up and putting them down?"

"Knocking them over or coming close? How could I forget it? She was a tornado."

"Did you notice if she took anything?"

"Took anything? Did she? Shoot, I wondered about that. She was so clumsy, touching everything until you came in there at the end. I kept wondering if she was sliding something into that big purse of hers. What did she take?"

"A bowl, a small bowl. I've got it back, no worries."

"Is anything else gone? I'm so sorry, Ms. Jayne. She was so hard to keep track of. I hope she didn't take anything else," Stella said.

"I hope not too, though I don't think she did. I'll be doing a bit of an inventory when I go home. Stella, this isn't your fault. I'm getting the sense that keeping an eye on Merilee would have taken an army of people."

"Yeah, I'm getting that sense too. Bash won't talk about this at home, but I'm worried about him. He's working so hard, trying to make sure this case is solid. I just got off a shift at the Star Café, and I'm taking him some lunch on my way home. I worry that he's not eating. Especially not since that post on the Goosebush Gossip site that showed him eating every five minutes. He really took it to heart."

"You're a good sister," Lilly said.

"Not so good," Stella said. "I need to talk to him, and I'm hoping if I feed him he will listen for a few minutes."

"Is everything all right?"

"Yeah, no, probably. You know about the issues around the Star, and the artist studios on the fourth floor?"

"I read the Goosebush Gossip site this morning."

"Really? You don't seem the type to read that trash," Stella said.

"Normally I'm not. But these are not ordinary times."

"No, they're not. You know who puts out the Goosebush Gossip, right? It's Kitty Bouchard."

"Kitty. I thought maybe it was her."

"Really? Man, nothing surprises you, does it? I just found out a little while ago, wanted to let Bash know in case it's helpful. Give him a heads-up before it's all over town."

"How did you find out?" Lilly asked.

"Well, this whole thing about the illegal studios? No one would have been any the wiser if Kitty hadn't tried to burn Cal's photographs."

Lilly pointed to the bench outside the police station and gestured toward it. "You mind if we sit?" Lilly asked. "I find standing too long to be exhausting."

The younger woman did as she was asked and sat beside Lilly. "That's better, thank you," Lilly said. "Now, start again. What photographs?"

"Well, you know that performance-art piece that Cal did?"

"The one with the ugly pictures of Goosebush?"

Stella laughed. "Yes, those. Those, and the dozens of pictures of naked women. Seems that Cal was inspired by the response his photographs got and decided to experiment with blowing a few of them up and entering them into some shows. He had a huge stack of reproductions in his studio and was looking at them. Kitty found out and tried to burn them. Problem was, the fire got out of control. Luckily, the artist next door had a fire extinguisher, but the fire department was still called. They realized that folks were working up there, and there were old sprinklers installed, but they didn't work. And so, this whole kerfuffle around the illegal use came up."

"Why would Kitty, if she is the gossip, put that on her site today then? If she was, is, the reason that this illegal activity was discovered?"

"Probably to divert attention from herself. Kitty would rather people be worried about Stan, and his illegal artist studios, than about why she would want to burn Cal's photographs."

"Why would she want to burn them?"

"Because she's in a lot of them. He's not just looking at doing solo shots; he's also looking at doing combo shots. One of them is called 'The Women of Goosebush' and features a lot of naked women. Everyone posed for him, and they knew he was taking the pictures, but still. I don't think people expected the photographs to be part of a show."

"Are you in one of those photographs?" Lilly asked gently. She reached over and took Stella's hand.

"I am," Stella said. "I don't know what came over me. He made me feel so special, like I was a piece of his art. He said I'd be his inspiration. But now . . . I don't feel like the photos are art anymore. Especially since Merilee's in so many of them. It feels so voyeuristic. And very opportunistic of Cal, which bums me out. I thought he was a real artist."

"He is a real artist," Lilly said. "But he doesn't always have a lot of common sense. Did you sign a release when he took the pictures?"

"A release? I didn't sign anything—"

"Leave this to me," Lilly said. "Cal won't be publishing any pictures, at least not without your permission. You mentioned that Merilee was in a lot of them?"

"Yeah, a lot. Most of the women, you can't tell who they are. But Merilee, she was so uninhibited. She didn't even try to pretend, try to hide who she was. In a way, I admired that, but I doubt Pete would."

"You're right about that," Lilly said. Stella got up from the bench, still holding on to Lilly's hand. She gave it a squeeze and reached down and pecked Lilly on the cheek. "Thank you so much for listening. Maybe I should hold off telling Bash about the pictures—"

"Well, I suggest you tell him about what happened, and that Kitty Bouchard tried to burn the pictures. The content, you can deal with that later. Though you may want to mention that Merilee Frank is in a lot of the pictures."

"I thought you were trying to get Pete off?"

"I am, I am," Lilly said. "But hiding evidence? That doesn't seem the best way forward. We need to let the light in on everything in this investigation and trust that the truth will come out of the shadows. Thanks for confiding in me, Stella. Your secret is safe with me for as long as I can keep it. And I will talk to Cal."

"Again, sorry about the bowl, and Merilee's sticky fingers. Man, I hate to speak ill of the dead, but she really was a piece of work."

"She was indeed," Lilly said. Stella went into the police station, but Lilly stayed put for a few more moments. She was considering her next step carefully. Things were beginning to become clearer to her, but they still didn't make much sense.

CHAPTER 34

Lilly decided to make one more stop before she headed home. She parked behind the Star Café, but this time, instead of walking all the way around, she went up the back stairs into the kitchen area. She'd never let herself in that way before, but she wanted to get a better sense of the store from this perspective. Besides, she was hoping not to go out to the front at all, but rather to just go up to the fourth floor and look around without anyone seeing her.

Those plans were thwarted, however, by the caution tape that blocked her from going up the back stairs. She'd need to try to go up to the theater instead. She maneuvered her way to the kitchen and went into the ladies' room on her way out to the front of the store. Oh my, she thought to herself. I really need to pay more attention to how I look in public. Between the gardening this morning, the riding on the Vespa, and the walking in Alden Park, Lilly was a mess. She was thirsty, had all sorts of leaves and detritus in her hair, and flecks of dirt everywhere. If she cared more, she would have turned around, hopped on her scooter, and headed on back home. But she was here now, and she wanted to see upstairs.

She spent a couple of minutes splashing water on her face, futzing with her hair, and trying to smooth her dress. She looked a little better, but not much. She walked to the front of the store and went to the left as if she was going up to the theater. That way too was blocked.

Lilly Jayne hated to be thwarted in anything she had set her mind to; it was all she could do not to harrumph out the back of the store in frustration. Instead, she took a deep breath and looked at the coffee shop at the front of the store. Someone had ordered a large iced tea and was sipping it slowly. Maybe that would help her feel a bit better.

"What can I get you, Ms. Jayne—I mean Lilly?" Stan asked from behind the counter.

"Stan, I'm parched, frustrated, and tired. You tell me what I should drink."

Stan laughed. "Well, we could be twins today. I felt the same way, and the new concoction that Stella made with her ginger tea hit the spot. A little bit of caffeine, but not too much. Sweetened with some fruit juices and a lot of lemon juice. It's both tart and sweet at the same time and made me feel miles better. How about if I get you a large glass of that and a sandwich?"

"Well, I'm going to go home and have some lunch. I just need a drink to tide me over—"

"A cookie then," Stan said. "One of the specialties of the house, a kitchen sink cookie. A little bit of this, a little bit of that, and a whole lot of those. If you've got any sort of allergy or are gluten-free or dairy-free, stay away from these cookies because I can't tell you what's in them. The recipe changes every day. But there's oatmeal, so they make you feel a little bit healthier."

Lilly laughed. "Sounds perfect," she said patting her pockets for her wallet. "Oh darn, I forgot my wallet in my scooter. I'll be right back."

"Lilly, how about if I start running you a tab, and you can pay it off every month? I do that for a few of my better customers. That way, if you forget money, or if you want me to order you a book, you can just pay it all at once."

"If you charge me for everything," Lilly said, giving Stan a stern look. "And I mean everything."

"I promise, I will. In fact, if you give me a list of folks who can charge things to your tab, I will let them. Like Delia, for instance."

"Perfect," Lilly said. Stan poured liquids from several bottles over a cup of ice, put another cup on top, shook it up, and handed her a very large, very icy beverage that was pink in hue. Lilly took a tentative sip and then puckered her lips slightly. It was tart, with a sweet aftertaste. "My, that is delicious. It tastes like one of Delia's concoctions, without the grassy finish. I feel better already."

"Well, take the cookie and have a seat. Get your energy back before you get back on your scooter. I know it's not summer yet, but it's really hotter out than it seems, and driving a bike can take it out of you."

"Stan, are you worried about me? That's the nicest thing anyone has said to me all day," Lilly said, taking the kitchen-sink cookie and giving him a smile. "Thank you so much." She looked around, but no one else was at the counter. She dropped her voice to whisper. "Everything okay around here? I heard there were some shenanigans."

"Were, and are. Delia suggested I call Ray Mancini to get some advice. He's on his way over to help me talk to the fire chief. Pat French will be at the meeting too. She's mentioned shutting us down, but I hope not."

"Well, I don't know the whole story, of course, but from what I have heard, it sounds like perhaps this is a bit of a distraction."

"Distraction? What do you mean?"

"Stan, don't you worry about it. I hear the sprinklers on the fourth floor don't work?"

"They did, but last winter must have taken its toll. Some pipes froze, and I thought I got everything fixed, but obviously not."

"Listen, tell Ray Mancini that I'm fronting you the money to get the sprinklers fixed and up to code. He can call me to verify it."

"You don't have to do that," Stan said. "I can get a loan."

"I'm sure you can. But Ray and I are old friends. Me lending you the money is code for him to back off and give you space. You won't get shut down; I promise you that."

"Now that's the nicest thing anyone has said to me all day. We should see each other more often so we can make each other feel better," Stan said.

Lilly laughed, gave him a wink, and went over to what she was starting to consider her table in the café. It was far enough away from the foot traffic to the back of the store into the restaurant, and was close by the books, with a bird's-eye view of a shelf full of sundries that were fun to look at. She noticed a fountain pen with flowers all over it. After she was done eating, she promised herself she would test it out. That may just go on her account here at the Star. This could be a dangerous arrangement.

"Lilly? Do you mind if I sit down?" Lilly looked up, and Rhonda Frank was looking down at her. Lilly continued to chew her cookie, which was a good excuse as she sought for a good answer to this benign question. Lilly had been able to avoid talking to Rhonda for over thirty years. Her intention, if she was being honest, was to continue that practice for another thirty. But it seemed as if life had other plans for Lilly these days.

Lilly noted that Rhonda hadn't presumed to take a seat, so Lilly finished chewing and took a sip of tea. She gestured to the empty seat across the table with her left hand and put the tea down with her right. She wiped any crumbs from her lips. She let Rhonda open the conversation.

"You have every right to hate me," Rhonda said quietly.

"I don't hate you, Rhonda," Lilly said. "I made a decision a long time ago that hate is more exhausting for me than it is for the object on which I would bestow that energy."

"You're a better person than I am, Lilly. You always were, I suppose. PJ thinks it would be a good idea for me to apologize to you for what happened all those years ago, so that we can, I can, let it go and move on. Maybe stop avoiding you every time I see you around town. So let me say this. I'm so sorry for what happened. I never should've had an affair with Pete while he was still married to you. I loved him, but that's no excuse. I'm sorry I hurt you."

"I accept your apology, Rhonda," Lilly said. And she did. She doubted she and Rhonda would ever be friends, but having somebody avoid seeing her around town was not the reputation that Lilly Jayne craved.

There was a pause, but Rhonda made no effort to get up from the table. "PJ mentioned that you thought that his new historically accurate, prebuilt, Goosebush-approved home-improvement pieces were a good idea."

"I do, as it seems like there's a market for them these days. He and Ernie are going to save a lot of people a lot of time and trouble, and some expense. That's a good thing."

"Yes, I suppose it is. I just worry that he's going to get folks riled up, people who can make trouble for him . . ."

"People like?" Lilly asked, but she already knew the answer. When Rhonda didn't answer, Lilly said the name aloud. "Pat French."

"And her minions. She's got a few people who think that she walks on water, and they call in code violations for her to fine. It's like a game to those people."

"It is remarkably mean-spirited, isn't it?" Lilly said. "Rather than taking care of each other, neighbors are turning each other in."

"It does seem like a dark turn for a town like Goosebush," Rhonda said. "I know we can get nostalgic amnesia, but I don't remember Goosebush being like this before. The only thing that's remarkably different in this town is that woman, Pat French. Where did she come from?"

"She was a distant relative of Edith Stone. Do you remember her?" Rhonda nodded. "She kept to herself for the most part. But she was a history buff, so I knew her from the Historical Society. Pat moved in to take care of her toward the end. Edith left Pat the house, and—"

"That's just the thing, what distant relative? At times like this, I wish my mother was still around, so I could ask her. I distinctly remember her talking about poor Mrs. Stone, who was all alone in the world, with no one to leave her money to. My father would joke that maybe they should lend her one of us kids, so we could get in the will. That used to be the way they tortured us. 'Keep it up, and we'll give you to Mrs. Stone, so she'll adopt you.' "

Lilly smiled but didn't laugh at the story. Rhonda's family had a cruel streak, and she'd had a tough upbringing, to put it mildly. Lilly was grateful that her family held kindness as a core value.

"Edith wasn't a very nice woman, rest her soul. Probably she'd written off Pat's branch of the family years ago, and Pat was able to make amends."

"Still, you have to wonder what the town of Goosebush did to deserve somebody like Pat French moving into it and taking over so many functions," Rhonda said. "They say that power corrupts. I'd say Pat is a prime example of that being the case."

"I've been in a bit of a fog these last few years, and hadn't really paid much attention to her or to what was happening around town," Lilly said. "These last few weeks, the fog lifted. Things are clearer. So yes, getting back to your original point, I think the work that Ernie and PJ are doing to help folks in town stay on the right side of the law is commendable. I'll make sure people know that I am behind him one hundred percent. Not that that will help much—"

"Lilly, that will help a lot. Your opinion matters in this town, always has. Thank you for accepting my apology. PJ also tells me you're trying to help Pete, which I find commendable, given the way he's treated you in the past. I'm not sure I could step up like that."

"Rhonda, I'm going to tell you something. I honestly don't think that Pete killed Merilee. I may be wrong, but I'm holding on to that belief. Seems like she really put him through hell these past two years."

"He could've left any time . . ."

"He could have, but he didn't. Pete needs to be married. Whatever the reason, he stayed with her. And he's upset by her death. I think he loved her, or did at one point. He's also in shock at some of what he's been finding out about the way she lived her life. It would probably do him a world of good to hear from you, Rhonda. He needs friends right about now."

"We were never friends," Rhonda said.

"Oh, yes you were. You and Pete suited each other, far more than he and I did. You were friends. You have a son together. Remember those two things, and give him a call."

To Lilly's horror, Rhonda's lips began to quiver, and a tear rolled down her cheek. Reading the situation well, Rhonda quickly got up from the table. She leaned down and gave Lilly's left hand a squeeze. "Thank you, Lilly," she said. She turned and left the store quickly.

Lilly took another sip of her pink drink. She hadn't imagined how it could be, but she did find that having spoken to Rhonda, her heart felt a bit lighter. Good to get that out of the way, she thought. She finished her drink, wrapped up the rest of her cookie, and went out the front door of the Star Café, taking the long way around to get her scooter.

CHAPTER 35

Lilly parked the Vespa in the garage and walked into the backyard through the side door. As always, her gardens worked their magic, and she felt much less stressed. She looked around, not only at the plants but at the sculptures in the different areas of the garden. Some people thought that Lilly had a rhyme or reason for the placement of the sculptures, but they were wrong. She placed the sculptures where they made her the happiest, or where the people who gave them to her could see them the most easily. The sculpture of car parts her godson Tyrone had created in his shop class? That had a place of honor in the center of the garden. Every time Tamara saw it, she smiled with pride. That small area with the Victorian mirror ball in the corner? It was Delia's section of the garden, complete with a meditation bench. Delia chose the plants and tended to them. Lilly made sure the plants lived. The area by the edge of the garden, where the grasses were growing? That was Ernie's area. He had brought the grasses over three years ago, claiming he couldn't sell them in the store and didn't want them to die, and asked Lilly to take them in. She realized later that he'd given her his late husband's favorite grasses, so Lilly transplanted them in a place of honor.

Lilly loved this time of year. In May, the gardens were just waking up. Everything was green, and nothing had been over-baked in the sun yet. Lilly smiled and took another deep breath of her garden.

She turned and walked up the back steps of her porch. She opened the screen door and immediately noticed that Delia was lying in her favorite place, on the hammock in the corner of the porch. She had built a contraption that acted as a desk and was tapping away on her computer keys when she walked in.

"I'm glad you're home," Delia said. "I was getting worried. From now on, we should probably set up a check in schedule."

"I'm sorry I had you worried," Lilly said. "I've had quite the day. How about you?"

"Surprising but not surprising, if you know what I mean." Delia went back to typing.

Lilly sat down and noticed that Delia had brought out a pitcher of lemonade. There were two glasses. Lilly poured lemonade into one and offered it to Delia. Delia shook it off. Lilly took a sip and sat back in the chair.

"Well, I went over to Pete's house like I said I was going to. Guess what I found there?" Delia didn't respond, so Lilly went on. "Remember when I said I was missing the bowl? Ends up that Merilee stole it the day of the open house. Not only that, but she'd sold it on an auction site. If she'd had a box that fit it, it would be in Kansas City right now."

"She trafficked in stolen goods?" Delia said. Lilly had her attention now.

"I'm not sure," Lilly said. "This may have been a one-off, an opportunity she couldn't pass up. Or she did this on a regular basis. Maybe people gave her things to sell. Who knows?"

"Gave her things to sell?"

"Yeah, that's another part of what I found. Merilee kept a planner and made notations of people she was meeting, with dollar signs next to their names."

"Maybe they were clients?"

"Could be. Some of these meetings were in the next few weeks, but the dollar signs were already written in. I took pictures of all the pages for you to look at. There wasn't a key in the book, but if anyone can figure it out, you can. If you have the time."

"You took pictures? How did you—"

"Don't ask. Those aren't the only pictures I took. I walked around the perimeter of Alden Park and took pictures of the fences along the borders. Some panoramas, some up close."

"Wow," Delia said. Now she was sitting upright. "I'm impressed. I was hoping to talk you into going there with me later this afternoon, but you saved me time." Delia held her hand out, and Lilly handed her her phone.

"Last thing. Well, probably not the last thing, but the last thing for now. I went to see Bash Haywood. He gave me the ground plans for the park, the ones he has been using for the crime-scene investigation."

"He gave them to you? Just gave them to you?"

"Well, I mentioned that I needed a map of the park. They are a copy of his copy. But, given our conversation this morning, I thought the more ground plans we had, the better off we'd be."

"You really were busy, weren't you?" Delia said. "No wonder you're running late. I'm sorry I was snappy. I was worried."

"Why so worried?" Lilly asked gently.

"Because somebody was following me."

"Following you? Are you sure?"

"No, but it freaked me out," Delia said. "Anyway, I figured you wouldn't notice if someone was following you, and who knows what they had in mind. It occurred to me that we may be stepping on some toes. Maybe whoever did kill Merilee doesn't want anyone to cast doubt on Pete doing it. Maybe that person would try to hurt you, to get you to stop looking. I just got worried."

"Delia, thank you for worrying about me. I don't know what I'd do without you. You're absolutely right; from now on, we have regular check-ins. Better yet, let's not go out alone anymore. Stronger together, don't you think?"

"I do; thank you, Lilly. Do you want to hear what I've been up to?"

"Of course."

"I went to the town archives and to the library. I requested records in both places. Alden Park for one, the Wheel, the lumberyard. I also asked for any deeds or transfers or variances to any of those areas in the last few years. The first part, the maps, they were able to get me at the town hall. But the record of the variances? They told me it would take a few days."

"Is that normal?"

"Yes and no. Usually when you ask for records, you can see them online, but then it might take a couple days to get your copy. They have to make sure it's okay to release them, I think. But for this? They didn't have any records of variances, sales, or property-line changes for the lumberyard or for Alden Park. Debbie, she's my friend down at the town hall, she was really confused because she couldn't find any record approving that road and those houses near the lumberyard. She promised to keep looking and keep me in the loop."

"Did you tell Debbie to be careful about who she talked to about this?"

"Oh, trust me, I did. Debbie's very cautious. I told her to talk to me, to you, or to Bash Haywood if she found anything. Nobody else."

"Good. That's interesting, isn't it?"

"That's not all," Delia said. "I asked Debbie if she could access the slideshow that they used at the last town hall meeting. She said she'd get hold of it and send it to me. I was just looking at the map of Alden Park. I was looking at my phone and realized I took a picture of it that night at the meeting. It's a habit I have. I always take pictures of slides for reference later."

"I'm glad you remembered you had the picture," Lilly said. She had learned not to let Delia see her exasperation, though sometimes she felt it. Delia had her own methods and was very, very good at what she did, even if sometimes it took a while for her to get to the point.

"So am I. I usually don't forget things like that. I need to be better about archiving my days. Anyway, it wasn't a very good picture, but it was enough to see this." She turned the computer toward Lilly and handed her the phone with the picture of the map. Lilly looked at both and shrugged.

"What am I looking at?" Lilly asked.

"Someone changed the slideshow after the meeting."

Lilly looked at Delia and then back at the picture and the slide. Sure enough, they were different. "Why would somebody do that?" she mused aloud.

"No idea," Delia said. "Let me look at the pictures you took today, this map, and the stuff I got. It's going to take me a couple of hours, but maybe I can come up with a report for you, let you know what all the differences are. Your pictures will help a lot," Delia said.

"I'm glad," Lilly said. "What should I do in the meantime?"

"Don't take this personally, Lilly, but I think you should go and take a nap. You look done in, and you know you need to be well-rested to think through problems."

"Well, I'm not sure of that, but I am going to go up and take a shower. There was a ton of poison ivy in Alden Park. It looked like it had been planted there. I want to make sure that I don't have any on me."

"Good idea," Delia said. "By the way, Ernie called, and he wants us to drive around Goosebush tonight, take some pictures of fence posts with him. I told him we'd go. I'm going to pack a picnic dinner; we're going to go down to the beach—"

"That was the other thing I meant to tell you, about Pete's house. He owns the house, but it's on leased land. They were trying to get building permits. You know anything about that?" Lilly asked.

"No, but Tamara is coming for the ride with us tonight. I bet she'll know."

"Does Tamara know she's going for a ride with us?"

"According to Ernie, it was her idea. She wants the company."

"It's not that I'm not having a good time, because I am, but why are we riding around instead of sitting on my back porch with a glass of wine?" Lilly asked. Tamara and Ernie were sitting in the front seat, and she and Delia were in the back. They were driving in Tamara's car, which had plenty of room, so it wasn't that she was uncomfortable. It was more that Lilly hated talking to people when she couldn't see their faces.

"Listen, Lil, our evening forays have made me oversleep these last couple of days, and I'm behind on work. I have to drive around to take some pictures of comparable houses for a few clients. Ernie needs to take pictures of broken fences, sad mailboxes, and ugly front doors so he can send the homeowners a flyer about his line of home-repair items. He and I need to hear about what you and Delia have been doing all day. So we thought we'd drive around, eat some food, strategize a bit." Tamara turned her blinker on. She pulled over to the side of the road, rolled down her window, and took some pictures of the house on the driver's side. She was using a digital camera, a nice one, which gave her more detail. She had a list of houses on a clipboard beside her and made a note of the time she took the picture.

While she was stopped, Ernie scanned the neighborhood. Sure enough, he saw a sagging fence post.

He got out of the car and took a picture. "All set," he said to Tamara.

Tamara checked the next address on her list and pulled out, after she'd turned her blinker on again. Tamara was driving slowly, and all four of them were looking at the homes of Goosebush.

"Such a pretty town," Ernie said. "I don't drive around here often enough. This is sort of fun. Can you pass me another pretzel?"

"And a napkin," Tamara said. "I'm asking you all to watch the crumbs. I'm picking up a client first thing in the morning, and I won't have time to get the car detailed before that."

"Sure thing," Delia said. "I tried to pack the least crumby food I could think of. These are soft pretzels. We have a portable vacuum at the house. I'll run it over the seats for you tonight when you drop us off."

"Tamara, the only person who hates crumbs more than you do is Delia," Lilly said.

"Delia, yet another reason I like you. We are kindred spirits. Please pass me a pretzel too. I figure we can drive around for another hour or so, while we still have light. I appreciate the company. I'm so tired I might drive off the road if I didn't have people to talk to."

"Would you mind driving down that new access road, the one along the marsh?" Lilly asked. "Delia and I wanted look at it and take some pictures."

"Take some pictures of what?" Tamara asked.

"Of the houses, of the road," Delia said. "Lilly and I are trying to put together a piece of the modern Goosebush town map. I've been trying to find the paperwork trail of some of the newer buildings."

"Tamara, how did they get a variance to build that road and those houses?" Lilly asked.

"You know, I have no idea," Tamara said. "I tried to find out while the houses were going up. I wanted to see if I could get the listings for them, but they were all presold before the first foundation was poured. I assumed it was the Frank family who sold the land."

"I couldn't find any records of the land being sold," Delia said. "Doesn't mean it wasn't, but usually those records are pretty easy to find."

"Maybe the land wasn't sold," Lilly said. "Maybe they leased it. Would they need a variance for that?"

"No, probably not. If they leased the land, then that's income for the town. Still, someone had to approve them building that close to the marsh," Delia said.

"Not necessarily," Tamara said. "The conservation agreement was nonbinding, and made by the Frank family. They could break it."

"So someone in the Frank family may have leased the land to build these houses?" Lilly wondered. "Or sold it? Why do I think Merilee's fingerprints are all over this?"

"Is that a thing around here?" Ernie asked. "Owning the house, but not the land?"

"There was a time in Goosebush history when leasing lots gave the town a revenue stream. I thought most of the leases were going to run out soon, which is causing its own set of problems. But new leases?" Tamara mused. "I need to do some research on that. For some reason, I really thought that the Frank family controlled those houses. I'm going to try to remember what made me think that."

They continued to drive around and take pictures. Tamara and Lilly told stories of prior occupants of the houses. Between the two of them, they knew a great deal of the anecdotal history of Goosebush. When the situation called for it, Delia added some facts to the story.

"Can you drive us past Pat French's house?" Delia asked. "I've been doing some research on that place and realize I've never really looked at it."

"It is off the beaten path," Tamara said. "It's on what folks would call the right side of town. But really, unless you are going to visit Pat, you don't drive down that road. Nothing but houses, and a dead end."

It didn't take long to get to Pat's house, and Tamara slowed the car as they approached it.

"Does it make me a terrible person that I hope her fence is off, and that her mailbox is the wrong color?" Ernie said.

"If it makes you a terrible person, then the car's full of them, because I was thinking the same thing," Tamara said. "Did I tell you that Portia Asher came by the office today? She looked like a ton of bricks have been lifted off her shoulders. Mentioned to me that Santa Claus had come six months early and given her a new mailbox. The best part was her grandson didn't even notice the difference. She's thrilled."

"Does she think you had anything to do with it?" Ernie asked.

"She may think I talked to somebody, but actually doing the work of digging a posthole? That's not my reputation," Tamara said. "My carefully honed reputation, mind you. She also mentioned that somebody had paid all her past fines and asked me outright if I did it. I could honestly tell her no, I didn't. Lilly, was that you?"

"No, not me. I was planning on doing it but didn't get around to it today."

"So there's another good Samaritan in Goosebush," Tamara said.

"No one else knew about Portia's troubles, except for the people in this car," Delia said. "Ernie, did you help her out?"

"I did," Ernie said, after a pause. "I don't want anyone to fuss over me about it. I don't have a ton of money, but I've got more than some. It broke my heart to think of that poor woman worried to bits because her freaking mailbox was the wrong color and the wrong size. People keep coming into the store, talking about the flagpole and how nice it looks. It gives them a spring in their step. We started a side business, the four of us. We're fixing things. I'm just doing my part."

Nobody spoke for a few minutes. Lilly thought back to how long she'd known Ernie and lamented that she hadn't become friends with him when his husband was still alive. She also wished that Alan had gotten to know Ernie better. They would've been good friends.

"Lilly, we're here," Delia said. "Should I take a picture of Pat's house?"

"Sure, why not?" Lilly said.

They had slowed down to a stop so that Delia could take a picture, but just as she was about to snap it, Pat French walked out of her front door and strode down her front path.

"Dammit," Tamara said. "I've got this. Take the picture, Delia."

Tamara got out of the car and walked over to Pat. Her three passengers watched as the two women spoke. Pat never opened the gate, and their conversation was brief. Tamara walked back toward her car and got back into the driver's seat.

"Wave, everybody," Tamara said quietly.

"What did you tell her?" Lilly asked.

"I told her a client's interested in moving into the neighborhood, and I wondered if she might be willing to sell her house."

"What did she say?" Ernie asked.

"She said she could never sell her house, but if any other houses came up for sale in the neighborhood, she'd let me know."

"She could never sell her house . . . ," Delia said quietly.

"Does that mean something to you, Delia?" Ernie asked.

Lilly looked over at her friend and then turned back to Ernie. "She's thinking."

"Oh, goody. I was hoping that Delia could make sense of this sooner rather than later," Ernie said. "Thank goodness it's sooner. We need to come up with a plan."

CHAPTER 36

They decided they all needed to get some sleep
and agreed to talk in the morning. Both Ernie
and Tamara mentioned meetings, but made Delia
and Lilly promise to call with any news. By seven
o'clock, Delia and Lilly were sitting in the library
with a pack of index cards, a pot of coffee, and their
computers. Both had been up late writing more
notes, and it was time to combine their thoughts.

Delia brought in the map of Alden Park that
Bash had given Lilly. She used painter's tape to at-
tach it to the bookcase to the right of the French
doors that led out to the back porch. She'd also
brought what she referred to as her toolkit: a tackle
box full of pens, pencils, Post-its, highlighters, mark-
ers, and other tools of Delia's trade. Delia was a visual thinker and often used different colors to help
her sort through information. Lilly didn't try to interfere with Delia's process. She let Delia pick the
colors and decide what they meant.

They combined notes and mapped out a timeline as close as they possibly could. Delia had been

writing on the cards and putting them on the French doors, occasionally moving them around so they made more sense to her, while Lilly had been reading from her notes.

"Is that it?" Delia asked.

"I think so," Lilly said, looking over her notes. She flipped back and forth between the pages and glanced up at the index cards to make sure everything she'd written down had a place on the wall.

"That's all I've got too," Delia said, checking her own notes against the wall.

"What are all those names you wrote in gray?" Lilly asked. She was referring to the entire row of cards to the left side of the French doors. They were visible, but not part of the overall conversation that the cards were designed to set up.

"Remember when I looked over all the videos and pictures I could get my hands on? I know it wasn't all of them, but there were a lot."

"I remember," Lilly said. "Did Bash's map help? Might there have been another way of getting into the park?"

"Your pictures helped," Delia said. "That, and the map. I think the map is optimistic as far as points of egress. I also cataloged all the pictures I could find of the day and tried to put them in time order. That gave me a good sense of who was in the park when, and where they were standing at different times."

"When did you do that?" Lilly asked.

"Here and there over the last few days," Delia said. "I'll admit, Lilly, I've been a little obsessed with trying to figure out who did that to Merilee."

"You? Obsessed? I can't imagine," Lilly said.

"Don't tease me," Delia said, smiling. "I know, I know, I can get pretty focused on things. But this is more than that. I'm the one who found Merilee. I saw her . . . like that. It was pretty terrible."

"I can imagine it was," Lilly said. "I should have kept checking in with you about that. I'm sorry, Delia. I can imagine it would have affected you; it would affect anyone."

"Yeah, even though I didn't like Merilee, nobody deserves that." Delia looked at the wall of cards and looked back down at Lilly. "This is what I could do to help. Research. Looking at pictures. Mapping data. I'm no good at talking to people; you're the one who is good at that. So, to answer your question. Those names in the gray, on the left? Those are names of the people who were there that morning. To the best I could figure out, they got there after you and I got there. Since neither of us killed Merilee, once we were there, I figure she was already dead."

"Maybe she met somebody in the garden shed while we were there?"

"No, most of the pictures show the shed. I didn't see Merilee at all once we were there, in any pictures."

"And no pictures of anyone going in and out of the shed?"

"No, nobody in or out of the shed on any of the pictures I could find."

"So where does that leave us?" Lilly said.

"Well, this makes our list a little bit shorter. Who was in the park before we got there or leaving the park before we got there?"

"You could tell that from—?"

"I was playing with the cameras at Ernie's shop by then, so that gave us a good viewing field. Plus, there's the camera outside the liquor store, and that gave us a different angle. It is not a long time span. From her fight with Pete to when you and I got to the park was about twenty minutes."

"So, Pete's still on the list," Lilly said.

Delia pointed to the card with Pete's name. There was a blue circle, a red star, and a green triangle on the card as well. "Blue circle says he was in the park, red star means he had a motive, and the green triangle means he doesn't have an alibi."

"PJ has a card—"

"PJ does, but there's a plus sign in the middle of his green triangle. He has an alibi."

"Stan's got a card," Lilly said.

"Yes, I'm trying to be objective about this. But he has a card. And he has all three symbols. No alibi. Even worse, he left the park before we got there, which could mean that he changed his clothes."

"Did anyone else leave the park and then come back, from what you can tell?" Lilly asked.

"Pat French and Kitty Bouchard seemed to leave and come back. At one point, they put jackets on. Pat put on a sweatshirt; Kitty put on a jacket."

"Anything else you noticed? Anyone else we should think about?"

"No, not really. Stella Haywood came in just before we did. She helped Stan bring stuff into the park. But I haven't figured out a motive for Stella. She should probably be on the list anyway though."

"Why is Pat French's star orange?"

"I couldn't figure out a good motive," Delia said. "I mean, of course they knew each other. Everyone knows everyone in Goosebush. But did they like each other, not like each other, do business together somehow?"

"Merilee and Pete were trying to build on to their

house," Lilly mused aloud, as if trying to jar something from her memory.

"Yeah, about that. You said you saw a notice about a hearing? I did a little research on those houses, and I sure can't figure out a way anyone would get a building permit. As you said, they own the houses, but they lease the land. There are very strict restrictions around the use of the land. Maybe, just maybe, Pete and Merilee could have built up, added a story to the house, but the footprint would have to stay the same. Those stakes you saw in the ground, they couldn't have been for a new foundation."

"Maybe I misread the notice or misinterpreted the stakes in the ground."

"Yeah, or maybe they got a variance. But they must have gone over Pat French's head for that, don't you think? I mean, if she won't approve a mailbox that is five inches too short and the wrong color, surely she would try to gunk up the works if Merilee wanted to break a building code."

"You'd think, wouldn't you?" Lilly asked. "You know, since our drive around last night, I've been thinking. I hadn't been out near Pat's house for years. I barely remember the original owner. She really kept to herself. I wonder how Pat reconnected with her?"

"That shouldn't be hard to figure out, should it?" Delia asked. "Can't you just ask her?"

"I could, but I'd like you to do little research first. Can you look at the history of Pat's house? Find out who owned it, and when and how the title was transferred? I'm remembering some story about it from back when I was a kid, but I just can't put it together. Would that be hard to do?"

"You think it's that important?"

"I'm not sure," Lilly said. "But either Pat's got a motive or she doesn't. I'm trying to be objective about this. If we can get her off the list, maybe we can concentrate more on the most likely suspect. And that looks like it may be Kitty Bouchard."

"Well, the data points to Stan, Pete, Pat, or Kitty—"

"Delia, sweetheart, I don't think Stan did it. We're trying to prove Pete didn't. We don't have a strong motive for Pat at this point. Kitty has motive, and you've just shown us that she had opportunity. But before we start accusing Kitty of anything, let's either get Pat French's star to be a solid red or get her off the list. Wait, what about Cal Pace?"

"Your friend, the poet?" Delia asked.

"The same," Lilly said.

"He's over here, in gray. He may have a motive, but he got there after we did. Besides, he had an alibi. He was over at the boatyard, taking pictures."

"How do you know that?"

"I saw his pictures on Instagram and went over to talk to Sally. She said he was there, taking pictures and drinking coffee with some of the folks who work on boats. New project," Delia said.

"Look at you, getting all Nancy Drew on me," Lilly said.

"Is that a good thing?"

"In these circumstances, yes. What are you writing down?" Lilly asked. Delia had opened another pack of cards and was scribbling notes and marking them with colors.

"More research questions. Some you gave me, some I thought up on my own. I'll update you once I know what I'm thinking. You know what I mean."

"I do. How long do you think it will take?"

"Give me an hour or so," Delia said.

"You got it," Lilly said. "I'm going to go out to the greenhouse, clear my head, try to think a little bit more. Come get me if you think of something I can do instead of repotting herbs."

"Knock knock," a male voice said. Lilly turned and saw Roddy standing at the back door to the greenhouse. Lilly had been going back and forth from her garden to the greenhouse, bringing in plants to divide, as well as some that needed tender, loving care.

"Roddy, come in," Lilly said. "What have you got there?"

"Some very sad flowers," Roddy said, looking down at the flat he was carrying. "I bought them two days ago and was going to put them in today, but I noticed they had wilted and looked terrible. I took a chance that you or Delia would be out here and could give me some advice. I know they'll perk up once I get them in the ground, but in reading more about them, I'm afraid that they're not going to do well in my garden."

Lilly wiped her hands on her apron and then held them out so that Roddy could give her the flowers. "Ah, these poor darlings. They just need some refreshment," she said as much to the flowers as to Roddy. She walked them over to one of her workbenches and put them in a shallow tub. She grabbed the misting hose that was hanging from the ceiling, with a cord on a coil that she could take anywhere in the greenhouse. She gently doused the flowers and murmured to them, promising they'd feel better soon. She went over to a shelf along the back wall and took an old-fashioned glass bottle from it. She double-checked the label and her handwriting providing a cryptic description of what was inside. She poured a small amount into her palm and walked back over to the tray of water, sprinkling the mixture in it.

"These will be lovely in the garden, but they do require some care. You want to make sure that you plant them in a very loose soil. There are a couple of options of materials you can mix in with the soil that will help it retain moisture. It's a good idea to do that for most things, but definitely for these. Summers are lovely here in Goosebush, but the sun does get hot in our backyards. These need mostly shade, which is challenging. The original owners of our houses didn't believe in big trees. Just gardens."

"I've noticed that," Roddy said. "Not that I mind, but it is odd not to have a big old shade tree in the back of such a big yard. What happened to the one in the middle of garden? I found the stump, by the way. They'd covered it up with this ridiculous wishing-well façade."

"The tree got toppled in a major storm about twenty-five years ago. A pity, it was a beautiful tree. I think that's one of the reasons your garden has so many issues now. A lot of it was designed to have shade, but the shade is now gone."

"I hate that wishing well," Roddy said. "I wouldn't have minded if it was really a well, but it's just a decoration, and a fairly ugly one at that. That was next on my list of things to remove."

"Well, I agree that it's not very attractive. But the stump was quite something. There is an artist who lives on the other side of town who uses natural materials to make beautiful sculptures. Look out into my garden. Do you see that carved wooden bucket? The one that looks like there is water going into it, also made of wood? She made that. Maybe she could think of something creative to do with your stump, to make it more of a feature and less of an eyesore."

"That's a great idea, I'd love to meet her. Tell me, is this flat of flowers going to survive?"

"Oh yes, but maybe you should leave them in here until you're ready for them. Bring over anything else that may need to be out of the sun until you're ready to plant them or replant them, as the case may be. They can stay in here; we'll take care of them."

"That's very kind of you," Roddy said. "I confess, I got ahead of myself on this gardening thing. I thought I'd be ready to plant by now, but alas. Getting the gardens ready, really ready, is taking much more time than I expected."

"It always does," Lilly said. "Besides, those gardens hadn't been tended to for years, so you've got to really convince your plants that you're serious about taking care of them. Otherwise some will never behave."

"I need to convince the plants?" Roddy said, smiling.

"Yes, you do," Lilly said seriously. "I always think of my gardens as a contract between myself and Mother Nature. I'll take care of them, good care of them. In return, I ask them to behave themselves. Stay within their beds, bloom when I expect them to, let me know what they need. So far, the relationship has worked out well."

"Very well, from what I can see. You know, the first time I saw your gardens, I thought they were impressive. But now, having spent this week working in my own, I am starting to understand how much work it takes to make them look so beautiful."

"And you're very kind," Lilly said, blushing. Blushing at her age. She didn't think that was even possible anymore.

"Your front-yard gardens are also lovely, though not as ornate," Roddy said.

"Well, I don't like to spend as much time in the front yard. Out in the open like that. Not my style. But with a front yard comes responsibility. Delia does most of the work out there. Which explains why the hedges are so perfectly cut."

"They are impressive. I was tempted to bring out a level to see if they were on the bubble; they certainly seem to be."

"Roddy, do me a favor. Don't bring a level over to the front hedges. I think that would make Delia's head spin. She already obsesses over edges, even though I keep trying to tell her that you are never going to get a bush perfectly square."

Roddy laughed. "I would never want to cause Delia concern. Tell me, how is it that on this main drag of Goosebush, yours is the only house with a substantial front yard? Or, for that matter, the only house painted yellow? I went down to the town hall to ask that woman, what's her name?"

"Pat French?"

"Yes, Pat French. Most disagreeable woman. Ernie suggested that if I wanted to do any home improvements, I run them by her first to make sure that they were within the code. Well, that was eye-opening. I have to wonder if it wouldn't have been better to go ahead and do what I wanted and deal with it later."

"From what I hear, that can get very expensive

for people these days. The town is adding more fines for going against the historic district codes."

"So I've heard," Roddy said. "When I went in, she was beside herself. Apparently, she'd just found out that Ernie was going to sell prebuilt historically accurate fences and other accoutrements. She was not happy about the potential lost revenue."

"Did she say something to you?" Lilly asked.

"No, she was talking to somebody on the phone. Said that she would need to redo the budget if those took off. Perhaps it was my timing. Right after she hung up, I asked what color green I could paint my house that was within the historical code. I thought she was going to pass out right there."

Lilly laughed. "Well, as you can see, my house doesn't meet any of the codes of the town. My family thought far enough ahead to buy a double lot, and the lot behind us as well, so we had plenty of room to grow. I suspect the original builder was also a bit ornery. From what I can tell, there was no reason to build it up and back from the street so far, except the family lore has it that he was a miserable person who didn't like to talk to people but was determined to keep an eye on what was going on around town. He'd sit up in his office on the third floor, look out over the boatyard. He took to keeping journals that tracked what was going on around town. They're quite fascinating. Part of the historical record of Goosebush now."

"I'm surprised you're here and not out ferreting out clues," Roddy said. "I heard someone mention your sleuthing when I was having dinner at the Star Café last night."

"My sleuthing? All I'm doing is asking some questions. Something about this whole matter doesn't make sense, so I came out here to tend to my plants. It relaxes me and helps me think."

"I'm sorry I disturbed you," he said.

"No worries. Your plant troubles have been a nice distraction. I've been thinking far too much about Merilee Frank lately."

"That can't be good for you," Roddy said. "I've been hearing stories about her as well, and while she doesn't sound like the sort of person I would enjoy knowing, I do wish I'd had a chance to talk to her. All of these stories can't be true."

"What stories?"

"Nothing specific, just hints of money troubles, affairs, and some disreputable business dealings. Come to think of it, that French women mentioned Merilee on her call. 'Now that Merilee's gone, we have to come up with a new budget.' Something like that."

"Huh. I wonder what that was about," Lilly said.

"No idea. I'm sorry, Lilly, I should let you get back to your plants, and to your thinking. Unless I can help with either or both?"

Lilly smiled at Roddy and pointed to the worktable full of empty pots. Then she motioned to the piles of grasses that were lying on another table. "Here, see those grasses? Divide each one into four and put them in those pots."

"These look familiar," Roddy said. "Didn't I see them around the flagpole in the center of town?"

"Did you?" Lilly said, smiling at him. "Grasses are fairly common around here. I'm constantly bringing them in and dividing them up. If you don't tend to them, they will take over. But the nice thing is that they stay green and hold on through even the hottest weather. A lovely natural border that is perfect for this climate."

"I should get some for my garden," he said.

"Please, I'm happy to give you some grasses. As a matter of fact, before you go shopping for more plants, let's look in here and see what I can send over. I'm constantly trying to find a good home for the plants I have divided—"

"You're never going to believe this," Delia said, bursting into the greenhouse. "She doesn't own the house."

"Perhaps I should go—" Roddy said.

"What do you mean she doesn't own the house?" Lilly asked. Roddy sidled his way out of the greenhouse, giving Lilly a wave, as Delia opened her laptop on the workbench. Lilly wanted to offer to let him stay but was grateful that he had left. She didn't want to have to catch him up on the conversation. She was afraid Delia would lose her train of thought if she did.

"Well, maybe she does own it. But there's just something hinky about the paperwork. You know, I've been doing some research on titles for Tamara— who owned houses when, all that stuff. Sometimes the title isn't clear for whatever reason, but usually you can figure that out. Somebody didn't sign off on a loan, or there was some sort of family dispute that got cleared up, but the paperwork didn't catch up. Anyway, because of my work for Tamara, I have access to all these databases. I started doing some research on Pat's house, trying to answer some of the questions you asked me. Sure enough, the Stone family owned that house for years and years. Old Mrs. Stone left it in her will to the Historical Society."

"But then she wrote a newer will and left it to Pat French," Lilly said.

"But did she? I need to go down to look at the records, but I have to wonder if that will was legitimate. Did anyone check the signatures? Was it properly filed?" Delia said.

"Why would they check signatures? It must have been notarized," Lilly said. "Pat French had been taking care of Edith Stone for years. Surely, that new will would indicate a change of plans."

"Yeah, well, it would. As I said, I couldn't find the will itself, not yet. I wonder who the witnesses were. I did look at the title. It isn't in Pat's name. It's still in Mrs. Stone's name."

"Really?"

"That's not the only thing. Pat pays all the bills for the house from an account that's still in Mrs. Stone's name. She's a joint signer."

"How do you know that?"

"You don't want to know—"

"I certainly don't," Lilly said.

"Well, I want to know," Ernie said, walking into the greenhouse. "What do I want to know?"

"You want to know how Delia found out that Pat French is writing checks on a dead woman's account."

Ernie whistled through his teeth. He'd been carrying a bag of garden soil and put it down on the floor. Lilly often felt that Ernie read her mind when it came to her gardens. He was always bringing her supplies before she asked him for them, but just as she needed them.

"Well, maybe she never bothered to open an account in her own name," Ernie said. "Those grasses look good, Lilly. Let me know if you ever have too many. I can sell some of these in the store easily."

"Can we talk about selling plants later?" Delia said. "I grant you, I haven't done a ton of research yet. But I can't find any record of Pat French."

"What you mean?"

"I don't know that much about her, so it's hard to be certain. But she once told me she grew up in Maine. I can't find any records of Pat French in Maine. At least not a Pat French who fits the description of our Pat French."

"Maybe she was married at one point," Ernie said. "Or she could have changed her name for a dozen different reasons."

"True enough," Delia said. "I'm just saying there's something odd about Pat French and her house. Or maybe not her house."

"Tell me, ladies, what were you talking about that started this particular conversation?" Ernie asked.

"It was earlier than that," Delia said. "We were listing suspects, motives, and opportunity. Lilly said that we should try to see if Pat French had a solid motive, and she asked me to look at a couple of things, so we could decide if she should stay on the list or if her name should be gray. It ends up that I'm still not sure she has a motive. But I am sure that I need to do some more research. There's something odd going on."

"The question is, does it have anything to do with the murder," Ernie said.

"That's hard to know right now," Lilly said. "But it does make me think. Yes, it certainly does that."

"You've figured it out, haven't you, Lilly?" Delia said.

"I think so. I have some specific things I want you to find answers to, but I think so. I'll tell you what, I think we should plan another performance event at the Star Café tonight. A performance with a very special invited audience."

CHAPTER 37

The theater at the Star Café had been opened by special permission from Bash Haywood, who sat at the back, watching the guests arrive. He had to hand it to Lilly Jayne. When she decided to do something, she did it. Bash had made it very clear that he could not officially condone this event, but neither would he try to stop her. Stella was the official waitress for the evening, but no one was ordering drinks.

The seats were set up in a semicircle around the stage area. The projection screen was down, and the light from the projector was shining blankly. The event was set to start at eight o'clock. By seven fifty-five, everyone was there. Pete Frank was the last to arrive, and he took the empty seat next to his son. At the last moment, Pete noticed that his ex-wife Rhonda was sitting on the other side of PJ, but to he did not get up and move, nor did Rhonda.

At the next table, Stan sat next to Delia. Cal Pace joined them. Tamara and Warwick were sitting with Roddy and Ernie at the next table. Kitty Bouchard sat alone at the next table until Pat French arrived and sat with her. Neither woman looked at the other, nor did they talk to one another. Ray Mancini sat in the back, next to Bash.

At one minute past seven o'clock, Lilly Jayne walked to the center of the stage area, looked around, and smiled.

"Thank you all for indulging me," Lilly said. "As I said on the phone, I wanted to talk about that Saturday when Merilee died, and Alden Park, and my plans for moving forward with the park."

"Isn't that in bad taste?" Kitty asked. "Poor Merilee—"

" 'Poor Merilee?' " Pat said. "Please. You hated Merilee Frank more than anyone else in this room."

"What are you saying?" Kitty snapped at her tablemate.

"Ladies, please. Let me get through my presentation, and then we'll all have time to talk. As I said, I want to talk to you about Alden Park. More precisely, the property lines around Alden Park."

"What the—" Pete Frank said.

Lilly lifted her hand up and pointed it toward the stage manager's booth near the back of the room. She hit a button, and the first slide came up. "This is an original drawing of Alden Park from way back in the day. As you can see, there were landscape items that created the border around the park. The boulder over here, and there was a tree over there, and then the street. Around the border, there was another hundred feet in all directions. Now look at this current-day drawing of the park." Lilly clicked again, and Bash's drawing that he used to outline the crime scene came up. "Look at the changes. The old boulder is still there, though the tree is

long gone. Let's anchor this picture, and the perspective, with the boulder and the road. You see
what has happened? Alden Park has shrunk."

Lilly looked around the room. People stared at
the park overlay, but nobody reacted.

"Now, here are some pictures of the park today.
As you stand on the street facing the park, you can
see the fence to the left that butts up against the
town houses that were built a couple of years ago.
Parallel to the street is more of the privet hedge,
with thorny bushes and some poison ivy to keep
people out. Behind there is a dog park for the town
houses and a loading dock for some of the stores.
To the right, another fence. That creates an alleyway for the stores along the Wheel." Lilly had
clicked through pictures, the ones she'd taken,
showing the new man-made boundaries of the park.

"You can see how the edges of the park were
taken away to be used for commercial or residential
rather than community development. That, some
may argue, was progress and to be expected. But I
noticed that it all has happened in the last few
years. Now, I'm the first to admit I haven't been paying as close attention as I might have for the last
four or five years, so I may have missed something.
But my friends Ray and Delia have both spent the
afternoon looking into this, and they can't find any
official documents that okayed that use of the land.
When Ray contacted the developer of the town
houses, he was assured that he had gotten a variance from town hall."

Lilly clicked again. On this picture, she showed a
copy of the variance approved with an official seal
of the town and the initials PF. "PF. Those initials
come up a lot, with official seals. At first, I assumed

that it was Pete Frank who approved these things. After all, he was on the board of selectmen at the time. Folks assumed that Pete Frank, PF, had signed off on them. But then I asked Pete if he had approved these variances, and he told me he hadn't."

"Of course he'd say that," Kitty said.

"I called the developer this afternoon and asked if any money had changed hands for this variance approval. Officially, no it had not. Unofficially, and off the record? There had been a cash payment."

"How did you get him to admit that?" Warwick asked.

"I will admit, I tricked him a bit by asking a direct question. One more thing about that cash payment. He said it was very cloak and dagger. He left it in an envelope, in a locker at the high school gym."

"What does that have to do with Merilee's death?" Cal asked.

"Well, that's an interesting question, Cal. At first glimpse, nothing. But then, as we were thinking about who had a motive to kill Merilee, knowing about this variance and who knows how many others, I thought about how Merilee was always looking for some quick cash. Was she the person behind this exchange of money? Or, more probably, did she find out that somebody was getting bribes to make things happen, and she wanted in on the deal?"

"So she started to blackmail whoever was getting the bribes?" PJ asked.

"I think she did," Lilly said. "Am I right, Kitty?"

"How should I know?"

"You and Merilee were good friends for a long time," Lilly said. "You know, I've been looking at that Goosebush Gossip site for the past couple of days.

Catching up on what I'd missed in the months previous. I'd heard you were the Goosebush Gossip, Kitty, but now I wonder if that was only half true. I think that perhaps you and Merilee started that website together. The posts have two distinct voices. One is far crueler than the other. Which one was you?"

Kitty had gone pale and had stopped talking. Everyone was staring at her, but she didn't take her eyes off Lilly.

"Kitty, I've made no secret of the fact that I blame you for a dear friend's misery and don't hold you in very high esteem. The way I always dealt with that was by pretending the people who fell out of grace with me no longer existed. I stopped paying attention to you several years ago," Lilly said.

"Man, that's cold," Stan said under his breath. Delia hit him on the arm and shushed him.

"That you, Kitty, and Merilee were good friends was not a surprise. That you had a falling out was also not a surprise. Surely, you couldn't have expected Merilee to be a loyal friend. Did she lose interest in the blog? When did she realize that she was the source of much of the content on Goosebush Gossip? You must have understood that eventually her laser focus would fall on you, or that she would hurt you in some way. I used to think that you hurt people with a total lack of compassion, but I've come to believe that that's not true. You are not a kind person, but you do have remorse. Merilee Frank, in my humble opinion, had no remorse. She was not a good person. That did not mean that she deserved to die, however."

"I didn't kill her," Kitty said. "I couldn't have—"

"Of course you could have," Lilly said. "Any of us are capable of murder, if pushed hard enough. Merilee certainly pushed. I don't, however, think that you killed her. No, I think you conspired with her to make people's lives miserable. You may even have blackmailed people with her. I think you hated her at the end, but I don't think you killed her."

"Okay, I'll bite," Roddy said. "Who do you think did it?"

"I thought back to that variance, and the seal with the PF initials. Initials that did not stand for Pete Frank. They did not stand for Pete Junior, I checked. Now, in Goosebush, there several other people with the initials PF, but who else has access to town records? I think the initials stood for Pat French."

"Are you accusing me of something?" Pat said, as she started to rise to her feet.

"Sit down, Pat," Bash said. "You don't want to miss the rest of the story, do you?" Even as he told her to sit, Bash stood up and moved to block the exit to the theater. Ray silently got up and moved in front of the other exit.

"It was the cash that made me think," Lilly said. "These days, such an odd thing to request, cash. Not a check, not wired funds, but cash. Who would want cash? Somebody who didn't want a trail, but it was more than that. Someone who lived on cash. There aren't many of those folks left. You'd be surprised how much they stand out when you start asking questions."

"You've lost it, Lilly. I'm not surprised, at your age, slipping a bit. I like to use cash, so that means I killed Merilee?"

"Pat, we've only had a few hours to do some research, but it turns out you don't like to leave any sort of a trail."

"From what we've been able to find, you don't exist," Ray said.

"Don't exist? I'm sitting right here," Pat said.

"You're sitting right here because Edith Stone vouched for you," Lilly said. "She said that you were a relative, and that you had come to take care of her. And then, of course, she got so sick people didn't see her in public much. When she died, folks were disappointed she hadn't left her house to the Historical Society after all, but they weren't really surprised. You'd earned it. You'd lived with her for five years and taken such good care of her. It made sense that you got the house. Besides, by then you'd ingrained yourself into Goosebush life. Taken over that thankless job of tracking payments of fines and taxes, and turned it into an important role. You didn't just do the paperwork, you found new sources of revenue, mostly by following the rules that our town elders had set up all those years ago and enforcing them with fines. Nobody noticed at first how much the cost of living in Goosebush had gone up. We got new garbage and recycling cans. Someone had to pay for that. Never mind that the companies underwrote the cost of the cans themselves. Ernie called them this afternoon and found that out."

"People in this town can afford it—"

"Not all of them, Pat, not all of them. Merilee Frank couldn't afford it."

"I never fined Merilee Frank—"

"Pat, you had me write her a ticket every day for six months because she parked in a place that you recently had marked as a no-parking zone," Bash said. "The tickets were twenty-five dollars a day. That adds up, especially since you added late fees."

"Hundreds of dollars," Pete said. "It really got Merilee's back up. She refused to pay the tickets, and then Pat booted her car."

"Merilee Frank never thought she needed to follow the same rules the rest of us did," Pat said. "Again, that doesn't mean I killed her."

"Here's what I think," Lilly said. "Pat, I think you and Merilee hated each other. I suspect you were used to tangling with tough people but had never run across somebody like Merilee before. Few had. She was spectacularly narcissistic. It must have been quite a challenge for you. Especially since she had it out for you and probably found your weakness. What was it? Did somebody want to confirm that Pete had approved some town business, and she knew he hadn't? Did she see you getting an envelope of cash? Did she talk to somebody else who you'd been blackmailing? Did she want in? Of course she did."

"You made a mistake when she decided to build on to her house and got you to walk through the paperwork," Tamara said. "Once Delia knew, that let me know what I was looking for, and it was easy to find it in the town records. It's an interesting combination, a crook who is also psychotically organized and in love with triplicate forms."

"You have no right to look at my paperwork—"

"A judge and a search warrant disagree," Bash said.

"You have no proof," Pat said. The color had drained from her face, but she did not look away from Lilly. Nor did she try to move. Kitty, however, did. She knocked over her chair in her effort to get away quickly and stood behind Ernie.

"The search warrant is also for your house," Bash said. "Tomorrow is trash day. You were smart enough not to throw anything away last week, when folks might notice. But this week? I just got a text that they found a bag with a sweatshirt in it. On the inside of the sweatshirt are what seem to be bloodstains. We'll see soon enough whether the blood is Merilee Frank's. In the meantime, Pat French, I'm going to caution you not to say anything that may harm your defense—"

Pat stood up calmly and looked around the room. "Tell me, honestly, is there one person in this room who is truly mourning that terrible woman? I did you all a favor, you know that's true. Anyone who knew Merilee Frank for five minutes wouldn't convict me. You all should throw me a parade."

"But why kill her?" Tamara asked.

"Believe it or not, I like it here," Pat said. "I care about this town. I felt settled, like I belong, for the first time in my life. I needed to supplement my income a bit, but of anyone, you'd think Merilee would understand that. If only she'd backed off and let me live my life. I even offered to cut her in a bit, but she kept wanting more and more. She wanted me to break my own rules, but I knew I'd get caught if I listened to her. I wasn't bothering anyone, not really. I'm part of the fabric of this town now. You have no idea how woven in I am." Pat gave out a bark of a laugh and swung around to look at everyone in the room, turning over the chair she'd been sitting in. Everyone jumped, except Lilly. Lilly stared at her and shook her head.

"Pat, stop talking. You need to get a lawyer to help you," Lilly said.

"You're the ones who need the help," Pat said. Bash moved to put his hand under Pat's elbow, but she shook him off. She started to walk out of the theater, back straight, eyes forward. Ray stepped beside her, and Bash stayed slightly behind.

CHAPTER 38

"Delia, that was outstanding," Ernie said, pushing his chair back slightly from the café table in Lilly's garden, lest he be tempted to dip into the pasta one more time. Between the soup, salad, homemade bread, and the pasta, Ernie was so full he felt he could almost burst. Almost. The promise of homemade ice cream and a slice of strawberry-rhubarb pie made him willing to take another bite.

"I second that," Warwick said. "I'm going to need to add five miles to my run tomorrow morning."

"Thank you all," Delia said, blushing slightly. She glanced over at Stan, who had smiled through the entire meal, enjoying the banter between the friends and the company of Delia. "It's the same old pasta I make almost every time we have an impromptu dinner party."

"Yeah, I don't think so," Tamara said. "This pasta had a little something added. Don't even bother telling me what it was. 'Cause that will make me try it at home, and I'll fail. Then Warwick will try it, and he'll fail. Then we'll need to wrangle another invitation to dinner, so we can have Delia's Pasta Nirvana again."

"Delia's Pasta Nirvana?" Lilly laughed.

"That's what we call it at the O'Connor house," Warwick said.

"We call her sauce Delia's Splendor Sauce," Tamara said. "Splendor for short. We've still got a couple of containers of that in the freezer, but I'm going to need more to help me get through the tangle of dealing with Edith Stone's house." Tamara sighed and took another sip of wine.

"Is that why you were late for dinner?" Lilly asked.

"It is. A few of us have been meeting with lawyers to figure out how to proceed now that we know Pat French forged the signatures of the witnesses to Edith Stone's will. Her house is worth a small fortune, so we need to cross the t's and dot the i's, even though the will she never filed made it clear she wanted to leave her house to the Historical Society. Lilly, you witnessed that one, and that made a difference."

Ernie let out a whistle. "Should you be telling us this?" he asked Tamara.

"It is going to be common knowledge soon enough," Tamara said. She looked over at Lilly and Delia and smiled. The three women had spent hours talking about the Stone house, trying to discern how best to move forward with Edith's intentions. "Edith signed the will, and Pat got it filed without a lot of scrutiny. Did she know what she was signing? That is up for debate. But what is clear is that Pat forged the witnesses."

"Were Pat and Edith really related?" Warwick asked.

"Edith thought so, but according to Bash, they weren't," Lilly said. No one questioned Bash confiding in Lilly. He had been in way over his head, but with help from Ray and Lilly, he'd done everything right in the investigation of Merilee's murder, and the case against Pat looked like it was going to hold up.

"Pat was a con artist, but none of us caught on," Delia said, with a slight rebuke in her voice. "Her real name is Stephanie Harris, by the way." She blamed herself more than she blamed the others. She should have paid more attention to the facts that didn't make sense but that everyone had glossed over. She'd gotten to know Edith fairly well, and Edith had always made it clear that her house was going to be home to the Historical Society. Why hadn't she looked at the will more closely?

"No, we didn't catch on," Lilly said, smiling at Delia. "Maybe if I'd been paying more attention, or you'd asked more questions, or . . . we could go on all day about this. Fact is, Pat was good at fooling folks and had made a living doing it. I'm just relieved that the results from Edith's exhumation confirmed that she died of natural causes."

"It's sad when finding out someone isn't a serial killer is a relief," Stan said. No one spoke for a full minute. Each was lost in their own thoughts, wondering what they might have done to change the past few weeks and coming up short.

"Well, how about I get these dishes in the house?" Warwick said, standing up. He leaned down and gave Tamara a kiss on her forehead and a smile. Then he started stacking plates. "We need some more water, and maybe another bottle of wine, or two. Stan, give me a hand. The squad needs to have an official meeting. Roddy has something to talk to you all about."

"The squad?" Stan asked, rising from his chair.

"I'll explain while we're deciding on the best wine to go with dessert," Warwick said.

"Cool," Stan said, gathering up plates with expert ease.

"Warwick, take off the coach hat, and stop telling us all what to do," Tamara said, handing him her plate.

"Warwick, don't listen to her, and don't ever change. I, for one, would be lost without your direction," Lilly said.

"Lilly, my friend, you are the last person who needs direction. But I figure you all should have a chance to talk before I light that firepit over there," he said, gesturing to the steel contraption that Ernie brought over for Lilly to test-drive.

"You sure that thing is safe?" Lilly asked.

"Oh, for heaven's sake. Do you think I would bring you something that wasn't safe? It's a way to have a fire while you're sitting outside," Ernie said. "Granted, it would work better in the fall rather than a week before the Fourth of July, but life has been a bit topsy-turvy lately."

"That's one way to put it," Roddy said. Stan and Warwick made their way up the back stairs of the porch. Warwick expertly opened the door with his elbow and gently kicked it open with his foot. With a practiced move, he hip-checked it open for Stan.

"I am sorry to interrupt your squad meeting. Whatever that may be," Roddy said. He smiled and looked around the table. He'd traveled the world several times over but couldn't imagine a place he'd rather be at this moment in his life. He'd found his home.

"We're a group of superheroes who don't have capes, but we do have garden trowels. And some of us—Lilly—have superpowers with plants," Ernie said.

"Others of us have superpowers with computers—right, Delia?" Tamara said.

"Roddy, Warwick mentioned that you wanted to talk to all of us?" Lilly said, ignoring the cacophony around her and focusing on her neighbor.

"I did, do. I know that many municipal initiatives have been put on hold while a forensics accountant figures out what Pat did with the town's funds."

"Another mess," Tamara said. "I still can't believe she kept three different sets of books and kept moving money around so that the monthly statements would look good."

"Well, she couldn't have done that without help from the accountant the town hired—" Delia said.

"On her recommendation—"

"Obviously, vetting mechanisms need to be put in place, and better systems for double-checking the financials," Lilly said. "Honestly, that's what breaks my heart the most. Goosebush always ran on a coffer of trust in one another. That trust is broken."

"Not for long," Roddy said. "Whoever the gardening Robin Hood is who's been going around gussying up the town has been doing a ton to make folks feel better."

"Small projects, nothing too huge, so far," Tamara said, looking down at her broken nails. The four members of the team had been averaging a job every third day. She was tired but had never felt so good about the work she was doing.

"I think it is remarkable," Roddy said. "I drove by a stop sign yesterday that had had a bed of weeds surrounding it. Today it has a few flowers, and some nice grasses. And the sign is straight. Small, perhaps, but it has impact. I would love to tell whoever is doing this that I appreciate it and am willing to help in any way I can."

The friends sat in silence. Warwick was the only person who knew what they'd been doing besides the four of them, and that was only because there had been some heavy lifting required lately, and Lilly had suggested he be brought into the fold. Roddy had been in the room when the original flagpole plans had been discussed, but he'd never been able to confirm that the four of them had done the work. He'd also never wanted to overstep and assume a level of friendship that wasn't reciprocated.

When no one spoke up, Roddy continued. "I need to ask your advice. I don't want to make this known around town, mind you. I feel a bit like an interloper horning his way in. But my understanding is that the Alden Park project is being delayed because of a land dispute?"

Lilly nodded. "Apparently, Pat—"

"Her real name is Stephanie," Delia reminded them.

"She'll always be Pat to me," Lilly said, smiling at Delia. She knew that her friend took Stephanie/Pat's betrayal personally, since it included a manipulation of data that no one had suspected, including Delia.

"I still can't believe she got the Frank family to agree to lease the land for those three houses to the town for free," Ernie said. "Why wouldn't PJ run that by anyone? They could have caught Pat right away, before the rest of this mess."

"Pat found out that PJ's grandfather owed some back taxes that had been overlooked for years. Once he died, she went after PJ for the money. You remember how hard it was for PJ back then; he had no extra money to spare."

"And Merilee was making noises about coming after the house," Tamara said.

"Right. Pat offered PJ a deal he felt he couldn't turn down. He thought that the lease money was going to the town."

"But instead it was going into one of the accounts Pat had set up as part of her shell game," Ernie said. "You've got to admit it, that took guts."

"You sound like you admire her?" Delia said. "She was a crook. Think of the pain she caused people. PJ Frank may go to jail."

"PJ isn't going to jail," Lilly said. "He's cooperating with the authorities, completely. He honestly thought that the land lease was on the up and up. So did the contractor who built the houses, though she admitted that she'd paid Pat a fee to move the paperwork along."

"But then there's the Alden Park mess," Ernie said. "I still don't understand how she pulled that off."

"Pat sold off strips of land on all three sides of the park. One to the town-house developer. One to the town, sort of, so that the business alley behind the Wheel could be sold. The third was the strip parallel to the street. Ends up that a group of the homeowners over there paid for the land and planted those awful bushes. PJ Frank was one of them and spilled the beans. They said it was for privacy, but it was more to keep their lawns free from dogs who were walking in the park."

"I still think there had to be more than that," Ernie said.

"I agree, but that's all they'll confess to now. Negotiations are delicate. Legally, they can make a claim on the land, especially since nothing has been done in the park for years. Squatters' rights."

"But they don't own the land," Roddy said.

"Maybe not legally," Tamara said, "but Lilly's right, a case can be made, and we don't have the funds to fight it in court. It's bad enough that Edith's house is being held up in probate while the will business is sorted out."

"But the Historical Society will get it eventually, right?" Delia said.

"That's the plan," Lilly said. "She'd made her intentions known, and there isn't any other family. I've asked my lawyer to look into it and try to move it along so the society can take it over. But as for Alden Park, that's a sticky wicket. Those landowners can make a case—"

"You don't understand me," Roddy said. "They don't own the land anymore. I bought it from them this week and am leasing it back to the town. Anonymously. The only agreement I made that must be adhered to is that there needs to be a fence built along the property boundary of the park to give the neighbors more privacy."

"The legal border or the Pat border?" Tamara asked.

"The legal border. That buys the park a few hundred more square feet."

"Roddy, that is so generous of you," Lilly said.

"Please, no fussing. That's why I want it to remain between us. I'm only bringing it up because I'm willing to fund the building of the privacy wall as well, and I want you to know that as you move forward on the plans for the park."

"The board of selectman will want to weigh in—" Ernie said.

"Not if another anonymous funder pays for the work on the park," Lilly said. "And creates a fund for its upkeep."

"You?" Tamara asked.

"Anonymous donor," Lilly said.

"They should start calling this town Lillyville in honor of the dozens of ways you take care of it," Tamara said, grabbing her friend's hand and squeezing it.

"Goosebush is a fine name in my book," Lilly said, squeezing Tamara's hand back. "Friends, it sounds like our next project has just been handed to us. I have two motions to put forth. One is to move forward on the Alden Park project. The second is to vote Roddy Lyden an official member of the Garden Squad. Those in favor?" Four hands shot up in the air.

"Roddy, welcome to the Garden Squad," Lilly said.

"What does that mean, exactly?" Roddy asked.

"You don't want to know," Delia said.

"You really don't," Tamara said.

"Hush, now. Roddy strikes me as the superhero type," Ernie said.

"The Garden Squad is a good thing. A very good thing," Lilly said. "Welcome aboard, and buckle up. We're in for quite a ride."

Gardening Tips

The joy of gardening goes well beyond seeing plants grow. Every step of it—from the planning over the winter, to the growing of seeds in the early spring, to the maintenance over the summer, to the enjoyment of the final gasps of the fall—nourishes the soul all year long. I have many family and friends who are amazing gardeners and have shared tips that I'm pleased to share with you. Special thanks to my sister Caroline, my Uncle George, and my Aunt Carol.

- Composting not only saves waste from filling landfills, but it is a nutrient-rich resource when preparing garden beds. Create a compost pit in which, year-round, you deposit coffee grounds, fireplace ashes, banana peels, fruit and vegetable peelings, eggshells, etc. No meat or dairy. Turn it over at least once a week during late fall and winter. When spring comes, shovel it out as fine dark brown pellets, and spread it liberally on the garden.
- Start plants indoors mid-February. For pots, you can use cardboard juice containers and cut off the bottoms, or paper egg cartons. Put them in a sunny window until it's warm enough to plant them outdoors in your garden soil. Keep them in the pots, as that keeps bugs out.
- To naturally repel mosquitos from your out-

door area, use strong-smelling plants, such as geraniums, marigolds, lavender, basil, rosemary, oregano, and citronella grass.

- Marigolds are also a great ally in the vegetable garden because they deter garden pests and attract bees.
- Spray plants that are prone to aphids with diluted dish soap and water to naturally control them.
- Hang highly fragrant soap around plants to keep deer from eating them.
- If you want the look of an oversized planter but not the weight, fill the bottom half with recycled Styrofoam or plastic containers from the recycling bin to promote drainage and make moving it around much easier.
- Don't cut your ornamental grasses too early. They provide beautiful foliage in the fall and give structure to dull winter gardens. Grasses can be pruned in late winter and early spring.
- Don't throw away decorative perennial plants once the season ends. Many, like geraniums and mums, can be overwintered inside and brought back out after the danger of frost is over.

Acknowledgments

A writer works alone, but getting published requires a team. I am so grateful to these folks for helping bring the Garden Squad to life.

Thank you to my agent, John Talbot.

Thank you to John Scognamiglio and the team at Kensington. I'm so grateful that the Garden Squad found a home with all of you.

Thank you, as always, to my family: my parents, Paul and Cindy Hennrikus, my sisters, Kristen and Caroline, my brothers-in-law, Bryan and Glenn, and my nieces and nephews, Emma, Evan, Chase, Mallory, Becca, Tori, Harrison, and Alex. My heart bursts with the love I feel for and the love I am shown by these remarkable people.

I have wonderful friends who double as a cheering squad. A special thank-you to Jason Allen-Forrest, my first reader. And to Scott Forrest-Allen, who always is there for title help. Courtney O'Connor, thank you for helping me reframe and think of myself as a writer. Amy Gauger and David Colfer, I'm so glad you are part of my cheering squad.

My life is full of gardeners, and I am the better for it. While writing this book, I thought of my grandfather George Stockbridge sitting on his wooden bench, digging in his garden. Other gardening inspiration came from my sister Caroline Lentz, my mother, Cindy Hennrikus, Pat Spence, Mel Spence, and Tom Dombkowski. Caroline Lentz, George Stockbridge, Carol Beadle Stockbridge, Lisa

Rafferty, and Susan Able helped me with gardening tips.

I blog with five amazing women, the Wicked Authors (www.WickedAuthors.com): Barbara Ross, Sherry Harris, Edith Maxwell, Liz Mugavero, and Jessie Crockett are friends, mentors, cheerleaders, and wonderful writers. I would not be on this journey without them and wouldn't want to be.

The mystery community is wonderful. I am grateful for my blogmates at Killer Characters, and to be a member of Sisters in Crime and Mystery Writers of America.